PRAISE FOR *MEET THE MOON*

"Jody Moran is an endearing guide—funny, smart, word-wise—through this sad and triumphant coming-of-age tale. There is such clarifying honesty here, about grief, friendship, resilience and faith. There is as well a keen and vivid sense of an era that seems more innocent than our own and yet remarkably timeless, perhaps because Kerry Malawista understands so well the enduring grace of family love."

—Alice McDermott, author of *Charming Billy* (National Book Award), *After This* (finalist Pulitzer Prize)

"A brilliantly faceted, life-affirming story about a girl and her family as they struggle to go on without Mom during a single year in the early seventies. Delightfully poignant and equally funny, this story reminiscent of Judy Blume will no doubt steal the hearts of readers of all ages—just like it did mine."

—Jennifer Richard Jacobson, author of *Small as an Elephant*

"I fell in love with the entire Moran clan in this beautiful portrayal of a family learning how to navigate the loss of a parent. In *Meet the Moon*, Kerry Malawista has created an emotionally complex story that's warm, funny and utterly real. I loved it."

—Frances O'Roark Dowell, author of *Dovey Coe, Shooting the Moon*, and *The Secret Language of Girls*

"*Meet the Moon* is a moving and captivating novel about the joys and perils of adolescence and family life—one of the rare books that appeals powerfully to both adults and children alike. I loved it."

—Susan Shreve, author of *More News Tomorrow* and *The Search for Baby Ruby*

"*Meet the Moon* captures a fractured world spinning out of control after the sudden loss of a funny and beloved mother who wanted her children to see the stars and beyond. Told through the eyes of thirteen-year-old, Jody Moran, one of four siblings, we go on a journey of hope and healing in Kerry Malawista's tender, funny novel of a family finding their way home again.

—Kerry Madden, author of *Offsides*

"In *Meet the Moon* Kerry Malawista's heroine, Jody Moran, brings us along as she stumbles from thirteen to fourteen, finding her way forward while grieving the sudden death of a mother whose love never seemed quite enough. This beautifully written, sharply observed novel takes us on a journey that is scary, tumultuous, yet grounded always in the love of family. Recreating 1970s America and the torture and promise of adolescence, *Meet the Moon* gives us a plucky narrator we want to enfold and never let go."

—Marita Golden, author of *The Wide Circumference of Love*

"Jody's just a regular teen, with regular teen things to worry about. But then in a blink, there's a wreck, a family in shock: Mom's gone, baby brother is in the hospital. Boyfriends, best friends, teachers, siblings, the neighbor across the street, all have a part in helping Jody adjust—but can they deliver? Jody loves her big rowdy family, but soon sees that sometimes Dads can be dumb, big sisters too bossy, teachers too nosy, and even best friends don't always get it. In the end, all the strength Jody needs is right inside her warm heart. Kerry Malawista knows that heart, and *Meet the Moon* rises full over the landscape of great reads for teens and grownups alike.

—Bill Roorbach, author of *Life Among Giants*, *The Remedy for Love*, and *Lucky Turtle*

"Kerry Malawista's novel *Meet the Moon* is beautiful and profoundly moving. She brings to vivid life a family dealing with the tragic and shocking loss of their mother and notably a father we'd all wish for. Young people and adults, alike, should find this book both engaging, humorous and reassuring."

—Linda Pastan, author of *Carnival Evening*, former Poet Laureate of Maryland

.

MEET THE MOON

Kerry L. Malawista

Fitzroy Books

Published by Fitzroy Books
An imprint of
Regal House Publishing, LLC
Raleigh, NC 27587
All rights reserved

https://fitzroybooks.com

Printed in the United States of America

ISBN -13 (paperback): 9781646032655
ISBN -13 (epub): 9781646032662
Library of Congress Control Number: 2021949154

Interior by Lafayette & Greene
Cover design © by C. B. Royal

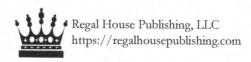

Regal House Publishing, LLC
https://regalhousepublishing.com

The following is a work of fiction created by the author. All names, individuals, characters, places, items, brands, events, etc. were either the product of the author or were used fictitiously. Any name, place, event, person, brand, or item, current or past, is entirely coincidental.

Printed in the United States of America

Dedicated to my siblings,
Kathy, Carol, Maryellen, Karen, and Bob

1

Although I'd begged Mom for dance lessons, I hated her for making me go to the Twinkle Toes class. I was stuck with my little sister, Mae, even though I was thirteen and as tall as Miss Dorothy.

The teacher tapped out the beat on the worn wood of the old Edgehaven firehouse, and as the floor vibrated, thoughts marched through my head. "Rum, pum, pum… Again, and one and two and…" How could Tracy not show up?

"Three and four and…" This leotard makes me look flat-chested. "Five and six and…" What kind of best friend bails at the last minute? No way was her nikkin' throat hurting that bad.

"Seven and eight and…" Now my scab keeps catching in that hole in my tights. Did Mom get me a new pair, like she promised?

The clock was high in the corner, one of those classroom things. Just five more minutes. I eyed the line of girls who followed me, each of them doing her own quirky version of a pirouette.

"Nice one, Cynthia," I said, patting Charlie's little sister on the shoulder. She turned, giving me a big smile. She had those same dark eyebrows as her brother. Pretending to adjust my ballet slipper, I glanced at the doorway, trying to look like I wasn't looking. Charlie sometimes showed up to walk Cynthia home.

"Jody, pay attention," Miss Dorothy snapped. "It's your turn."

I twirled across the floor one last time, hoping I looked more graceful than gangly, and when I reached the other side I flipped my hair over my shoulder. Damn, no Charlie.

Miss Dorothy gave a final rap with her wooden staff, signaling the end of class.

Mae and I pulled our stretch pants over our tights and leotards, gathered our things, and stepped out into the early spring heat. Mae with her freckles and strawberry braids was our very own Pippi Longstocking, just not as skinny.

A zingy feeling itched at my nose. Even though the sky was blue I could feel a storm was coming. As we trudged uphill toward home, lugging our blue-plaid book bags, I could hear Mae's flute case banging against her thigh.

"My stuff is too heavy," she whined. "I don't want to walk home."

"Me neither. But Mom had to take Annie somewhere. It's *mandatory*."

"Is that today's word?"

"Yep." It should be *disgruntled*. Tracy bailed on me. Charlie never showed up. And Annie and Billy were probably home already having Mom's shortbread cookies. My new thing was trying long words, the weirder the better. In the *Oxford English Dictionary* I kept next to my bed, I learned that a sesquipedalian is a lover of polysyllabic words, which are words with lots of syllables. Every night, digging, I discovered a newer and bigger and weirder word, wrote it in my notebook, and the next day I challenged myself to see how many times I could use it. I wouldn't go to sleep without finding a good one. Two nights ago, it was *incomprehensible*, meaning impossible to understand or grasp. One night ago, it was *longevous: live to a long age*. A good one, right? It gave me a feeling of power, knowing words that others didn't.

"What's mandatory?" asked Mae.

"It's something you *must* do. Required, like going to school."

"Why didn't Mom have to pick us up? That should be *mandatory*." Mae was three years younger and sometimes she could be pretty smart.

"I guess a ride's only mandatory for Annie," I said.

Mae liked that.

We skipped across Abbott Avenue, passing the tiny stream that ran behind the ruins of a house. If I'd had my net and jar, we would have stopped for tadpoles. My last catch had all died and I was aiming to watch at least one turn into a frog. I'd read that it takes fourteen weeks to transform from tadpole to frog. I was hoping it might work the same for humans, but in years. At fourteen I would transform from a skinny kid into a girl in need of a bra, and some of those other things that our big sister Claire was already into, now that she was fifteen.

A dark blue Plymouth pulled up beside us, someone inside waving—weirdness!—but it was only our neighbor, Mr. Geiger, without his wife, Mrs. Geiger. At least I thought it was that Mr. Geiger. His identical twin lived in their basement apartment with his wife, also Mrs. Geiger. What would it be like living with someone who looked exactly like you? I wondered about their wives. Could the two Mrs. Geigers tell their husbands apart? At the dinner table? In *bed*?

Mr. Geiger leaned way over and rolled down the passenger window. I was pretty sure it was the upstairs Mr. Geiger, Walter, and not the basement Mr. Geiger, Fred. Walter's black hair didn't pouf up like Fred's.

"Hi, girls. I'm sorry to bother you. But it's important. Your dad, um. Your dad asked me to pick you up from ballet. Sorry I'm late. Hop in."

We'd never been picked up by a neighbor. Maybe Dad knew it was going to rain. I looked closely, making sure it was the right Mr. Geiger—Walter. The other one didn't have kids and seemed kind of creepy. He never looked you in the eye. Mom said you should always look a person in the eye.

Mae was frozen. When grown-ups talked to her, she pulled her head back into her shell like a turtle. It was up to me to be the boss. I pushed her into the back seat as the first drops of rain began to fall. Perfect. As soon as Mr. Geiger pulled into his driveway, I saw Mrs. Geiger in the living room window, curtains pulled to the side, waving us inside with her cigarette hand. Barely moving his lips, Mr. Geiger said, "Yeah, why don't you two come on in for a snack?"

A snack! In the seven years we'd lived on Randolph Court,

I had never once been invited in for a snack. The last month had been weird: snow the day before Easter and another man aiming to walk on the moon. Now this.

We sisters followed Mr. Geiger inside.

I was shocked to see our older sister Claire in her new green bellbottoms—now that she'd turned fifteen she wore *only* bellbottoms—perched on their gold couch. I wish I looked like her—long, red hair and the bluest eyes, like Mom's. Mine were drab green on a good day. The soft cushions pitched me into her as I sat. She'd been out in the rain, and her hair was still damp.

Far from taking charge, Claire whispered, "What in Fred's name is going on?"

"Like I know," I said, pushing my glasses up on my nose.

Claire sprung off the couch, started pacing, her coppery braid swinging behind. I looked around the room, afraid to touch anything. The house was so clean: a couch, two chairs, a coffee table with a single copy each of *Family Circle* and *Ladies Home Journal*. Not a sign that three kids lived here.

And where was my snack? Muffled voices from the kitchen. Mrs. Geiger didn't even come out to check on us. I watched the wall clock: tick, tick, tick.

The Geiger's oldest, sixteen-year-old James, tramped in the door, sweaty from Edgehaven High School baseball practice. The star second baseman. His T-shirt outlined his wide shoulders. Scruffy hair on his cheeks. He had the same shiny black hair and milky white skin as his mother. His father's light blue eyes. He looked like his two parents had been smushed into one face, a really cute one.

Claire hated that she wasn't with James in school. If we lived one town over she would already be in high school. But ninth grade in Edgehaven? That was part of nikkin' middle school, and James was a sophomore.

"Hey," he said, clearly surprised to see us there. A look passed between him and Claire, but I was the one who blushed. He gave my big sister a wide grin. My skin heated, my embarrassment plain to see.

"James," called Mrs. Geiger from the kitchen.

Claire feigned disinterest at his leaving. She gazed out the front window. Our house, yellow and apparently Dutch Colonial, was directly across the street, black shutters and white front door like a face.

I looked over at Mae, who balanced on the edge of the couch, not moving, as if she had been put under a spell.

Suddenly Claire straightened, all the flirtiness scared out of her: "Jody, come look. Dad's van's in the driveway." It's large white lettering, *Moran Tile and Marble*, printed on the side.

"Uncle Mike is there too," I said, pointing at his station wagon.

"What the hell is going on?" asked Claire.

"Something's definitely wrong," I said.

"Incomprehensible," said Claire.

"Hey," I said.

"Word of the day," she said, giving me a nudge.

Mr. Geiger ducked in, all serious. He said, "Come on, girls, I'll walk you home."

Walk us home? Across the street? Claire and I shared a look, eyebrows raised. But it wasn't funny. Mr. Geiger marched us outside into the pouring rain, hoisted a gigantic umbrella. We took shelter, the three of us, a solemn parade crossing the street to our house.

I led the way up the steps, ten of them, often counted. Mr. Geiger held the screen door open, practically pushing me after Mae, then Claire, inside. "Okay, girls," he said.

Inside were my grandparents and a blur of other faces in the living room. Definitely not our usual Chicken Delight Monday. Our sister Annie, in an old Halloween princess dress, perched on our neighbor Mrs. Katz's lap. A tiara crowned her curly golden hair, accompanied by an array of brightly colored barrettes. Annie always had a notable way of decorating herself. She hopped off Mrs. Katz's lap and ran to me, wrapping her tiny arms around my leg.

I hoisted her up onto my hip, said: "Where's Mom and Billy?"

My question hung in the air for a second, as if everything were all moving in slow motion. The adults turned and stared at me, but none of them answered. The hairs at the scruff of my neck were prickling and I jutted out my chin a little.

Finally, Dr. Katz cleared his throat. "Your dad's waiting for you."

Mrs. Katz led us upstairs. Why were the lights off? She opened the door to my bedroom, mine and Claire's, dark except for a thin slat of light. The curtains had never been closed before. Dad sat on Claire's bed, work shirt hanging loose on his shoulders, his hands in his hair. Mae hopped on the bed beside him. He seemed small. Apple-cheeked Annie and her precious Roo climbed up, too. Claire and I huddled close. Everything was normal—our pajama-bag dolls, Claire's Polaroid snapshots that surrounded her dresser, my *Oxford English Dictionary*, our matching lamps, fringed shades, everything normal but Dad.

He put his hand on Mae's chubby leg. "Girls," he said. "Girls...I..." He slipped his Clark Kent glasses off, wiped his eyes. I rarely saw him without his glasses on; his eyes looked different—smaller, and tears welling, unheard of.

"Girls, I have very sad news."

"Are you crying?" Annie said.

"Daddy?" Mae said.

"There's been a terrible accident."

2

If I had paid closer attention those three weeks before the accident, could I have seen what was coming? Or was life that uncertain, precarious? *Precarious: dangerous; dependent on chance.*

First, there was the unexpected, a blizzard on Easter weekend. Even our crabapple tree, bursting with early blossoms, was confused. That Saturday the snow kept falling and falling. I woke early and crept out of bed to be the first to see it, every surface blanketed in a thick layer, at least five or six inches on the mailboxes and not a snowplow in sight.

I wasn't first: Mom and Dad snuggled close at the kitchen table, drinking their giant morning mugs of instant coffee. Mom's golden-red hair puffed out around her round face like a lion's mane. She had built the table with her own hands and painted it the same pea green as the cabinets. Dad had laid the mosaic floor tiles, which were a matching speckled green and black. They were reading the *Edgehaven Record.* The headline read: New Jersey Gets Dumped On, The Blizzard of 1970.

"You guys! Snow," I said.

Mom was already dressed, black stirrup pants and a white turtleneck. Lowering her glasses, she looked up as if she'd been waiting for me. "Hey, eat your breakfast and let's go!"

"Go where?"

That crooked smile. "Sledding," she said. "Just you and me. Here's your chance." Finally.

I poured myself a bowlful of Cheerios, sugar, and milk, and spooned them in rapid fire. Dad put on a sad face, like he was being left out, but we knew he didn't care. Mom loved anything that went fast, like roller coasters and ice skates, bikes and planes. Dad did not.

We had to pull my coat out of a box full of winter things ready for the attic. And off we went, just the two of us.

❧

I expected we'd have the sledding hill to ourselves, but as we rounded the corner at the end of our street at least a dozen early risers whooped and hollered. All three Geiger kids. This was even better, the neighborhood kids seeing just me and Mom having fun.

Prospect Woods had two trails to choose from. With sleds flying, walking to the top was death defying. Mom and I hiked up along the old rickety wooden fence that ran along the McClearys' property. Brittle branches snapped beneath my feet. The hills were steep, with a couple of moguls that, if you hit just the right spot, sent you airborne. Halfway down, the two paths met, making your timing a crucial calculation.

"Yo, Moran," Timmy Geiger, the middle Geiger kid yelled to me, as a snowball hit me in the head. I stopped to pack my own snowball, but by the time I was ready to pitch it, Timmy was long gone.

Mom, seeing me turn, began expertly packing her own. I chucked one at her back, accidently hitting the side of her head. "Hey, foul ball," she called.

A couple of high school boys were doing tricks, surfing upright on their sleds, arms stretched out wide, the metal blades glittering in the sun. A gaggle of high school girls stood nearby, nudging each other, pointing and giggling. *Gaggle: a group of geese* or *a noisy or disorderly group.*

"Yo, James," yelled Rose Voss, one of the pretty older girls. "I bet you can't do that on one foot." Claire would not be pleased. I looked at Rose's lip-glossed lips and her pink cheeks. Her maroon wool hat had a cool flower on it. Suddenly, I wished I could put her hat on my head and feel what it would be like to be Rose, even for a morning.

When we reached the top of the hill, Mom lay down on the sled. I stretched out on top of her, my belly against her back. She called this pancake sledding. "It's lucky you're so light," she said. For once, I was glad to be skinny.

"Ready for blast off," she called.

"To the moon," I said. I snuggled into her neck, breathing in the smell of licorice and cigarettes.

"And back," said Mom. "Now hold tight."

I hugged her throat. I remembered last year, sledding pancake style, with Charlie Coggins. Since we'd played around in his basement and kind of kissed, he wouldn't even look at me.

"Not that tight!" Mom shouted, laughing.

I never knew how close to get. Mom wasn't a hand squeezer like Dad.

We took off down the hill, unimaginably fast, the cold soft snow blowing raw against my face, my heart pumping, the bare oak trees a blur of brown soldiers standing at attention against the morning sky. Mom leaned to the right and I leaned with her, Mom twisted to the left and I did the same, in sync, my stocking hat flapping like a flag in the wind. Faster and faster.

Right before the finish we hit a sharp bump. I flew into the sky, Mom tumbling beneath me, my heavy boots hitting her in the stomach. "Ow," she yelped. "What the Sputnik!"

"Sorry, Charlie," I cried.

I wiped the snow off my glasses, saw Mom with snow covering her hair and eyeglasses. Our cat-eye frames almost matched. Mom's giggle started slow, then grew to one of her unstoppable laughs, and it was as if she loved me not only as much as the other kids but maybe a little more. Trudging back up the hill, Mom took hold of my hand to help me climb, as our boots mashed into the deep snow. Our prints would be evidence that we'd been here together, large prints and small. When Mom and I had watched Neil Armstrong walk on the moon, the news guy had said that with no wind or water his footprint would be there *forever*.

"Me in front," I called, already starting up the hill. When I reached the peak, I saw she was chatting with Mr. Geiger.

"Come on," I yelled, as I stretched up, trying to locate the roof of our house.

Michelle, Claire's best friend bumped my back. "Where's your bitch sister?"

"Where do you think," I said. "Sleeping."

"Well, tell her to get her ass over…" Mom appeared giving one of those 'I heard that' looks—a raised eyebrow and corresponding right-sided crooked smile. How did she do that?

"Sorry, Mrs. Moran," Michelle mumbled. I snorted.

Mom said, "Well, someone might be getting their *tush* spanked." Michelle had been at our house enough times to know she was kidding. Mostly.

The kids at the front of the line made way for Mom. She gave a little bow, and stepped to the front.

"*Mom,*" I mumbled. "Don't cut."

"Age before beauty," she said. I rolled my eyes, trying to hide my pleasure at jumping the line.

"And I'm not getting any younger," she said as she positioned herself on the sled.

As we set off, Mom pointed ahead, warning, "Keep an eye out for those little kids." Her arms encircled my body, feeling like a warm hug. I wasn't afraid.

Laurie, the youngest Geiger, was just ahead of us on a flying saucer. I waited, then pushed us off.

A perfect moment. Trouble was, our sled was faster than Laurie's. As we caught up, she spun out of control and fell off right in front of us.

Mom shouted, "Turn. Turn! Your left foot. Harder." I steered to the left, barely avoiding Laurie, all of us shouting. A near miss.

We careened over the last part of the hill and landed with a swoosh.

"Smooth move," said Mom as I threw my arms in the air and yelled, "YES."

Mom stood, took off her glove and touched my cheek. "You're turning into an icicle, Jody."

"I'm fine," I said and pointed to her dripping nose. "And you're getting snotsicles." I slogged back up the hill, my boots scooping up wet snow.

"Okay, one more run and then we get some hot chocolate."

At the top, she said, "Let's go for the big one—pancake style again." She nodded toward Dead Man's Curve. The trail was narrow, lined with fir trees, a sharp turn halfway down the hill. If you veered off course, you risked running into a tree.

Oh, Mom liked to go fast. She lay down on the sled and I climbed on top, trying not to squeeze her too hard around her neck. "Ow," she said. "I guess you kicked me harder than I thought."

"I didn't mean to!"

"Of course you didn't."

And off we flew. Like a race driver, Mom took the turn perfectly, whooping. The wind caught her knit cap, whooshing it right off her head, the gust carrying it away. Her thick hair flew in my face, blinding me.

When we reached the bottom of the hill, Mom's hat nowhere to be found, we plodded for home.

A new layer of snow covered the ground, our earlier boot prints had already disappeared.

3

A week later I lay in bed, enjoying the rare silence in our house. My eyes landed on that familiar indentation on the wall. The tiny gouge looked like a rocket ship lifting off, the chipped paint the exhaust of the fuel boosting the ship up, up and away. Every night before I fell asleep I'd stare at that spot, imagining the capsule growing smaller, disappearing into the atmosphere. When I was really little I'd pretend that my rocket ship had brought the Man in the Moon up into space.

Claire's and my single beds lined up end-to-end, forming one lengthy bed that ran under the windows. Mom had sewn one long bedspread, which was so annoying—my half was appliqued with the Scorpius constellation for my birthdate and Claire's had roses. Claire didn't care anything about the moon and stars. I couldn't make my bed if Claire wasn't making hers at the same time. Was that the point?

Dad knocked once and bounded in. "Rise and shine," he said. "You two marshmallow heads, hear the bluebirds sing." Dad's nicknames for us were mostly based on food. I was skinny like a string bean, and Annie with her rounded belly and chubby bottom was pork chop.

"Go away. I want to sleep," Claire answered, pulling the covers over her marshmallow head. I sat up, put on my glasses, enjoying this ringside seat, ready for the sparring.

"Church in an hour," Dad said.

"We went last week," Claire moaned.

Dad and I shared a grin. He said, "Nope, actually you got lucky last Sunday with the snow." He tousled her blanket. "Come, on, Claire-Bo-Bear. Up and at 'em. I know it's hard to go sometimes. But listen to this: you'll have something to look forward to. After lunch, we'll go to Hudson Park."

"Oh, whoop-de-do," said Claire. I stifled a cheer, didn't want to act like I cared about going if Claire didn't. But the park! As Dad moseyed out, the grizzly sat up and growled.

I rifled through my hangers and found my honeydew orange Easter dress that Mom had sewed and I never got to wear last week because of the snow. Four years before, a reporter and photographer from the *Edgehaven Record* came to our house to write about Mom's talent—and to take our photo next to the crab apple tree for the Sunday Easter issue. The reporter called her a master seamstress. Mom had sewed each of us matching short-sleeved dresses—white with navy-blue polka dots. Over the dresses we wore the navy-blue coats she had sewn, lined with the same polka dot fabric of the dress, and fastened with big white buttons. Even four-month-old Annie wore a matching outfit. I imagined we looked as good as the Kennedys.

Billy, he wasn't born yet.

This year I was hoping to get noticed—noticed by Charlie.

My best friend Tracy Bernard said he was a brainiac and too quiet. That was what I liked about him.

Tracy and I were an inseparable pair—a pair of opposites, but still—ever since we were five and moved to Randolph Road. Dad called us "the twins." But no one took us for twins. Tracy had dark eyes, hair, and skin, and was short and curvy, while I was tall and scrawny with light green eyes, fair skin, and sandy brown hair. Me, one of five kids, and Tracy an only child. Her mom, Amelie, was from France, beautiful, exotic, and with a French lilt to die for. Like her mom, Tracy had no trouble getting noticed. If she liked Charlie, she'd walk right up to him and start talking, probably with that phony French accent she sometimes used. She was such a flirt—and spoiled too!

Claire plucked a flowered smock dress out of her closet and pulled her pajamas over her head. Out popped her prodigious boobs. Prodigious a few pages back in my word notebook. *Prodigious: remarkable, impressively great, abnormal!* I stared as she put on her bra. Was I weird to look? I wanted to ask her what they felt like when she walked around, but knew better. Maybe I'd be one of those girls who stayed flat-chested her whole life—no boy would like me. When I first got my period, last January, I thought they had grown. But they hadn't really. Mom said, "They just feel like that each month."

I turned my back, got dressed.

Entering St. Paul's Church, I led our line of seven—Dad, Annie, Mom, Billy, Mae, and Claire—up the aisle and into the pew. I always fixed myself in a seat next to Dad. All the St. Paul families had their usual time and pew and stuck with them. We always sat in the middle right of the church, sixteen rows back from the front, when we could be exact, which I preferred.

The plump old lady who drove a big Cadillac to church each week, Mrs. Appleton, sat next to me, her flesh close to mine, hair in a tight white bun. She smelled like onions which made my nose itch.

"My, my, don't you look nice," she said as she gave my knee a pat. I scootched away.

"She dressed herself," Dad joked.

Mrs. Appleton clucked, not unkindly.

Light streamed in through the gigantic stained-glass windows. Bored, I stared at the one of Heaven and Earth. Did people ever think of the moon as heaven?

Turning around my eyes landed on Rose Voss. She looked like one of the glossy-haired Breck girls who brushed her hair 100 times a day, the way they tell you to do in *Seventeen*. Her gold hoops sparkled. Maybe Mom would finally say I could get my ears pierced.

An eagle's claw gripped the back of my neck, Mom reaching over Dad and Annie. She mouthed, *Eyes straight ahead*. A few moments later she said, "And don't bite your nails."

I pulled my finger away from my mouth. How did she know I was biting my nails? And why did she even care? They were my nails.

Father Sullivan's voice boomed, "Jesus rose from the dead for our salvation." I used to believe everything he told me. Now I had lots of questions. How could someone die and then come back? Some of this just didn't make sense. I was pretty sure Dad would agree.

Claire was busy admiring the way her nail polish shimmered in the light. I pulled a stashed Easter Kiss from my pocketbook, popped it in my mouth. After some singing and some more babble from the priest, Mom, Claire, Mae, and I went up to receive communion, while Dad stayed back with Annie and Billy. He gave my hand a squeeze as I scooted out past him.

Returning, I slipped into the pew, the paper-thin wafer sticking to the chocolatey roof of my mouth. Tapping my foot lightly against the kneeler, I watched Mrs. Appleton waddle back. As she wriggled in beside me, her hands in prayer, she slowly lowered herself onto the bench, trapping my foot underneath the kneeler.

"Excuse me," I whispered. "Mrs..." Her head was bowed. Was she asleep? My foot was getting scrunched. I started to feel clammy as the pain got worse. I didn't scream but dots flashed in front of my eyes before everything went black.

The next thing I knew we were packed in the car and on the way to the park.

Hudson Park was a twenty-minute drive. When Dad was a boy, Grandpa took him fishing at the pond there, just blocks from their apartment. Mom grew up one town over. Both families were sandwiched between the Holland and Lincoln tunnels.

The day was bright and sunny. Between bites of black licorice, Mom led us in a round: "Ob-La-Di, Ob-La-Da." We shouted the "BRA" part extra loud.

Dad parked in a shady spot, and Mom handed each of us an item to carry: a blanket, a kick ball, a jump rope, bubbles, and a big bag of sandwiches and snacks for Dad to tote. Claire, her Polaroid camera slung over her shoulder, took hold of Annie's hand, leading her through the cars toward the open grass. Mom tried to wrestle Billy, dressed in his Batman head mask and cape, into the stroller, but he squiggled away from her, shouting, "No! I'm Batman. I fly."

"Jody, make sure you drink extra water after fainting like that. You hear?"

"That was so awesome," Claire whispered.

I'd gotten us out of church! Things were still fuzzy, but Mae told me that Dad had boosted Mrs. Appleton off her kneeler and carried me out of the pew to the back of the sanctuary.

We followed that same familiar meandering path down to Duck Pond, named by some super imaginative person. Billy, ahead of us, was trying to catch a butterfly.

Wet leaves, that was the smell. I readily fell behind as Dad picked up skipping stones along the way. I reached for any chance to be with him. I was still thinking about the morning's mass, the priest's words echoing in my mind: *Jesus rose for our salvation!* Did anybody really believe that stuff? Nobody comes back from the dead.

"Do you believe in God, Dad? Or are you an agnostic?" The Catholic church was like carpet in our family, always there but never talked about.

Dad laughed. I was always surprising him. "Where do you get all these words, Jody? I'm not sure I know what half of them mean."

"Agnostic means you aren't sure." I glanced down at the shadow he cast, how it blended with mine.

"In that case, I'm agnostic because we can never be sure about things we don't understand."

Dad slowed his pace, ran his hand through his hair. His hazel-green eyes were boring into mine, his brow grew furrowed: "Well, I guess I don't believe there's a God looking down, a sort of old man with a beard, deciding things for us, if that's what you mean. Like I always tell you, we make our future, not God. He just wants us to be good."

"Does it worry you if you do something wrong you'll go to Hell? That's what Father Sullivan says."

"Me? Do something wrong?" Dad said with a smirk, giving my shoulder a nudge. "And, well, I'm not so sure you can trust a guy who wants to live with a bunch of men and hang out with altar boys."

"Dad!"

And of course, he had to get all serious: "Remember, Jody,

heaven is what you make it on earth. That's what my dad told me. Heaven is right here, right now. Is your foot hurting? Looks like you're wobbling."

"It's okay," I said. "Just a little."

"I thought Jesus made the lame walk," he said. "You go to church and come out limping."

A Frisbee soared by, almost hitting us. Dad leapt, leaned, picked it up, and tossed it back to the two boys playing. "Forget I said any of that, stringbean."

I zipped my lips.

Mom laid out our blanket on the broad expanse of mown grass, at the same time keeping a one-handed grip on Billy to keep him from running off.

Annie called back, "Hurry up!"

"We're coming," Dad called, but we didn't hurry any more or less.

I stopped to pick one of those dandelions that had turned into a white fuzzball. I closed my eyes and blew.

"Wish big," Dad said.

Charlie Coggins, I thought.

I flopped next to Claire on her towel, strategically laid out away from the family. "Jump rope with me," I said as she groaned.

She'd taken off her church sweater and rolled her dress up to her thighs. She hadn't told Mom, but before we left she had sprayed Sun-In in her hair. Lifting her shoulders, she shaded her eyes. "I don't *want* to jump rope."

"Why not?"

"Cuz you might pass out."

"You might fall over 'cause your boobs are too big."

"At least I have boobs. *Ha Ha.* All you have are mosquito bites with Band-Aids to cover them up."

"Who wants lunch?" Mom called. We all lined up, except Claire.

Mae yelled, "Watch out," as a teenage boy barreled toward us, almost knocking into Mom. He was looking over his shoulder at the bright red kite trailing behind him. Or Claire.

Dad took the sandwiches from Mom, gave her a quick kiss. "I'll protect you," he said and began handing them out.

"My hero," she said.

Dad said, "Dominus vobiscum," as he handed one to me.

"Ha ha," I said, trying to sound like Claire. This had been Dad's joke for years, even with the mass no longer in Latin. When the priest said those final words at the end of church, Dad had told us it meant, "Time to eat."

Mom felt my forehead. "You feeling okay, Jody?"

"I'm fine," I said, brushing her hand away.

Billy found a stick, turned it into a rifle, pointed it at me and said, "I shoot you."

"Aauugggh, you got me," I cried.

"No, you have to fall down," yelled Billy. I did a spiraling death drop onto the grass. Mae fell the exact same way.

"He didn't shoot you," I said. I hated when she copied me.

"Billy, put down that stick," said Mom. "You're going to poke someone's eye out."

"No, it's mine," he said. "Pow, pow. Now I got you."

"I want to feed the ducks," said Annie.

"Me," yelled Billy, dropping the stick. "Gimme some bread."

Dad pulled out the Wonder Bread bag filled with stale bread. "Casting bread upon the waters," he sang as he took hold of Annie and Billy's hands and wandered down to the murky green pond.

Gripping my sandwich, I followed them to the pier, which jutted out from the grass. I kicked off my Keds and let my feet dangle in the water, splinters from the pier's rough edge poking at my legs. A flotilla of brown-speckled birds swam by, one with a shimmery green teal head and golden amber eyes. *Flotilla: a fleet of boats.* I loved when I found new ways to use one of my words of the day. Two old guys were fishing off the end of the pier.

"Catch anything?" Dad called over to them.

"Nah, they ain't biting," said the man in suspenders.

Dad leaned over and whispered, "Someday I'll tell them why."

I tossed my sandwich crusts in, and Annie, who stood next to me, squealed when a duck plucked up the bread. A young couple pedaled nearby in a paddleboat. "Hey, ducky," Annie scolded. "Don't take the baby duck's food!" When she leaned over the pier, I held tight to her skirt so she wouldn't fall in.

Mom and Mae, lying on the blanket, were eating their sandwiches and chatting. Where had Claire disappeared to? She'd probably followed the kite—or the boy attached to the kite. "Dad! Dad!" I cried. "Tell Annie the duck's names you told me when I was little."

"Let me take a look," Dad said, pretend-scratching his chin. "Well, yes, there he is. Mr. Kennedy."

"Which one?" asked Annie.

"The one with his chest all puffed up. That's him."

"And who is that one?" I said, playing along, pointing at another.

"Pope Sullivan," Dad said. That was a new one. Usually it was Mr. Eisenhower.

"*Joe*," Mom said, pretending shock, a shoestring licorice hanging from her mouth. We hadn't heard her and Mae come up behind us. Dad chuckled.

"And who is that one?" asked Annie.

"Why that one is Margaret."

"Daddy!" Annie said, giggling. "That's not Mommy."

"The most beautiful duck of all," Dad said. Mom rolled her eyes, but she loved it.

When the bread ran out, Dad pulled a flat stone from the collection in his pocket, patted down the cowlick on the back of his head, hooked the edge of the skipper with his index finger, and flicked his wrist. The stone lightly kissed the water, then tap...tap...tap...tap...tap...thunk.

I said, "Not your record, Dad."

Dad held his hands up and shrugged. "I don't want to show off, stringbean!"

Dad handed Billy a flattie. Patting down his hair, like Dad, Billy launched one as hard as he could. It landed with a plop. "Hey, you're scaring the fish off," said the old guy. "Joe! Don't let him stand so close to the edge," Mom called sharply.

"Dad's right here," I said.

Dad gave my hair a tousle, called, "Okay, let's get packed up and head over to the playground." As Dad and Mom walked down the pier, Dad said, "Come on, Billy. Stay with me."

Mom said, "Everyone grab something."

"Wait," Mae said, "I have a little more bread for the ducks," and she tossed in the remaining crust.

Billy was still pitching pebbles, close to the edge, watching them plunk in the water. I laced up my sneakers and grabbed hold of Annie's hand. As I reached for the blanket behind me, I heard Billy shriek and then a splash.

"Joe!" Mom shouted.

I spun and galloped back to the water, so much for my limp.

"Wait for me," yelled Annie, following behind.

Mae, still on the pier, hollered, "I'll save him!" She knelt, holding on to the wooden post with one hand and reaching for Billy with the other. In she went. Dad jumped in, too, the water reaching his chest, and gripped Billy by his shirt. Billy shrieked, then seeing Dad and Mae in the water, yelled, "Swimmie."

"Daddy, here," cried Annie, who leaned over to offer her hand. In she fell! Worried the water was over her head, I jumped in after her, gasping at the cold water. Annie was fine, treading water doggie style, her billowing dress like a floaty.

Giddy, Mae and I splashed each other. Dad tossed Billy into the air. "Toss me, Daddy," said Annie. Dad passed me Billy, then whisked Annie into the air.

"Ready for blast off. Five, four, three, two, one, blast off. Rocket away," he said and tossed Annie into orbit.

"Get outta there, you're spooking the fish!" the fisherman hollered. "Don't you see the sign. No swimming!"

"There haven't been fish here in twenty years," Dad called back.

Claire sauntered onto the pier, a high-and-mighty look on her face.

"Come on! Jump in," I said.

"You are *all* pathetic," she said. "*And* embarrassing me." But I knew she was tempted.

"We had to save Billy," I said, splashing her.

"When in Rome," Mom said. She was grinning, and I watched her leap in the air and bring her legs to her chest, cannonballing into the water.

Claire pulled her Polaroid camera from behind her back. "Say cheese," she said.

4

On Friday we filed into the Edgehaven Middle School multi-purpose room, where just an hour earlier we'd eaten lunch.

Two large television sets on wheeled carts were parked on the stage. Mr. Fryberger, the principal—the Big Mac—cancelled classes to have us all watch the Apollo 13 splashdown. I squiggled in next to Tracy, my butt resting on the ear of the bulldog mascot that was embossed on the cold floor. The rest of our gang—Jennifer, Meg, Kate, and Bettina—plopped down behind us, abuzz with the thrill of getting out of class. I wished everyone would be quiet so we could watch.

"Move in closer," called the Big Mac. "Fit everyone in." Jennifer scooted next to me, giving my hair an affectionate pull. I looked back at Bettina. Perfect skin, silky, long blond hair. Why couldn't I look like her?

I remembered what Mom had said at breakfast. How something had gone wrong with the rocket and now the astronauts were at risk of burning up on re-entry. Like me, Mom loved anything to do with the moon, the planets, the stars. She started blathering on about Laika. Again. She never got over the Russians sticking that poor dog into a capsule and sending her off into outer space. To be honest, I was sad about him too. She said how much she wanted to see the moon up close but was queasy with worry about the astronauts dying. I pictured those astronauts' kids watching the splashdown in their own schools, their faces frozen in terror. For a second, I tried to pretend it was my dad in the space capsule. All eyes would be on me.

Mr. Stan leaned on his broom in the doorway, glowering as usual. We were messing up his newly shined floor.

The television picture shifted from a cloudy purple sky to a large room filled with men in blue-and white short-sleeve dress shirts sitting in front of computers: Mission Control, Houston, Texas! Something had gone wrong, and now they were heading home. Forget landing on the moon, they'd be lucky if they got back to Earth safely.

"Why did they give it such an unlucky number?" I said to Tracy. She wasn't listening. She was too busy flirting with Rhys Finley. She liked his British accent, his *real* British accent.

Walter Cronkite told us that the astronauts only had twenty-four hours of oxygen remaining. My heart raced. No oxygen. Like when I stayed under water too long in the pool, or worse, that time Claire held a pillow over my face and I thought I was going to die and she didn't even care.

Cronkite continued: "Now it's a question of whether we can get the astronauts home safely. It's a grave emergency."

Houston said, "There will be four minutes of reentry blackout. Standing by."

Tracy threw her head back, giving one of her stupid fake laughs.

"Apollo 13 has entered the Earth's atmosphere... They are hitting max G."

"Quiet down. Quiet," came the calls from the teachers stationed around the room.

"Three more minutes of blackout. Stand by."

My palms sweated. My fingernails were destroyed. I lifted my glasses off my face, not wanting to see the crash.

"You look good without your glasses," said Tracy, whisper-shouting in my ear.

"*Really*?" I said. "Now?"

"They are coming in faster than expected," Walter Cronkite told us. "Faster than any spacecraft has returned from space. Just about now they are going through maximum heat. We don't know if the heat shield will hold."

I clutched Tracy's arm.

"They'll be fine," she said, shrugging me off.

"Fine? They could be dead already!" I said. "Look what happened to Laika!"

She raised her lip and scrunched up her nose. "Ca nest pas

grave," said Tracy waving her hand. "They wanted to go. They knew the risks." I ignored her. She was only saying those stupid French words to show off for Rhys. She didn't even like him

Houston said, "Contact lost. We have lost contact." All the men on the screen—bald guys with glasses mostly, like a bunch of science teachers—appeared terrified. One was biting *his* fingers.

"Thirty seconds of blackout with Apollo 13. Ten seconds... five. We will continue to monitor—"

I looked away from the screen. I saw Tracy clutch Rhys's arm. Now she was pretending to be scared. What an actress!

The television camera centered on the blank sky. I held my breath. *Hail Mary full of Grace.* The image shifted back to the ocean, then back to the empty sky. Where were they?

I scooted closer and closer to the front of the room and the TV monitor. The camera panned the vast Pacific Ocean—no astronauts in sight. Nothingness.

Walter Cronkite said, "The time when the astronauts were expected to come out of blackout has come and gone. All we can do is listen and hope."

A sudden silence swept across the room.

Hadn't Mom told me that three astronauts had died three years before? What if Lovell, Swigert, and that other astronaut burned up on re-entry? Their families were at home watching this on TV. Lovell's four kids! My lips started to tremble, so I bit down on them. Hard.

"Houston, do you read me?" Houston kept repeating.

"Okay, put your head down and I'll tell you when you can look," said Tracy. I buried my face into her sleeve. I crossed my fingers. *Hail Mary.*

Then, finally, the whole world heard one of the calm astronauts say, "Okay, Joe."

The control room cheered. Houston said, "We have received signal. *Odyssey*, Houston. Stand by."

"It's okay, you can look now," said Tracy.

A new countdown appeared on the screen. What! They weren't safe! They hadn't splashed down. They only made it through the blackout. Why didn't they stop this? I felt lightheaded, like water was gushing through my brain.

Houston said, "We are awaiting splashdown." Sailors in white caps stood at attention on the deck of the navy's recovery ship. Hundreds of kids in the auditorium counted down the numbers on the clock as they continued to tick, tick, tick down.

On television, the capsule broke into the blue emptiness. I gulped breaths. Tracy gripped my hand and gave a squeeze. Suddenly three red-and-white parachutes opened, butterflies from cocoons. And the capsule floated oh-so-gently down to Earth. Wild cheers exploded in Houston and in our school auditorium. I didn't cheer. I didn't even smile or breathe. What if they had never made it back to Earth? What if they had blown up? How could everyone cheer when the astronauts had all been so close to death?

Houston said, "*Odyssey*, we're glad to see you."

"You're okay, right?" asked Tracy.

"Yeah, they're safe." A calamity avoided. Their families would get to welcome them home.

They let us out early but instead of heading off to the blacktop to hang out with Meg, Jennifer, and Bettina, I said I was going home.

"I'll go with you," said Tracy.

In the kitchen, Mom sat in front of the small TV, smoking a cigarette.

"Jesus, Mary, and Joseph! Did you see all that?" said Mom.

"What the Sputnik!" I said.

Mom looked up, laughing to hear her own words in my mouth. "Are you nikkin' imitating me?"

"Good one, Mom," I said with a groan and eye-roll to Tracy.

Mom said, "I'm just so glad those men made it back. Jim Lovell has *four* kids, so does Fred Haise! That would have been a crime."

"Well, they knew they were taking a risk," I said.

"Ha," said Tracy. "She was a wreck!"

"Well, she comes by it honestly," Mom said. She got up to empty her ashtray, filled from her anxious afternoon.

5

Three days later, there was no near miss for us.

Hours after Dad told us about the accident, about Mom, I tiptoed down the hall, barefoot in my PJs, past Mom's quirkily painted version of the *Mona Lisa* and that curvy old table leg she decoupaged and hung from the wall.

In the kitchen, a bit of moonlight edged in through the yellow lace curtains. Dad took a long gulp of his coffee and stared off into space, exhaling loudly. I coughed from the doorway.

"Stringbean!" Dad startled. "I didn't know you were there." He patted the seat of the chair next to him.

I scooted the orange vinyl seat close enough to smell the cedar and cinnamon of his Old Spice, our Father's Day gift. I said, "Lovell and Swigert's kids got their dad back. How could they go all the way to the moon and come home safely and Mom crashed? It's not fair."

"Some things make no sense," said Dad. His usual combed-down black hair was messy, as if he had been running his fingers through it over and over.

"I heard you tell Uncle Mike that the priest gave Billy last rites. What's last rites?"

Dad spun his wedding ring on his finger. He spoke more softly than usual. "That's a blessing the priest gives to someone sick."

"Could Billy die?"

"No." Dad picked the newspaper up from the table and dropped it on the kitchen floor, and I jumped. "Sorry," he said, as if he hadn't even heard the noise. "No. Billy is *not* dying."

"Is that why you sounded mad telling Uncle Mike?"

"I didn't like Father Sullivan doing that without asking me. Billy didn't need that."

"Did he give Mom last rites?"

"I don't know, Jody." He waited for my eyes to reach his. "Though likely, yes. Look, I'm going to head out. Go see Billy. Grandma and Grandpa will stay till I'm home, but I'll check in when I get back. See if you're asleep."

"Can't I come?"

"No, he'll be sleeping, bean. He needed surgery to repair some deep cuts."

After Dad left, I lay on my bed, staring at the ceiling. I picked up my *Oxford English Dictionary* and flipped through, trying to find a word of the day, but my mind couldn't land anywhere.

I looked up "last rites." It read: *rites administered to a person who is about to die.* An electric current shot through my body. This was not going to be a word I use. *Extreme unction* was when the priest… Keeping my finger on the page, I flipped to the letter *u* to find *unction.*

Claire came into the room, carrying the photo of Mom from the living room side table—Mom in a shimmery cream dress and a corsage on her left wrist. Claire placed the photo on the dresser next to her and plopped down on the bed, which squeaked under the sudden weight. Mom smiled down on her. I sat up. Claire's eyes were glassy, her face raw and red. She had been crying since this afternoon, making me feel guilty that I wasn't. If I let myself cry, it would mean it was really true. Then I would need Mom and she wouldn't be here.

"Why'd it happen?" I asked.

"*Why?*" Claire snapped. "There's not a reason. Why do you think it's called an *accident?*"

"Sometimes she drove fast," I said.

"Don't blame her! It wasn't her fault." Claire yanked her shirt over her head. It was the pink bra today, her boobs burgeoning over the cups. *Burgeoning: to grow or increase rapidly.* She climbed back into bed and rolled over to face the wall. I shut off the light.

"I know," I said, sounding sorry. "But Billy. He's so little. He won't understand. He'll think we left him there."

Claire moaned, "I can't believe she's gone." Muffled words

came from beneath her blanket. "We didn't even get to say goodbye."

I pulled my pillow over my ears, trying to silence Claire's sobbing. What if this was all my fault? I cringed, remembering that night, last month, when I'd snapped at Mom.

I'd drawn the short pencil in a round of hide-and-seek, and everyone scattered, Mae and Annie falling over each other trying get to the best hiding spot. Claire moseyed along, as if she were completely uninterested in this silly game, then I saw her grab a couple of Mom's shortbread cookies and rush off to hide. I closed my eyes and counted silently.

Billy, an astronaut helmet on his head, scampered after them. Mom gave him that helmet. Sock-footed on the hardwood floors, unable to get traction, unable to stop, Billy started to slide, then the weight of the helmet thrust him forward. Finally, at the end of the hall, he crashed into the wall, jostling the crucifix that hung overhead, setting Jesus atilt.

"You're okay, Billy," said Mom, pulling off his helmet. "Go and find your hiding spot."

I covered my eyes and began to count in the loudest voice I could muster. "Three, two, ONE. Here I come!"

I took off down the hallway, making sure to call out, "Where's bubbala? Where can he be?" Anytime we played hide-and-seek we knew where to find Billy.

"I can't find him anywhere!" I called.

Annie, tiny for her age, was the easiest to find, a bit of her rounded belly and chubby bottom sticking out from under her bunk bed, along with Roo, his bottom sticking out, too.

"I found you, pork chop," I shouted.

Delighted to be found, Annie pointed up to the top bunk. I yanked back the blanket, and freckle-faced Mae popped up.

"Annie, you told!" Mae said.

"No, I didn't," Annie said, her hand guarding her mouth, always proof she was covering up a lie.

"Jody, you don't find me," hollered Billy from the hall bathroom. "Jody, Jody!"

Claire was standing in the hall closet, our phone stretched to the length of its cord. Her voice was all breathy. James. She put a finger to her lips. I'd never tell.

"Could he be in *here*?" I said, leaping into the bathroom.

There stood Billy, his tiny fingers covering his eyes, leaving plenty of space for him to peek out and watch me not seeing him. Recently turned three, he believed if he couldn't see me, then I couldn't see him.

"Nope, he's not in the bathtub."

He spilled over in giggles. "Here I am!" he yelled, and climbed out of the tub.

That left Mom. And Mom always hid in the same place. Her bedroom closet door was slightly ajar. "I know you're in there, Mom. I smell licorice."

I drew back the hangers, parting the line of clothes. There she stood in the back corner, putting the last strand of black licorice into her mouth.

"You're it," I said, and pushed aside the clothes for Mom to come out.

We gathered at the end of the hallway, near the door that led to the basement rec-room. Mae, still pouting, gave Annie a poke. With a stern eye on Mae, Mom started the countdown.

As Mom counted, eyes closed, she was holding on to the brass doorknob of the basement behind her back, then for some reason she leaned forward, unwittingly pulling the door open. Spotting the gap, I seized my chance and scooted behind her through the narrow opening. I tiptoed down the remaining stairs and headed for Mom's sewing room.

I heard Mom yell, "Five, four, three, two, one. Ready or not here I come," and the basement door closed. Brushing aside a container of Christmas ornaments, some puffs of dust and an old shoebox filled with bows and ribbons, I burrowed in, wrapping myself up in one of Aunt Sheila's hand-crocheted afghans. I tried to make myself small, like a fox in a den. The smell of mothballs pricked at my nose.

A squeal broke through the silence. Through the wall vent I heard Mom shout, "Annie, I see you." Two more shrieks followed, for Mae and Claire. I was going to win!

Upstairs, Mae called, "Jody, come out, come out wherever you are." But I was not giving up.

Minutes passed, with no one coming for me. I scrambled out of my hiding spot, allowing my eyes a few moments to adjust to the light, and climbed the stairs to get a better listen.

"Maybe she's in the basement," Claire said.

"No, she can't be," Mom said with certainty. "I'd been standing right in front of this door counting when everyone was hiding. I didn't move once."

Annie said, "Maybe she was stolen."

"Jody. I want Jody," Billy cried.

I was Tom Sawyer hiding in the back of the church listening in on his own funeral. Maybe they really thought I was gone for good. Mom would start weeping, realizing that all along she had loved me more than Claire or Mae, who Mom said was "the best cuddler." The last time I sat on Mom's lap, she said, "Ouch, Jody, you're hurting me. Your bones sure do stick out." Those words still stung.

"Jody!" Mom yelled. "That girl is too clever by half," she said, and she sounded annoyed.

I returned to my hiding spot, next to Mom's sewing machine, when the basement door finally opened and footsteps came down the stairs. I imagined Mom's shock and amazement when she opened the sewing room door and out I popped. Instead, I heard the TV turn on.

Annie said, "We need to find Jody." I had wanted to win, now I wanted to be found.

And Mom said, "I'm done looking. She'll come out when she's good and ready."

I could starve to death down here, and she didn't care! Mom would find me shriveled up in the corner. Dead. Then she'd be sorry.

"It's chilly down here," said Mom. "Who wants a blanket?" She'd forgotten all about me.

The sewing room door opened, and Mom clapped a hand to her chest. "Sweet baby Jesus!"

"You gave up! You didn't care if I died!" I pushed past her.

When I got to the basement stairs, I grabbed the bannister and hissed, "Well, I don't care if you die either!"

If only I could press rewind, like a film on our school projector, take back those words.

Billy. He had to be all right. God, I promise I'll be good if you make Billy okay. I lay in bed, staring at the ceiling, then stroked the rocket indentation on the trim next to me, but it was no help.

I was still awake when I heard Dad arrive home.

The doorknob slowly turned, light shining in. I sat up as Dad slipped in and sat on the side of my bed and patted my leg, whispering though Claire's snores.

"Can't sleep, stringbean?"

"Is Billy okay?"

"Getting better."

"Can I go see him tomorrow? He's there all alone."

"He's in good hands, bean. You get some sleep, now."

He squeezed my palm three times, a secret message, *I love you*, one squeeze for each word. He leaned over and kissed my forehead, his cheek scratchy against mine.

The next afternoon, friends and relatives and people I'd never seen before gathered at our house. They brought their kids and a lot of food: platters, casseroles, Jell-O molds. Father Sullivan, in his black frock, arrived in a cloud of holiness, and he patted Mae on the head like a dog. Why was he here? Then he patted his big belly. Dad ushered him to the buffet.

A gang of us headed to Claire's and my bedroom to play team Sorry: Claire, Mae, three of my cousins, Toby, Jesse, and Carol, along with Tracy, who brought me her favorite shell, a big sacrifice, and Claire's best friend, Michelle, who brought her the new Beatles album, *Abbey Road*. We had set up a card table in the center of my bedroom, two chairs to a side. When we drew cards to pair up, I picked a twelve, the highest number, and chose Toby. Toby, two years older, had big soft brown eyes and sandy hair in coils like springs. He had an enormous bag of

M&M's and gave me all the reds, knowing I liked them best—and him. Was it kinda creepy to like-like a cousin? Well, it's not like we were getting married!

We were all singing along with John Lennon: "Oh, darling, I'll never make it alone." It was strange, as if my bedroom, this one room in the house, had time-traveled back a week and no one knew Mom had died.

We were our usual frenzy of competition, maybe more so. Drawing a *Sorry* card, I picked up Jessie and Michelle's pawn and waved it in their faces with glee, "Oh, I'm so soorrreee!" I mocked. With three pawns at Home, Toby and I were in the lead. I was lost in the game, and I expected Mom to come in at some point and tell us all to cool it. Then I remembered all over again.

Someone farted. "Ewww, Jody passed gas," said Claire. The gang all laughed. Was it okay to laugh?

"Did not," I said.

"Person who smelt it dealt it," said Tracy.

"You're so funny," said Mae. She was Tracy's *Sorry* partner and kept hanging on her arm and every word.

"I'm starving," I said. "What if I go get some food and bring it back?"

"What if Father Sullivan ate it all?" Claire said.

"Bring me back a sandwich," said Jesse. "Roast beef if they have it."

"Toby," I said, "you can take the turn for us. But if it's not a clear move, don't go without me."

"I won't go anywhere without you," Toby said, giving me a wink.

"Tell me if James is out there," said Claire.

As soon as I left the bedroom, the hallway felt like falling through the looking glass, everything distorted and strange, lots of dead ends, no clear way out. I flew down the steps, two at a time. A smoky haze filled the house and even though my feet were on the ground I was disoriented, floaty, like I was walking on that cloud of smoke. Someone was in the bathroom, someone waiting to be next. The living room was packed with grown-ups puffing cigarettes, eating, drinking, yakking—kitchen and dining room too. I saw my science teacher. I saw Dad's worker, Al. Tracy's mom, Amelie, makeup streaked with tears. There were babies in arms. I hated them all. No James, no James slouching anywhere. Dad was whispering with Dr. Katz. Something welled up in me, like the sudden thrust forward in time had scrambled my brain.

Suddenly I shouted, "Just get out!"

A hush fell over the room. I tore off my glasses so I couldn't make out any more of the faces. I heard the clatter of silverware and dishes and felt an arm across my shoulder. It was Mrs. Geiger in a black dress, with her thick fake eyelashes all clumpy from crying. I felt the sweat under her armpits. "Honey," she said, "your mother is in heaven with God."

I shouted again: "Yeah, right! Heaven is just a fancy word for fantasy."

"God bless her," said Father Sullivan. Then, "God bless you, child. You're overwrought."

With that, everyone went back to talking and eating. I pushed my way to the dining room, my head down, my heart pounding in my chest. I took the liquor bottles off the side tray, picked up a plate and piled it high with American cheese, cold-cuts, and slices of Wonder Bread and filled another with cookies and brownies. A neighbor mom reached for my free hand. "I'm so sorry you lost your mother. She was a wonderful woman," she said.

"We didn't lose her," I barked, leaving the laden tray on the counter.

I rushed outside, bright sunlight, beautiful air. The thick grass pricked at my bare feet. I paced the front lawn like a Bronx Zoo lion, collected some small white pebbles from around Mom's crabapple tree, whipped them with force at the garage. It was satisfying to hit the strike zone, the center panel of the door, and hear the pinging sound—more pebbles, more strikes, and before long the pebbles were gone.

Tracy and Toby were upstairs playing Sorry! Waiting for me. They were probably starving, wondering what happened to me.

Let them wonder, I thought. I couldn't go back. Mom was gone.

On the sidewalk lay the *Edgehaven Record*, neatly rolled, delivered by stupid little Willie Roorbach who lived up the street. There were always pictures of friends in there, maybe Charlie— the soccer team had won regionals. I unfolded it and—oh no, right on the front page, there it was. Maybe I knew. A picture of our new Country Squire, glass shattered, hood smashed in, an enormous accordion pressed closed. I could almost smell those dark-red leather seats. Caption: *Woman, thirty-six, killed in Hampton Hills*. Subcaption: *Toddler survives*.

According to Sergeant Paul Manger, Mrs. Moran was driving south on Rosedale Avenue when she collided head-on with a delivery van. The van driver suffered only minor injuries.

"Oh, sweetie."

I jumped.

It was the new neighbor, house next door to the Geiger's, all bun tight in a white nurse's uniform. I hadn't met her yet, only heard of her. Her ID tag read: Juliette Landau.

"You don't want to see that," she said, reaching for the paper.

"Mommy," I said. Pressed inside that jagged wreck.

Mrs. Landau took the paper from me and I leaned into her arms, steadying myself.

"I know," she said. "Sweetie, I know."

I staggered over to the crabapple tree and barfed and barfed again, a warm hand at my back.

"Let me get someone," she said.

The next morning was Wednesday, not that it mattered. All the days were the same. No smell of vanilla. No syrup warming on the stove. No stack of eggs on the counter that Mom had cracked in half with one hand. No French toast. No stinky cigarette smoke. No Billy begging to play. No Country Squire in the driveway.

I could read in peace, the only thing I could do. I slipped into the hall and heard a sob coming from my parents' bedroom. Peering through the left ajar, I saw Dad standing at Mom's closet, her clothes draped over his arms, others strewn across the bed. "Maggie. Maggie," he moaned, over and over again.

I couldn't watch. I returned to my bedroom, opened *In Cold Blood*, and started reading: Mountains. Hawks wheeling in a white sky. Mountains. Hawks… The words repeated, over and over.

Finally, Dad called, "Gang, come to breakfast."

Book in hand, I crept down the hall, down the stairs, to the kitchen, where I sat in my usual seat.

"Morning, stringbean," Dad said.

"Hey, Dad," I kept my eyes glued to the pages of my book. Mountains. Hawks. I didn't want him to know that I had seen him sobbing like that.

"How you holding up, kiddo?" he asked. I wanted to say, *How are you holding up?*

He flipped the eggs, from the pan, right on to a piece of toast. I'd never seen him do that before. "Want some eggs? Toast?" he asked as he turned the heat up under the kettle.

"No, cereal's okay," I said, still not looking up, pretending to be lost in my book.

"Always reading," he said.

"Yeah," I said. I placed *In Cold Blood* on my lap, below the tabletop. The story of an entire family bludgeoned to death didn't seem like the way to go. I headed him off at the pass: "What happens today?"

"Well," he said, "I have to go to the funeral parlor to take care of some things."

I was about to ask him what things when Claire wandered in brushing her hair.

"Claire Bo-Bear," Dad said, attempting a hug.

Claire stiffened, wriggled out of his arms. "I'm brushing my hair!" she protested.

"I was just telling Jody that I need to go the funeral home. Grandma and Grandpa will be here soon."

"What time is the wake?" asked Claire.

"It will be two to five and again after dinner."

"I'm going to both," said Claire.

"I don't think it's a good idea," said Dad.

"Well, I do."

"Claire, I'm sorry, but you don't want to remember Mom that way."

Claire slammed her hair brush against the countertop. "Don't say what I want!"

Dad stumbled back, then folded his hands in front of his chest. "I talked to people at the funeral parlor who know about these things and they said I shouldn't bring you kids."

"Well, I'm not a kid. And neither is Jody." She was dragging me into her fight and when I didn't answer, Claire said more strongly, "Are you?"

I shrugged. I hated not taking her side, but seeing Dad sobbing had scared me. I didn't want to make anything harder for him.

And the idea of seeing Mom in a casket was even scarier.

"Claire, that's not how you want to remember Mom." His voice so soft I could hardly hear him. "You girls can choose how you want to remember her."

Dad won that argument. Maybe Claire hadn't wanted to win. She nabbed a piece of Dad's toast off his plate and dug in.

While Dad was at the wake and Grandma watched us, Mae, Claire, and I played our twentieth round of Yahtzee at the dining room table. Annie sat nearby, orange crayon in hand, her tongue sticking out of the left side of her mouth, the way it always did when she was concentrating. Her hair was filled with tiny colorful plastic barrettes, each clasping a tuft of hair, making her look like a crazy person. There was no convincing her to take them out.

"Claire, quit shaking the dice so much," I said. "It's *so* annoying."

"What, like this?" she said, rattling it as hard as she could near my face.

"Cut it out," I said, pushing her hand away. "You are such a, such a v*exation*." *Vexation: something that causes annoyance.*

Claire laughed cruelly.

"Stop fighting," said Mae. "It's my turn."

Grandma Moran was puttering around in the kitchen. She had come home early from the wake to get dinner started. "Girls," she said appearing in the doorway. "Girls, girls!" It was strange to see her wearing Mom's apron, the one with ruffles along the bottom edge, doing what Mom would be doing. "I'll have one of the casseroles from yesterday warmed up and ready for you in ten minutes."

I groaned. I hated leftovers. I hated casseroles.

Claire said, "Can't we order a pizza?"

"Nonsense!" Grandma said, waving a dishtowel in the air. "No pizza!" She said the word *pizza* like it was a booger hanging on the end of her finger that she was trying to shake off. "We have perfectly nice food right here. We don't want it to go to waste." Grandma only ate "American food." Dad thought he was being adventurous when he nibbled the crust off one of our slices of pizza.

"What should I draw now?" asked Annie.

"How about a house?" I offered.

"I already did that! See? Here's my house. And here's Daddy, Mommy, Claire, Jody, Mae, Billy, me, and *Roo!*" she said, happily pointing out each of the stick figures pictured.

An anxious look passed between Claire and me.

"Why is Mommy so big?" Claire asked. "Like seven times bigger than Dad?"

Annie began to cry. "When's Mommy coming back?" Mae started erasing the numbers on her Yahtzee pad, making them neater.

"That's a great picture Annie," I said, trying to distract her. "You gave me beautiful big eyes."

The neighbor's dog started barking, then two more dogs down the street started howling.

"What a racket!" Grandma called from the kitchen. I wasn't sure if she meant the dogs or us.

Keys in the front door jangled. It was Dad. "Hey, girls. Hello, Mother."

He fell into a dining room chair and slumped over. Not his usual soldierly posture. Grandma rested her hand on his shoulder. "Son," she said, "can I get you a nice cup of tea? It's a comfort."

"No, thanks, Mother. I'm okay. Maybe some water." It looked like it took all his energy to speak. Grandma scurried to the kitchen and returned with a glass. "How's Billy doing?" she asked, so very softly.

Dad gulped down the entire glass and then cleared his throat. I could see he was weighing what we kids should hear. "Better. Better. They moved him out of intensive care."

"What's *infensive* care?" Annie said.

"Not infensive. *Intensive* care is where they take extra good care of little kids, like Billy," I said. "To make them all better."

Before he could answer, I said, "Can I go too? Please."

Dad looked cornered. "Maybe. I'll check with the hospital in the morning, but, yes, maybe. Mother, maybe you and Dad can go after lunch, then I can take the three older girls over after the afternoon calling hours. If you can watch Annie."

Grandma patted Dad's shoulder and returned to the kitchen.

"I wanna come too," Annie said.

Dad scooped Annie up, sat her on his lap and planted a kiss on the top of her head. "Show me what you're drawing, pork chop." I wanted to crawl into his lap too.

Annie said, "It's us, see."

"I see that. That's a very good drawing of our family. And Mom looks very tall and nice. We can put it up on the refrigerator."

Mae was still erasing her score card. Without looking up, she said, "Dad, what did Mom look like at the wake?"

"Peaceful," he said, no doubt as planned. "Like she's asleep."

"Why do they call it a wake, anyway?" I said.

"What was she wearing?" Mae asked.

Claire was suddenly all attention.

"Well, sweetie. I…well…" This answer he had not planned. "I brought them some of her clothes. Her white blouse and the black skirt that she likes…liked…"

Someone had dressed Mom. Dressed her dead body. Claire said, "You should have let us pick."

"Wait," I said. "Did the funeral guys see her *naked*?"

Dad's mouth started to open, then closed tight. He shook his head, as if he were trying to clear the fog from his brain. His eyes filled with tears.

"Don't ask stupid questions," Claire said.

Dad took a deep breath. "Girls, *please*. Stop sparring."

"Is she wearing her glasses?" asked Mae.

"Where is she?" asked Annie.

He was looking out the window, like Mom might, any minute, pull up in the Country Squire. I broke the silence. "How will we get to the funeral?" I suddenly saw myself like Eloise at the Plaza Hotel, chauffeured by a driver in a black cap, black suit and tie, bowing to me as he opened the car door. "Thank you, Jeeves," I'd say as I sat on a velvety, cushioned seat.

"Oh, I don't know. So many details. I'm talking to the funeral home," Dad said.

"Don't they sometimes have limousines?" I tried to seem all casual, like this thought had just occurred to me. I opened the refrigerator to grab some milk.

"Why does that matter?" He sounded genuinely confused.

"All *you* care about is the limo," said Claire, spitting out the words.

A sick, hot shame wrapped around me like a heavy woolen coat: "No," I said. "I was going to say don't get one."

"Well, we will need a large car," Dad said, not mentioning what we all knew—that our station wagon was gone, smashed. "We'll need to go from the church to the cemetery, all of us. I'm not sure how that will all work."

I noticed he hadn't changed his clothes. Sweat stains spread out under his arms. His face was unshaven, his eyes puffy and red. His voice had a gruff, rough sound. He rubbed his face, then said, "I'll figure it all out. We'll figure it all out."

Mom was the one who figured these things out. Dance class, softball practice, school play, who goes where. But Mom was dead and it was her funeral we had to figure out.

6

Stupid Easter bunnies with baskets of colorful eggs hopped along the tiled gray walls of the hospital corridor, trying to make the place look jolly. Easter was over, you idiots, I wanted to say. We waited at a certain door till a nurse ushered us in, whisking aside the pale curtain. And there was my three-year-old brother, with his tiny face covered in a hundred jagged cuts, his eyes swollen shut, cheeks dead white, bandages wrapped around his head and another under his jaw, tubes sprouting from his chubby little arms, one hooked up to a bag of clear liquid, the other to an array of machines, pinging and whooshing. Poor Billy.

"Hi, bubbala," I said.

He squealed at the sound of my voice, reached for me to pick him up, but there was no moving him through that tangle of tubes and wires.

I ruffled the patch of Billy's unbandaged hair, still the color of ripe apricots, and pulled *Green Eggs and Ham* from my bag. "Look what I have for you," I said. Heat rose up off his soft skin.

"Boom. Boom. Crash," Billy cried, wanting me to know something, the something that had happened to him. Like a punch in my gut, the image from the newspaper, the smashed car, flashed in my head.

Dad's face drained of color. "Now honey," he said.

Claire opened the Hess firetruck that we bought in the hospital gift shop and showed Billy how the ladders moved. I wished I had brought him his fireman's hat.

"I want Mommy," Billy said. And he said it again, and again, louder and louder, until he sounded like a fire truck.

Mae started to cry.

"Mommy can't be here," I said. It was like a refrain in my

head from somewhere, something I'd told myself when I felt she'd forgotten me. When had I started that?

A gray-haired nurse hurried in, pursed her red-painted lips as she injected medicine into the tubes in Billy's arms. I grew dizzy, as if the liquid was seeping into my arm. The hospital was weirdly familiar, especially the fear of being here alone.

"Mommy," Billy cried. And he said it again, but more softly. "Billy-boy," Dad kept repeating, as he rubbed Billy's head. "Bubbala boy, it's okay, Daddy's here."

That line, too, I'd heard in a hospital before. In a few seconds, Billy was asleep, and the nurse nodded, ushering us out. Visiting hours would have to wait.

I was glad Claire took Mae's hand so I could take Dad's, and we lagged a little behind as they darted to the elevator. "I feel like it's me here, when I was in the hospital," I said.

"That was a different hospital," Dad said.

There was the Madeline book, where she has her appendix out, and I could see myself on the page of that book. I was puzzling through the confusion about what I'd read or lived.

Dad said, "We were so worried. Mom was about to have Annie. We all worried it was something worse." Then, as if this explained everything, he said, "That's when I taught you how to play Rummy."

The next morning my sisters and I stood outside the church in outfits Mom had made—a three-quarter sleeve dress for me with blue, green, and gray stripes and two big blue buttons on each sleeve and both pockets. I loved pockets. When Mom showed me the dress, weeks earlier, I told her I didn't like it, that the fabric was scratchy. Maybe I'd said I despised it. I wished I'd said I loved it, even if I was lying. Against my neck I could feel the label she'd sewn into the collar that read, *Made Expressly for You by Mom*. She had other labels that she affixed if she made something for a friend or neighbor; those said *Made Expressly for You by Maggie*.

A perfect day, clear blue sky, soft breezes. Unfair. Wrong.

Dad accepted hugs and handshakes from everyone that passed, his cousin Eddie, Dr. and Mrs. Katz, and our pediatrician, Dr. Hamilton. There were lots of people I had never seen before. I noticed the gash on Dad's chin. He must have nicked himself shaving. Father Sullivan approached and put an arm around his shoulder. Dad shrugged him off, not wanting to hear any of his words of sympathy. Mom would have killed him!

As people entered the church, I kept a look out for kids from Edgehaven. It would be weird to see them in school next week after all of this. Tracy gave me a long hug. When she stepped back I saw she was wearing the blue plaid dress Mom sewed for her. A few tears came when she took my hand and touched it to her sleeve. The Geiger family arrived. Claire's eyes brightened. James gave her a nod and a sad wave.

Mrs. Porter, Mae's best friend Lisa's mom, approached. Her pancake foundation was as thick and cracked as one of the decoupage projects Mom used to do. She patted Mae's arm and said, "She's in a better place." A better place! What did that say about us?

Charlie appeared. His mother was holding Cynthia's hand. He smiled shyly—perfect white teeth—and handed me a Hershey's Easter kiss. A kiss!

The hearse pulled up to the curb. There were no stretch limos. Four men in black suits and sunglasses slowly slid out the casket, a long rectangular white box. They looked all serious; two of them like they were about to cry. It wasn't their nikkin' mom who had died.

My eyes followed, as they placed the box on a stretcher and wheeled it up toward the beige stone church. What if they'd closed the casket and she really wasn't dead? What if they made a mistake and she was in there with no air, food, or water? She'd be like one of the astronauts, trapped in a wooden capsule, tapping on the cover, trying to get out. Mom, I thought. Mommy.

The church bell chimed. My uncles and two neighbor friends of Dad's latched on to the handles, lifted the casket off the stretcher, and carried it inside. Dad signaled for us to follow. Every row in the church was filled. Our whole town was there. There were hundreds, maybe millions of people. With all eyes upon me, I felt an uncomfortable pleasure as I marched solemnly behind the casket. A few of my teachers were there, even some from elementary school. Jennifer, Meg, Kate, and Bettina, of course. And all the neighbor moms, all sorry for me. Grandma Cupcakes joined us from a side door. She was Mom's mom, and didn't mind the nickname. She put her hands on our backs. The casket holders stopped at the end of the church aisle, letting Mom rest on the wooden platform. I inched closer, in case she was tapping or breathing. But all I could hear was the whooshing in my ears.

Grandma Cupcakes let out a moan from somewhere deep inside her. Her legs buckled. She reached for the casket to break her fall. Dad caught her before she hit the floor. Her daughter was in there. I looked away, fearing for a moment that I, too, would collapse.

We settled into the front row bench, Grandma Cupcakes at the far end of the shiny pew, then me, Claire, Mae, Annie, and Dad on the aisle. Claire took my hand—maybe the first time ever—and squeezed. Huge flowers of every variety and color lined the altar. The lilies were so perfumey, making me sick.

"I hope we don't need to carry Grandma out too," whispered Claire.

"That's terrible," I said, but laughed anyway. Claire shook my hand away.

I turned around, scanned the room, and spotted Charlie on the other side, halfway down. For a moment our eyes locked, then his mother bowed his head for him. I turned around, smiling.

I watched as Grandma Cupcakes pulled out a hankie along with her red rosary, her fingers hesitantly touching the beads. Usually Grandma's fingers rolled quickly along the row of gems, making that repetitive clicking sound. Today they were silent. I started tapping my nails on the pew, trying to see if I could make that familiar sound. With each click of my nail, I recited,

Hail Mary, Full of Grace. Maybe this was all happening for some important reason. Maybe I was meant to do something really valuable, something God was preparing me for, something big. Like the Kennedys: they had lots of tragedies and then did important things.

I pulled the kiss from my purse.

Claire clamped my arm so tight, I nearly yelped. "How can you be eating chocolate! Mom would *kill* you."

"Charlie gave it to me."

"Even worse!"

Dad leaned forward, put his fingers to his lips.

I popped the kiss in my mouth, letting it slowly melt. Staring straight ahead, I felt everyone's gaze on the back of my neck, heard weeping and sniffling, and protesting toddlers. No Billy. Dad had said he might bring him home later today. He said little kids heal really fast. But he only said he *might*.

Annie climbed over Mae, who was hanging on every word, wiggling in between me and Claire, trying to keep her feet up high so she could admire her new patent leather shoes, bright white.

I spun the button on my sleeve, barely listening as Father Sullivan recited all the familiar prayers. When he finished, some gray-haired lady sang about returning home to God. Annie sat there making up her own words. "Return ye home, good dog!"

When would the funeral part start? I snapped to attention when Father Sullivan said Mom's name, deep tones rising: Margaret Louise Moran. Dad spread his long arms across our backs. *Maggie.*

Astonished, I watched as Father Sullivan slowly made his way down from the altar. The steps were covered with large white lilies. Jesus hung on the cross above. Was Father Sullivan coming to us?

He stopped at the end of our pew, arms folded. Mae stiffened as if preparing for a blow. I stared at the missal lying open across my wrinkled dress. I was in danger of crying. I will not. I will not. I will not, I told myself—a new prayer. I didn't want to hear the priest say that Mom was dead. I didn't want anyone to say that. If Mom was dead, gone, all the happiness would be sucked out of our atmosphere. I closed my eyes, trying to will him back up to the altar. I ran my hands up and down my thighs. My eyes started to fill, and I feared they might overflow, so I tried to think of the names of the planets in order. With each planet, I gave my blue button another spin. Mercury. Spin. Venus. Spin. Earth. Spin. Mars. Spin.

Before I reached Pluto, Father Sullivan clasped his hands, slowly moving his watery blue gaze over each of us. I could smell incense. I was so happy to be at the far end of the pew. Finally, he spoke. "Your mother, she was a beautiful flower."

My mother was not!

"Your mother, she was such a very special flower—one of the most special. She was so special, your mother, that God picked her for Himself. God takes the most beautiful and precious flowers for His garden. To have with Him at home, in heaven."

Through my teeth I messaged Claire: "Home!" I twisted that button.

"So, he goes around crashing cars," Claire hissed back.

"Yeah, with babies in them," I said.

"What a load of crap!" Claire said, her voice rising.

Father Sullivan stepped back as if he'd been slapped. His jowls quivered.

"Claire, enough," Dad said calmly.

Father Sullivan recovered—everyone watching—raised his hand to give a blessing.

Suddenly, the button on my sleeve popped off. I cried out as it dropped to the floor and rolled under the pew. Mom had sewn it on! I slid to the floor, crawled under the pew, retrieved it. I stared at it in my sweaty palm.

"Mom," I cried, so everyone in the church could hear. I didn't even care. Who would sew my button back on?

Father Sullivan blessed Mae, blessed my father, blessed Grandma, pointedly did not bless me or Claire, muttered a few words about Billy. "Our dear Billy is a bud that will get to blossom."

Back at the altar he looked out across the congregation—we Morans were no longer there, not to him—his job was done. "The Mass is ended," he atoned. "Go in peace. Amen."

"Amen," echoed from the pews.

"Bunch of sheep," Claire said. She clutched my hand again, something between a pinch and a caress. "Baa. Baa. Baa."

I followed along, "Baa, baa, baa."

Dad squeezed both our necks, guided us out, but he was suppressing a smile too.

Graveyard guys in overalls stood off to the side, shovels ready, a high pile of earth nearby. The smell of raw dirt. Dad encircled us in his arms and led us to our spot beside the gaping hole. Mourners crowded up around us. My dress itchy against my skin and missing a button. I watched the four men open the back doors of their hearse and, once again, drag the casket out. The one in front grunted, and in unison they lifted Mom and carried her over to the nearby tarp.

Father Sullivan followed her into the hush, coughed a few times, gave me and Claire a long look, recited some prayers, first Latin, then English. I wasn't going to listen to him ever again, never. I stared at the casket and made humming sounds in my head like I do at the scariest parts of scary movies.

Using long black ropes, the black suits from the funeral home inched the long box into the ground. The hole was so deep. If someone fell in they would keep falling forever. A black hole. Once in, you never escape. *Nihility: Nothingness, nonexistence.* It might suck me in. Not wanting to see Mom reach the bottom, I stared off into the distance, my eyes roaming the tree tops and blue sky, checking for any sign of her spirit floating up to heaven, but all I saw were some birds hurrying away.

Aunt Sheila, Mom's sister, handed me a red rose and pointed to the hole. I looked down at the stretch of grass between my black shoes, the mud on the tips, and the dark wall of bare earth off to the side. She'd suffocate under all that dirt. I was afraid to approach, afraid to stand too close. For a moment a gush of spit filled my mouth, and I feared that I might barf, but I pushed it back.

I retrieved the blue button from my pocket. Slowly I stepped forward up to the edge. As I was about to toss the rose and button in, Claire laid her hand on my arm, startling me. My front leg slipped out from under me and into the hole. I screamed, flung the flower, flung the button, and they fell, and fell.

"What the hell?" Dad cried, but caught my arm, pulling me to safety. Father Sullivan shook his head, raised his eyes to the heavens.

Claire laughed into her hand.

"Mom!" Annie cried out. "I want Mom."

Mae started to cry.

Mud covered my bare leg and dress—just perfect! I thought. Behind the shocked faces, I saw my cousin Toby, his eyes on mine at last. He was cuter than Charlie, cuter by far, but he was my cousin.

"I will talk to you later," Dad said to Claire.

But he wouldn't. We knew he wouldn't.

The next day was just as awful as the funeral. Was every day from now on going to be heartbreaking? Dad drove up to the house in the Moran Tile and Marble van. He came around the passenger side and carefully gathered Billy out of the seat, wrapped in the blue blanket Mom had spent weeks knitting. Billy's bare feet and sailboat pajamas stuck out from the bottom. We all watched from the dining room, my nose, Claire's, and Mae's pressed flat against the window.

Dad carried Billy in through the screen door. The side of his face was swathed in a white bandage. His thumb and blanket were in his mouth. Mom wouldn't be happy seeing him do that. She'd gotten him to stop months before. He smiled crookedly as the rest of us surrounded him, patting him, tousling his hair, gingerly tickling.

"Hi, bubbala," I said, hoping he'd come to me.

But he shook his head, scanned the room. Suddenly his face

collapsed. "Mommy," he cried. Then louder: "Mommy!" He flailed, he screamed, "No! No!"

I worried his surgery stitches would rip out.

"I'm not leaving," Dad said. "I'm here."

Annie held Roo out—a big sacrifice—but Billy whacked it away.

"So sweet, Annie," I told her. "Billy's too upset right now. Maybe he'll like Roo later. Don't be sad."

But we were all sad. Annie began to cry, then Mae. Billy batted at Dad with his tiny fists, then batted his own head, banging and banging. Claire held his arms down so he wouldn't pull off his bandages. Annie threw Roo on the ground, then herself.

I picked up Annie off the floor, heaved myself onto the couch, held her against my chest: "I'm here, sweetie. I'm here."

"Mommy," Annie cried. "I want Mommy. Where's Mommy?"

"Mommy," Mae cried.

I, too, thought, *Mommy*, even as I hugged Mae.

Claire said, "Oh, Annie bananie. Were you expecting Mommy? Not just Billy?"

I said, "Annie, remember Mommy is up in heaven now." And hated myself.

"She's one of God's flowers," Claire said evenly. I was her audience of one.

Suddenly I knew how to speak. "Yes, God's favorite flower. He wants her there in heaven."

"And Billy is his bud," Claire said.

"Girls," Dad said.

"I want her home," Annie demanded, crying harder. "Get Daddy's ladder and get her down."

Suddenly Billy went limp, like a rag doll, sniffling and gulping air, his thumb moving in and out of his mouth.

"Please, girls," Dad said. "Please be grown-ups here. You and Claire. And take the little girls up for a game of Chutes and Ladders. I'm going to lie down with Billy."

"Jody," Billy cried, raising his arms for me to pick him up.

"I'll take him," I said, lowering Annie to the floor.

Dad looked like a wounded soldier, relieved to be leaving the battlefield, even if he were grievously wounded. Claire hugged Billy hard, then harder, all the rebellion flooding out of her. Dad picked up Annie, carried her to the kitchen, Mae under the other arm, Claire following along. I carefully carried Billy to his bedroom. He felt lighter than before the hospital. The warmth of his body radiated against me and sped up my heart. I didn't want to let go.

Lowering the crib railing, I rested Billy on the mattress and lay down next to him, my face nestled in his neck. I bristled at the gauzy smell, hospital smell too, and some vestigial smell of Mommy. *Vestigial: A very small remnant of something that was once present.* I never thought I'd have to use that word of the day.

"I won't leave you," I said. "I'm here." And I kept saying it. I remembered when I was eight and spent a week in the hospital, Mom left me. I thought she had forgotten me. She was having another baby, Annie, and couldn't come be with me. I was always fighting that jealousy, but I came home to Mom and Billy didn't.

Across the room, Billy's hat stand cast a shadow over his bed. His recent favorite, the astronaut helmet, lay on the floor nearby.

Billy was an astronaut, alone in space. We all were.

7

That summer was like forever. My sisters and I shed our layers of clothes, spending most of our days in bathing suits at the Edgehaven swimming pool. I wore my new two-piece blue-and-white-polka-dot bathing suit. The fringe on the top made it look like I had more up there.

At the pool, the usual moms lounged on plastic beach chairs, blabbing, with half an eye on their kids. Mom used to be right in the center of it all. Instead, we had Jessica, a college student home for the summer, keeping an eye on Billy and Annie. Bikini clad, she lay, tanned and oiled, on a beach towel, basking in the sun and the teenage boys' attention. A perk for Claire and me. Really just me. Claire spent all her time hanging around James, who was lifeguarding.

With her silky, straight blonde hair, everyone thought Jessica was pretty. Once I asked Grandma Cupcakes if I was pretty. She said, "Pretty enough for all normal purposes." What was a normal purpose?

In the evenings, covered in mosquito bites and calamine lotion, I'd hang around Randolph Court. The street had sixteen identical houses, differing only in their color and the number on the door. Ours was yellow, the color of a box of Chiclets; the number forty-two stenciled in black. Forty-two was perfect—it was even and if you doubled the two you got four. I liked even numbers best; they seemed friendlier. The only other homes that mattered to me were the ones with kids. The Geigers lived at forty-three. My best friend Tracy lived at forty-five. While she didn't have an even number, I liked that four and five were consecutive. Charlie was two houses down from Tracy, number forty-nine. Claire's best friend, Michelle, lived at the end of the cul-de-sac, number fifty-six.

We'd play kickball, listen to music, gossip and argue over

who liked whom. Claire, Michelle, and James would sometimes join in. Claire and James had been going steady. I liked seeing her happy again. Looking at us, no one would know anything terrible had happened. Billy never mentioned Mom and Annie rarely did. Or not really. Both had called me Mom more than once, when I read to them or they were sleepy. How long before they wouldn't remember her? The wound was scabbing over and none of us wanted to pick at it and risk ripping it back open. I guess anything in life can become ordinary.

But at night, when I lay in bed, I imagined all six of us lying in our beds, eyes wide open, thinking about Mom.

One cloudy afternoon in August, Tracy, bored enough, agreed to ride bikes to the library with me. I was the one who loved the library, everything about the place: the light from the huge windows, the weight of a book in my hand, the way the paper felt against my fingertips, even the musty smell that filled the stacks. And the quiet!

Tracy, wearing a cropped halter top and shorts, took off for who knew where, and I marched off for the fiction section. On the end of the aisle were shelves marked: Popular Adult Fiction. That was the spot. There was *Love Story*, which I had already read, super goopy, very sad, another young woman who dies for no good reason. Next to that was *The French Lieutenant's Woman*, creepy fingers on the cover, holding a creepy camera. Definitely not sexy. I picked up *The Godfather* and read the back cover: "Nico Puzo takes us into the violence-infested society of the Mafia and the gang wars." I'd had enough murder with *In Cold Blood*.

Behind me I heard stifled laughter—Tracy talking to a high school boy. How did she do that?

Then I spied *Valley of the Dolls*, with its sexy cover of pills and panties. I had heard Claire and some of her friends joking about it: dolls were pills. First line on the back cover: "Cutthroat careerism, wild sex, and fierce female protagonists."

Yes!

Older-than-Moses Mrs. Breslin was parked at the checkout desk. She never said anything other than "Shush" or "Quiet down over there." Acting normal, heart pounding, I handed her my book, cover down.

"Well," she said. "This is a grown-up book. Should I check with your mother?"

My mother had got me my library card. I remembered standing at the exact desk, same old lady.

I was supposed to say, never mind. But I stood taller, said the awful thing: "My mother died. But she liked me to read current bestsellers." It worked—using Mom's death to get away with something. Not another word, Mrs. Breslin stamped the card in the book, slid it away from her.

The next morning, I was so tired. I'd read till two, the entire book, trying to find all the sexy parts. When I finished reading I hunched over my OED leafing through for just the right word for sexy.

It took a while, but I found the perfect one: *Salacious: inappropriate interest in sexual stuff.* I opened my black and white marbled word notebook and recorded the word and its meaning.

My OED was like my own universe, each word another star, with more than I could ever see or know.

The next day I went with Dad on a tile estimate. I was the only one who liked to go on jobs with him. I'd often gone when I was little, when he first started the company. But that was before. I realized it had been at least a year since I was his helper, and so I was keen to go when he asked me along to look at a job.

Dad believed that if you wanted to accomplish anything in life you first had to have intention. Catholicism was Mom's religion. Dad's was intention, and he was devout. His intention with Moran Tile and Marble was simple: work for himself, make more money. The first thing he did was to write what he called an intention card. Grabbing a pen and an old business card, he jotted down his aspiration on the back. He then placed it in his wallet, where it remained until the goal was achieved: *Moran Marble and Tile will be a great success.*

And it was. Now he had a lot of guys working for him. Our cars had gotten newer and newer, right up to the Country Squire wagon. There'd even been talk of a new house, a room of my own.

Not anymore.

We gobbled breakfast, which for him was two cups of coffee. We rushed to the car and climbed in. He patted my knee and said, "Change your thoughts and you change your world."

We drove to the main road, where Dad leaned over me, opened the glove compartment, and dropped the book of maps in my lap. "Okay, navigator," he said, "find 29 Livingston Avenue in Forest Glen."

I flipped through the pages, narrowed in on the right coordinates. "Got it," I said. The houses got nicer as we drove into Forest Glen. Driving down Mayer Court, Dad said, "We make this deal, kid, we'll stop at a diner, get some lunch. Use the ole terlet." Dad pronounced toilet as "terlet." Even though he grew up only a few towns away he had his own weird accent, "vinegar and erl" goes on the salad and the furnace was in the "berler room."

"Ralph's!" I said.

"Ralph's, it is!"

Pulling up to the job site, Dad looked at his watch. "We're early. Let's do some canvasing." He handed me a stack of flyers. "You cover that side of the street and I'll cover this side."

Off we marched, mansion to mansion, putting a postcard in each fancy mailbox:

Moran Tile and Marble

When you're ready to make your home beautiful, give us a call!

Back at the van, I straightened Dad's tie. He stuck a pencil behind his ear, retrieved his clipboard and tape measure, and we headed to the front door. He knocked like a TV cop, knocked again.

"How nice you have a daughter to help you," the lady said. She wore a perfectly neat plaid dress and high heels. On a

Saturday! "You're a lucky man." The biggest chandelier I'd ever seen hung over our heads.

"Yes, I am. And I have three more at home, *and* a son."

The husband lumbered unhappily down the steps. "What's this gonna cost?" he said.

Dad shook the man's hand. He loved the challenge. "Joe Moran," he said. "I'm like you, Jim. These days, we always have to consider the bottom line."

I planted my feet at the far corner of the enormous bathroom, holding fast to the end of the tape measure while Dad jotted numbers. He balanced on the lip of the tub, calculating, erasing, calculating, licking the tip of the pencil. The shelf had Ponds cream and Revlon Brush-on Blush, same as Mom's.

Finally, the calculations were done and the estimate sheet filled out. I was getting butterflies. Dad leaned close, and in a soft voice, he said, "I'm going high on this one. That guy's a grump, so he needs to pay for the aggravation he's gonna cause me!"

We laughed as he showed me the figure: So much money!

Back in the fancy kitchen I hovered in the background while Dad spoke to the lady. The husband scowled. The wife shushed him. The husband sighed and nodded. Dad lost no time shaking both their hands. The deal was done!

Walking to the van, seeing our name printed there, I was puffed up with pride. Dad said, "You're such a big help, maybe one day you'll take over the business." It was the happiest I'd seen him since Mom's accident. Would I have to take over the business? For him? I had wanted to be an astronaut, a librarian, a teacher, the president, but never a business lady.

We climbed into the van, and after Dad drove a block, he beeped the horn and said, "Milkshakes all around!"

Ralph's was so good. I had my usual burger and salty fries. Dad asked me, "Whatcha reading these days, stringbean?" He was always proud of my reading, though he didn't read much himself.

"*Valley of the Dolls*," I told him.

"Still with the kid books, huh?"

I didn't tell him dolls were pills and that the women in the book had sex in all sorts of weird ways, or they seemed weird to me—lying on your tummy, or sitting in a car, even standing in an alley.

I didn't think Dad was ready to hear all that.

8

The last Saturday in August, like most other Saturdays that summer, Grandma Cupcakes took the number fourteen bus from Hoboken, to see us. She announced her arrival with her usual two-tone whistle, then she hurried up the sidewalk in front of the house.

My sisters, Billy, and I went running, flinging ourselves around her ample waist. "Look, Grandma, I'm Popeye," said Billy, who was wearing his sailor cap.

"I see that," said Grandma. "That must mean you eat your spinach."

"I'll carry that," Claire said, grabbing for Grandma's bag.

"Me, me!" said Mae.

Grandma Cupcakes was the star of the Hostess Cupcake factory assembly line. She sometimes injected cupcakes with creamy filling, other times packaged them, but best of all, she inspected them, rejecting the ones with a white squiggle too close to the edge or maybe a dent in the icing. She tossed aside enough to fill the bag she was carrying.

Grandma said the same thing she always said, her blue eyes twinkling, "Why do you want that bag? I just have some old dish towels in there. You don't want those, do you?"

In unison we yelled, "Yes!" and hurried inside behind her.

She laughed. Her skin was so pale it was almost translucent. "All right, all right. Now give me a second to get my jacket off and collect my beans."

And then she presented the bag, turned it over, and the little cakes tumbled onto the kitchen table.

"Give me some," said Billy.

I ripped open the cellophane and carefully pulled back the icing, giving pieces of the cake to Billy and saving the chocolate icing for me.

"Milk," said Mae, chocolate crumbs circled her mouth.

"Yummy!" said Annie, who was licking the vanilla filling off her fingers. Claire leaned back in her chair, placing her feet up on the table. Grandma swatted them off.

Grandma puttered around the kitchen, her shoulders stooped a bit, and got busy making our favorite dinner—pasta with canned brown beans and fried eggplant—enough to freeze for another night. Her thick support stockings bagged around her ankles, giving her legs an orange tinge.

"Enjoy them now, you ragamuffins, because I'm out of there come October!" We groaned.

"You little rats! You want your old grandma on her feet all day? I've been working ever since I lost my Charlie." Charlie. Did I know my grandfather was also a Charlie? Maybe this meant Charlie and I were meant to be together.

Suddenly, as if just hearing what Grandma said, Mae asked: "Can we still call you Grandma Cupcakes?"

Annie hugged her waist and said, "And bring us cupcakes!"

Grandma paused, mid-tying of Mom's apron around her waist. "Of course. I'll always be Grandma Cupcakes. Right?" It surprised me to see there was a bit of worry in her eyes.

I picked up the batter-covered fork, dipped the thin-sliced eggplant in a beaten egg, then laid it on a plate of bread crumbs. Grandma flipped it into a skillet of hot oil that spit and smoked and smelled so good.

"Grandma, we'd love you, even with no cupcakes," I said.

Grandma put down the spatula, looked me in the eye, and slowly nodded.

ॐ

That night—and many other nights, in fact—I got Billy ready for bed, a challenging round of teeth brushing before tucking him in for *Green Eggs and Ham*. Claire was helping Annie, wrestling her through teeth brushing and pajamas, which was trickier than trying to catch a bar of soap in the tub.

As Billy finally drifted off I ran my fingers through his mop of thick hair and inspected his scar, a thick cord that ran from his lip to the base of his neck. The scar tugged and stretched his lower lip, giving him an endless half frown. Three-quarters of his adorable mug was perfect, and now the lower quarter was, ugh, *freakish*. The police had had to smash the window to get him out of the car, which had been in danger of catching fire. My sweet little brother often woke in the night shouting. He remembered the crash, glass smashing. He loved to crash his toy cars, a noisy game of booms and shouts. He remembered doctors. He didn't seem to remember Mom, who had been there next to him in the wreck, killed. He no longer mentioned her.

How long before she disappeared from my mind too?

Was memory like a puddle of water in the sun that evaporates? I started calculating. He was three years old and had forgotten her in four months. I was almost fourteen. If Billy is forty months old and I'm 165 months, I'm nearly four times his age, which if it works the same way, I'd forget her in four times the four months it took him. Sixteen. In just sixteen months she would be on the dark side of the moon. That would be only August 1971!

I kissed Billy goodnight and tiptoed down the hall to the bathroom.

Claire, hair in a ponytail, was washing her face. She swore that a ponytail kept her hair from frizzing when she slept. I filched one of her ties and pulled mine back.

"Next time let's swap. You read to Annie and I'll read to Billy," said Claire with a sigh.

"Billy's no easier. You can't get through a sentence without him talking," I said. "Scoot over." I covered my toothbrush with paste.

"At least he isn't covering his mouth and making fart sounds the whole time and giggling," said Claire with a laugh. Grabbing a cotton ball, she gently wiped the mascara from her eyes. Without her mascara, she still looked like a kid.

"At least it's only the noise," I said, the words garbled around my toothbrush. Claire nudged me, reaching for her toothbrush.

"I'm not done," I said. She flicked the water at me.

"Hey," I said, toothpaste spitting out of my mouth. A big glob landing on Claire's arm.

"Ewww," she squealed as she reached for the toothpaste. She squeezed the tube and squirted some right in my face. We collapsed on the floor in giggles.

At the end of the summer over a dinner of take-out Chicken Delight, Dad got all bright and said, "I do believe you three girls are in need of haircuts."

School was starting up in a week and he was finally noticing we were a shaggy crew.

"No way. Not me," said Claire. "I take care of my own hair." She'd been telling me that my hair looked like a rat's nest. And it was true, my tangles had grown into knots and I had given up trying to get them out.

A spiraling pole, red-and-white striped like a peppermint stick, hung next to the front door. A bell tinkled and the smell of disinfectant—and not the peppermint candy kind—filled my nose.

"My girls are starting school this week and are in need of a haircut." As soon as Dad said the word haircut, Billy started wailing. Ever since the accident, he was terrified of anything to do with cutting or scissors. Avoiding a meltdown, Dad lifted Billy into his arms and headed for the door, saying he was going to run some errands and return soon.

Pointing at me the barber said, "You're the oldest, you go first." He was bald! He pulled a comb from the tall glass jar on the countertop and parted my hair down the center and began cutting. When he finished chopping, he picked up a large electric razor, and began running the blade up and down my neck. A prickly feeling vibrated down my spine. With a flourish, he whipped off the cloth, spun me around to face the mirror, and shouted, "Voila!"

I gasped. A perfect bowl of hair. I couldn't speak. This man wasn't a barber, he was a butcher. Mae and Annie dutifully took their turn, each getting the same haircut.

Until that haircut I imagined that on the outside we appeared no different from every other kid, that no one could see we didn't have a mother. Now we looked like girls without a mother, and that is just what we were. That night, leafing through my OED, I found the word of the day: *Disconsolate: sad and depressed.*

Mae and I waited on Broad Avenue for the 23 bus to the Westpark Mall for new school clothes, with Annie tagging along. I would have preferred going with Tracy or Claire, but Tracy was at her grandmother's beach house and Claire was off somewhere with Michelle.

Searching for my headband, I had found Annie laying perfectly still atop her bed covers. Her eyes were tightly closed, her arms crossed on her chest. She was holding her breath.

I said, "Lumpkin, what are you doing?"

She let out her breath, like air releasing from a balloon.

"I'm seeing what it feels like to be dead," she said. "Play dead with me."

What the nikkin'!

Laying down next to her, I placed my arms across my chest, closed my eyes and tried not to move. Relaxing. No way was this like being dead. I shivered and flew off the bed.

"Annie, I gotta go."

"Where?"

"Mae and I are going to the mall. School shopping."

"I want to come." She popped up and leapt off the bed.

"No, it won't be any fun. You stay here with Miss June." Miss June was the Irish lady Dad hired when boy-crazy Jessica returned to college. She was no Jessica. Old, with sagging skin and swollen ankles, she toddled like she didn't trust her legs to hold her up.

"Please, pretty please, Jody."

I couldn't resist that adorable face. "Okay. On one condition, that you put on some clean, matching clothes and take out some of those barrettes. Oh, and leave Roo at home." Since Annie was starting kindergarten and couldn't bring Roo with her, I figured she better start getting used to not having him with her everywhere she went. Mostly, I didn't want her to be teased.

The bus was stuffy and hot. Passing one man asleep and another reading the newspaper, we slipped into a middle row seat. Annie squeezed in between Mae and me, careful to not get too close to the five rowdy boys draped across the back bench, their legs hanging over the seats in front of them. One super tall boy with curly black hair was drumming his hands on the ceiling.

There were two women in the row across from us, speaking Spanish. Were they a mother and daughter or two sisters? Then I saw the older one gently brushing the other's hair from her eyes and I decided they were a mother and daughter.

As I stared out the window, Annie rested in the crook of my arm, watching the blur of familiar sights as we drove through Hampton Hills. The bus fumes gave me a sick feeling.

At the first stop, an old woman with groceries boarded. She slowly made her way down the aisle, smiled, and lowered herself on the bench behind us, lifting her bundle onto her lap. Grandma Cupcakes sat on the bus that same way.

At a traffic light the bus screeched to a halt. Suddenly, from the last row I heard, "Hey, Moron Tile and Marble," echoing up the bus seats. Another boy yelled, "You lost your marbles."

Cringing, I looked over at Mae. There wasn't enough air in this stuffy bus.

"Hey, morons," the black-haired guy said.

Mae whispered, "How do they know us?" I didn't want to look behind me, but I peeked. I didn't recognize any of them.

"They don't," I said and sank further into the seat. Sweat seeped through my clothes. Why were they being mean?

Without a plan, I jumped up and pulled the cord. "Annie, take my hand. We're getting off."

"Where are we?" asked Mae.

I read the street sign—Rosedale Avenue! The street where Mom's accident had happened. We climbed down the side steps. Maybe Mom had made this happen, so we would get off the bus right here.

Annie pointed at the billboard. "That's our name."

"Oh, Moran, moron," said Mae. I should have known, boys called each other names since second grade.

Moran Tile and Marble—*When you're ready to make your home beautiful, give us a call!*

Did Mom see this sign when she was driving? Was this the last thing she saw?

&

We waited in a huddle for the next bus. It came within ten minutes.

At the mall, we strode past the dress shop Mom always dragged us to and made a beeline for Spenser's. I held tight to Annie's hand.

I noticed a couple. It's tricky figuring people's ages, but I guessed they were in their twenties. They were holding hands, yakking. At one moment the woman was laughing so hard at something the man was saying she couldn't keep walking. I sped up, trying to catch a glimpse of their fingers, to see if they were married. His left hand was in hers, blocking my view. I came up on her side.

"Slow down," called Mae.

Finally, I caught a glimpse. Yes, a wedding ring. I studied them, forgot my sisters. I was trying to understand the mystery of what makes two people love each other. They seemed so perfect together. Comfortable. Maybe Dad could be a couple again. Or, maybe, it was really for me to figure out how someone would love me. Charlie, for example, meeting me on the blacktop. Holding hands. I needed the perfect outfit.

"Slow down, Jody!" Mae's voice brought me back from my thoughts. I took hold of Annie's hand.

At Macy's I found just what I was looking for: a woolen miniskirt with a matching long-sleeve turtleneck. The brown perfectly matched my hair and the price was right, leaving me enough money for the best part of the outfit—leather boots—

and still some change for Dad. No one else in eighth grade would have boots like these!

Mae got herself a new purple shirt—all her shirts were some shade of purple—and Annie was happy with Silly Putty.

At home, I tried on the whole outfit, from top to tights. Pulling the beaded necklace out of the little white Spenser's box, I slipped it over my head. I started to toss the box in the trash, but stopped, deciding it might come in handy. I cleared a space in the top drawer of my bureau and added the box.

I slipped my feet into my new boots, one-inch heels— my first. Lovingly, I zipped up the sides and stood. I would definitely dominate eighth grade! And I sang, loud as I could, strutting and shimmying back and forth in front of the mirror: "These Boots Are Made for Walking."

"I'm home," I heard Dad call.

I burst from my room to show him.

"Jody, that is terrific! You look *beautiful.*" Oh, my insides felt warm, my heart welling. "A great winter look!"

Wait. "Winter? Not, the first day!"

"Too hot," he said jovially.

"No, it's perfect!"

"You'll roast!"

"It's my choice!"

"Yes," he said. "Okay, make your own mistakes. If I listened to what people said, I never would have started the tile business. And look at me now."

I saw the billboard: *Moran Tile and Marble.* I wish I had an axe to cut that sign down.

9

Grandma Cupcake's railroad apartment was on the second floor of a three-floor row house. The front door opened into a small galley kitchen that connected to a string of three consecutive rooms, one after the other, like cars on a train. The living room, or the parlor as Grandma called it, led into her bedroom, which was more like a passageway to the dining room.

The dining room for me was a room of riches. Here I could find almost anything I needed—Grandma never threw anything away. The dining room table took up most of the room, but in one corner was her sewing machine, and in another corner was a card table, where we played Canasta and Pokeno. There was an area with empty gift boxes, folded used wrapping paper, and ribbons.

Sitting at the dining room table under a large stained-glass chandelier, I was organizing buttons into plastic food containers while Grandma fixed lunch. There were hundreds of buttons of every variety. If any of us lost a button, Grandma Cupcakes could always find the perfect match.

This day I sorted them by color, other times I did it by size. As I rummaged through the collection, I found the most beautiful button I'd ever seen. It was a bottomless blue and looked like it was made out of glass.

"Grandma, can I have one of your buttons?" I called. I loved coming on my own to spend the night.

"Sure," she said. "Take two." It was only this one I wanted. I put it in my front pocket to bring home with me.

Tiring of the buttons, I went and settled myself on the windowsill and watched the cats darting along the fire escape at the rear of her building. Electrical wires and clotheslines zigzagged between the alleyway, the bras and panties swaying like flags in the wind for everyone to see. I felt my face redden.

"Grandma," I called again. "The cats are hungry."

Grandma handed me a bowl of milk to put out on the metal grid. Mom used to say if there was a stray cat within ten miles they would find Grandma Cupcakes.

On the ground below, two cats, a tabby and a calico, were making an awful racket. "Grandma, that cat's hurting her."

"Oh, that's Stinky. They're doing that doo-dah-doo-dah business." I knew what this meant, though it looked like fighting to me.

Grandma made a pss-pss-pss sound and the cats came running. One slunk up, rubbing against Grandma's arm, encouraging her to pet him. She cooed and sang, "O lovely Pussy! O Pussy, my love, what a beautiful Pussy you are, you are!"

When I tried to make that same pss-pss-pss sound and pet the tabby, she skittered away.

I moved into Grandma's bedroom and stretched out on her bed. Noticing the mirror, I got up to look at my new haircut. Mirror, mirror on the wall, who is the ugliest one of all? Grandma said it looked much neater, which was the most boring compliment ever.

A paper was wedged between the frame and the mirror—a mass card. I pulled it down. It was for Mom. Why wasn't I given one of these? I wanted to keep it, but I knew Grandma wouldn't give it up.

A ceramic mother cat and three kittens perched atop Grandma's chest of drawers, and I hid one of the kittens in her jewelry box, planning on playing a game of "Hot and Cold" later.

The apartment was filled with old things from when Mom was a kid. Grandma never talked about her, but she was willing to tell me the stories behind what she called her "tchotchkes," like the miniature old-fashioned lantern that Mom had gotten as a Campfire girl and a spelling bee award that Aunt Sheila won back in middle school.

In the parlor below the tall front windows sat a pull-out couch, where I slept, giving me a bird's-eye view of all that was happening in the street below. The couch was the only upholstered furniture that wasn't dark and covered with a lace doily, which was probably why Mom had so much color in our house and not one doily.

We ate our tomato soup and grilled cheese in the dining room. After lunch, Grandma said, "Let's mosey up to the Avenue," which I knew meant Washington Street.

It was like Billy's *Busytown* book, every inch packed with people, one man fixing a street light, another jackhammering the pavement, and a policeman directing traffic where the streetlight was out. And that was just on Grandma's block. I rushed ahead.

"Keep your girdle on," Grandma Cupcakes called after me.

On the Avenue, our first stop was John's Bargain Store, where Grandma gave me three dollars. The narrow aisles were crammed with dusty cubbies filled with everything from soaps, candles, and stockings to hammers and wrenches. There was the changeable holiday aisle that was already packed with Halloween stuff.

I set off for the nail polish. Carefully I sifted through the bottles, hunting for the perfect color to go with my new outfit. I chose a shade the older, popular girls were wearing—frosty white. Only $1.05.

"Almost time to go, Jody," called Grandma. I snapped up the polish and scooted over to the jewelry area, quickly eyeing the selection. Forget about the pierced earrings. There was a peace necklace, the medallion a rainbow of colors in its own white box. I grabbed it and dashed for the cashier.

"Go back and get a normal color," said Grandma.

"White is normal. Lots of kids wear it."

"Not my granddaughter." I swapped it for pink.

Back at the apartment, wearing my new necklace, I painted my nails.

After dinner, our usual pasta fazool and fried eggplant, Grandma and I leaned back on her front stoop chatting with neighbors. Grandma's friend Maria called her my *abuela*. Here Grandma picked up the latest bits of gossip, like a discard pile in Canasta. Each lady spun a story Grandma could hold on to until the perfect moment came to lay hers out on the table for the win.

We stayed, chatting and watching strangers pass by until it was time for bed. Once upstairs I helped Grandma put sheets on the old foldout couch. I changed into pajamas and started to put my new necklace back in its box. Instead I pulled out my blue glass button and gently laid it in the box, admiring how it sparkled on the white cotton. I asked Grandma if she had any other jewelry boxes and she gave me two more.

Grandma asked me to massage some lotion on her back, to places she couldn't reach. Her shoulders were sore from years on the assembly line. Scrunching up my nose, I tried not to smell the cream, a burning minty smell. As I rubbed the balm I looked around the room to avoid seeing her loose and saggy skin. In the corner, my grandfather's ratty brown La-Z-Boy remained forever empty, more like a tombstone than a chair. He had died when I was four, but I remembered him anyway, lounging in that recliner, smoking a cigarette. His left leg was gone from the knee down, the empty fabric of his slacks looking like a flattened paper bag. Claire and I were scared of him and his missing leg.

Staring at the chair, I suddenly remembered how he used to line up his coins, in equal piles, on the table next to him. Maybe things you think are forgotten are still there, you only need a reminder.

"Grandma, do you miss Grandpa?" I asked. I never got the sense that she missed him. I didn't need to ask about Mom. Her, I knew, she missed.

She shrugged. "He's in heaven with God."

"What did he die from? Not sugar." When I was little she told me that sugar was the cause of Grandpa losing his leg. I thought that meant he had eaten too many Hostess cupcakes.

"Diabeedeez," is how she said it.

Finally, I said, "If God is so great, why would he let Mom die?"

"We can't know the reasons for what God does," she said. She pursed her lips together like she was trying to keep herself quiet.

Grandma glanced at the book resting next to me. "Don't read too long, it's bad for your eyes, chickadee. G'night."

I pictured Mom bending over giving me a kiss goodnight, her saying, *I love you to the moon and back.*

"Grandma, do you love me?"

"Oh, pssh, love, why do you ask such silly questions?" She rubbed my head the way she stroked the cats; her way of saying she did. "Now say your prayers."

"Wait, Grandma, do you have a dictionary?" I wasn't sure I'd be able to fall asleep without finding a new word.

"A dictionary? Why would I have one of those? I already speak English."

From Grandma's room the deep voices of radio talk show hosts wafted through the air.

Sounds of neighbors drifted up and down through the floor vents. In the apartment below lived the Super, who played opera, sometimes so loud that Grandma banged on the floor with the stick end of the broom. Mrs. Puccini in the apartment above yelled out her window, "Tony, Tony, get in here!" Then a little while later, "I said get in here. Am I going to have to get the belt?" Outside, a police siren blared.

I lay there imagining all the lives in those other spaces. What was happening in their apartments? Eating, watching TV, reading, smoking, going to the bathroom. Sex, maybe. Probably. It gave me a queasy feeling to think of all the different people. Two apartments on Grandma's floor, three floors in the building, so six apartments, and the super in the basement.

My brain went even fuzzier as I considered all the apartment houses down the street, ten of them, all filled with more people, say six apartments each, so sixty people. Seventy with the supers. If there was an average of three people per apartment, more than 200 people lived on Grandma's block alone! Then the next block, and the next one after that. It was like a flood, a never-ending flow of people. Without even having my OED I found the perfect word: *Infinity: an uncountable number.*

In the morning Grandma Cupcakes was already dressed, her hair pulled back tight in a little bun, a glittering red brooch pinned to her best church dress. I didn't want to spoil the visit, but I dragged my feet getting ready and dawdled while eating my three-minute eggs—it was Saturday! Why would anyone go to mass every day when Sunday was torture enough?

Clasping my hand, Grandma led me down the street to Our Lady of Grace. Entering the church, I dipped my fingers into the holy water, touched my forehead, then ran my fingers down my chest and across my heart. This was only for her eyes. We continued up the aisle—between great pillars forming arches to the ceiling, beneath dangling lanterns rimmed in gold—Grandma's black pumps tapping on the old marble tile.

Once seated, she pulled out her red rosary beads. Her fingers, like speckled marble, rolled quickly along the row of them as I watched her lips mouth the words. The clicking-clacking sound of each bead against the other gave a familiar rhythm.

10

Dad hovered over my bed in his well-worn khakis and blue plaid button-down, sleeves rolled unevenly up to his elbow. "Rise and shine, stringbeanski. Hear the bluebirds sing," he said. "First day of school." He rustled my blanket, found my feet, and started tickling.

"Stop, Dad." I laughed and ducked my head under the covers. "Stop!"

Dad tugged on Claire's comforter till her tousled hair appeared. "Hey, Claire-Bo-Bear. Rise and shine. It's back to school."

When she didn't budge, he started on his rendition of reveille, complete with bugle sounds: "It's time to get up, it's time to get up, it's time to get up in the morning!" My sister growled, yawned, and rolled over. For Claire and Mom, Dad's cheeriness in the morning was as appreciated as a nose zit on prom night.

Outside, it looked like rain.

Dad went full Dad: "If you don't get up, you'll get the ol' feet-tickling treatment."

At least with Claire still in bed I could use the bathroom in peace. I pulled on my new wool miniskirt and turtleneck, ran a small dollop of goop through my stupid hair, turned from side to side to see myself in the mirror. I could hear Mom saying, "Fantabulous." I could hear diabolical Debbie Doidge, the meanest girl in school too: "Dorkwad."

Each of us found our way to the kitchen. "Spin for me, Mae," Dad said as he noted her flowered purple top and checked skirt. "Well, I guess that works." Only Annie, dressed in her kindergarten uniform, didn't require any inspection.

Dad looked me up and down. "You're committed. I'll give you that," he said.

My stomach started to hurt. Mom's not here to take us to school. No first day of school pictures. Forever, every special day would be filled with missing Mom.

Billy showed up last in his military hat and blue shirt, his bottom bare.

"I guess you don't need pants to eat," Dad said, lifting Billy into his booster seat, pee-pee and all, and buckling the belt around his round tummy.

"Pee-pee," Annie said.

"Jody, please get Billy a sippy cup of milk," Dad asked as he sprinkled Cheerios in Billy's plastic bowl. I snapped the bib around Billy's neck. Immediately he started tossing the cereal on to the floor.

"Mae, help Annie pour that juice! *Quick*, she's gonna spill it," urged Dad. A box in each hand, he circled the table pouring cereal into our bowls as I trailed behind with the milk.

Where was Claire?

Dad started making that "aahh" sound that came right before he sneezed. Dad's sneezes were like explosions, and ever since the accident Billy was terrified of loud noises. As soon as Dad's shoulders started to rise up, he made a mad dash to get away before he detonated, then stepped in a puddle leaking from Billy's discarded Superman big boy underwear. The rest of us roared—Dad looked like he was dancing. Billy, caught up in the excitement, started tossing his Cheerios into the air. Annie laughed so hard, sounding like a hyena. Even goody-goody Mae was in hysterics.

"Okay, very funny, girls," Dad said, wiping his nose. The excitement had halted Dad's eruption mid-sneeze. "Jody, hand me some napkins."

Crouched down, Dad wiped up the pee. "Young man," Dad looked up at Billy. "Yes, I'm talking to you. You need to use the terlet and keep your pants on."

"A-okay," said Billy, giving a salute.

Claire shuffled in. A long sleeve shirt covered her pink crop-top—a shirt I was certain was coming off the minute she walked out the front door.

"Claire, grab yourself some cereal," said Dad.

"I'm not hungry." She poured herself some juice. "What's for lunch?"

Dad tugged an assortment of bags out from the cabinet. Taking a crayon from the junk drawer, he wrote each of our names on a bag: *Claire, Jody, Mae,* and *Annie.*

He snapped up the bread, butter, and cold cuts from the refrigerator, rolled his sleeves up further and announced, "Now watch the maestro at work," as he laid out two rows of Wonder Bread on the green laminated countertop, four in each line. He tossed the heel aside. Only Mom ate the heel, or tried to hide it inside your sandwich. I could hear her voice. "You don't know what you're missing!"

Grabbing a knife, he smeared the bread with butter, draped it with bologna—his favorite lunch, the one Mom used to pack for him.

"Dad, bologna?" I asked.

"Peanut butter, then?"

"Yuck, I hate peanut butter."

"I'm sorry, stringbean." Plainly distressed, he pleaded: "Bologna, yes? You can eat it for today, right? We're all out of ham, okay? No turkey either."

"Sure," I said. At least it wasn't liverwurst.

"I'll find something to eat at school," Claire said.

This seemed a good time to start my campaign. "You know, Dad, if Grandma Cupcakes lived with us it would really help you out. She could make our lunches."

"Who wants a cupcake and who wants a Twinkie?" Dad asked.

"Twinkie," said Claire, tapping Dad's left shoulder and stealing one from his right.

"Dad, come on. Why not?"

"Why not, what?"

"*Daaad,* you know, Grandma!"

"Stringie, Grandma has her own life. It's not fair to ask her to give that up and come live with us."

"She wants to," I said. "And she's retiring in October. So

work won't matter. And you wouldn't have to worry about dinner."

"Let's wait and see."

Jubilation. It wasn't a no.

"We have Miss June now, who's a big help. Isn't she?" No one answered.

Dad tossed a flawed Hostess cupcake into each of the three bags. Then, a can of Mott's PM for each. The can said it was an apple flavor "mixed with a medley of fruits." In my mouth, it tasted more like a medley of nuts and bolts, oily and metallic.

Dad clapped his hands as if he were just remembering something. "Hey, gang," he announced. "You remember that tile company that gives trips to their top customers? Guess what?"

"I guess Roo," said Annie.

"Not Roo," Dad said with a chuckle. "But good guess. This year I earned a trip to Rome." That got Claire back in the kitchen.

I remembered Mom talking with Dad about a trip. She pictured walking through the European art museums, seeing famous paintings that she'd only seen in books.

Claire brightened. "We're going to Rome?"

"Not so fast, my friend. But almost as good. *I'm* going to Rome, but get this: Miss June said she can stay here with you kids that week! Not till October, but exciting, right?"

"I'm moving in with Michelle," said Claire.

"You're going on a plane?" asked Mae, verging on tears.

"Why can't Grandma Cupcakes stay?" I asked.

"Well, as I said before—" Dad said.

"I want Grandma too," said Mae.

"She's got her job," Dad said. "She's got her life."

"Grandma would be way better than Miss June," I said.

"A dog with rabies would be better," said Claire.

"I just wish your mom could go with me," Dad said.

With him? What about us?

On the counter sat four lunch bags in a line, one crumpled brown, another a Wonder Bread baggie, and two of them some tile company. None of them the bags Mom would have packed.

ᕦ

We'd had our tragic summer. Now it was time for me to go back to Edgehaven Middle School, without Claire. The cement halls, the same barf-beige walls, the same prison-gray steel doors. The smell of chalk, pizza, and zit cream permeating the halls. The cafeteria was definitely serving pizza and beef macaroni, off to a great start as usual. Stuck-up Anthony Marano, the new ninth-grade president, was strutting down the halls like he owned the place. And I was wearing my new outfit, chin high.

Tracy and I strutted onto the blacktop. A popular ninth-grade girl asked, "Love the boots. Where'd you get them?"

"Oh lá lá," said Tracy with a snigger. It bugged her when I had anything better than she did—which happened almost never!

The bell rang, signaling the end of third period. Math, with Mr. Loew. All the kids charged out of their classrooms, mobbing the halls like a prison break. I stopped at my locker and fiddled with the combination. Why didn't they give you the same nikkin' locker as the year before? No way was I rushing. I needed to run to the bathroom to check how stupid my haircut looked and cool off. I was sweating like one of those ladies on the cafeteria lines. *Hyperhidrosis: excessive sweating.*

Mr. Loew would just have to understand: I was tragic.

At the end of first period, Miss Vitter, my science teacher, had called from the front of the room. "Jody. Just a sec." I wended my way back through the crowd to her desk. "How are you and your family doing?" Her eyes, all downcast and pity-droopy, were magnified by Coke-bottle glasses.

"Fine," I'd said, doing a quick about-face.

Calling after me, she said, "Well, if you're having any trouble or need extra time on an assignment, just let me know." Embarrassing. I closed my locker and scurried down B Corridor for the girl's restroom. In my head I heard Dad's warning about how hot I'd be. No way would I admit he was right. Debbie Doidge sauntered out of the bathroom, trailed by the smell of cigarettes. This year's dark eyeliner added to her perpetual look of scorn. I stepped aside to let her pass.

"Oh look, it's the Ironing Board," she said.

I gasped, like she'd punched me in the stomach, which she might as well have. At the sink, I splashed cold water on my face and patted down my hair. I stood sideways and stuck out my chest so it wasn't completely flat.

Mr. Loew didn't say a word when I traipsed in after the bell. This could work in my favor.

Fourth period, I met Tracy outside the cafeteria. She was buying lunch and dessert—another perk of being an only kid. I followed along, Wonder Bread bag behind my back. In the cafeteria, we spotted our friend group at one of the long white tables—the best one, by the big windows—and took our seats.

"Remember when we used to walk to my house for lunch?" I said to Tracy as I opened my sandwich wrapper. I chucked the nuts-and-bolts juice.

"Maggie made the best lunches," said Tracy biting off the corner of her pizza. "Sorry."

Lowering my voice, I said, "Miss Vitter called me over after class. So lame. She was all, like, 'I hope you're doing okay.'" I took a sip of Tracy's milk. "And then Loew didn't even care that I was late. When your mom's dead they cut you slack."

"You're lucky," said Tracy. I tightened and raised one side of my mouth.

"Okay, not exactly lucky," she said. "You know what I mean."

After talk of boys and teachers, we went out on the blacktop. I shimmied up the brick wall, which snagged my wool skirt. Sweat rolled down my back.

Tracy said, "Scoot over," as she hoisted herself up next to me.

Tugging a long twig off the tree above, I dug it into a crevice between the bricks and watched to see if the army of black ants marching along the wall would follow the road I was carving. They did. They were lugging some kind of food on their backs. In science I had learned an ant can carry fifty times their weight! When I accidentally swept a few off the wall, the others were thrown off by their friends' disappearance and began walking in chaotic circles, then returned to formation and continued on their trek. At any moment, they could be crushed by a flick of a stick or a shoe landing in the wrong spot. Their lives were so fragile.

"Hi, Jody. Hey, Tracy," Jennifer said. I hadn't seen her since the end of last school year. My armpits smelled like a swamp. She said, "Your hair's short."

"Don't even try to say it looks good," Tracy said. "She'll bite your head off."

Jennifer smiled. "Those boots are great. Did you and your mom...I mean...you and your sisters get them at the mall?"

"Yeah, Bakers," I said. I peered down at my boots. Damn, there were already scuffed from sitting on the wall. A fly buzzed around my face. I swatted at it.

"Sorry I said your mom. It must be really hard," said Jennifer. "With her gone."

It was a relief that someone had said it out loud. It threw me off balance for a minute, but when the bell rang, I followed everyone inside, a trail of ants going to fourth period.

After school, Tracy and I crossed behind the Ambulance Corps parking lot to sashay along the ledge—a barrier about three feet high with woods behind it. I was looking for a reason to dawdle, hoping Charlie would pass by and we could walk home together.

But no Charlie.

"Let's stop quick at the library," I said as we set off. "I need to swap my book."

Tracy groaned. "How can you read so much? I'll wait here."

I pulled my library card out of my wallet. "I'll be right back."

"*Allons*," she said with a wave of her arm. "My mom is taking me to get new sneakers."

"I'll be fast," I said. Geez. I was learning French despite myself. "We can cut through the gas station and get home just as quick."

Once inside I made my way to the fiction aisle. Passing a large table strewn with papers, my eyes locked on a book: *Death and Dying* by someone named Elisabeth Kübler-Ross. Was this Mom again, leaving me a clue? I swiped it off the table, strode off to a secluded area, and flipped through, my eyes catching the sentence: *We cannot look at the sun all the time, we cannot face death all the time.* Maybe this book had some answers.

Aiming for the checkout desk, I paused. I didn't want one of those pitying looks, and I didn't want anyone to know I was thinking about death. About Mom. Then the urge hit, I didn't know why exactly—I'd steal it.

Heart thumping in my chest, I rushed towards the girl's room, terrified someone would notice me going in with the book. Once in the stall I took out *The Valley of the Dolls* to return and stuffed the death book into my satchel. I buckled the strap tight.

As I made my way to the return cart, I heard footsteps behind me. A shiver went down my spine. Was I caught? Would they arrest me? Handcuff me?

"Hi, there," a voice said behind me. I almost dropped my bag. "I'm Miss Wendy, the new teen librarian. Here's some welcome punch." She handed me a plastic cup. She had big owl-like glasses, curly strawberry-blond hair and a warm, open face, as broad as a cat. Her glasses hung on the tip of her nose. She looked just the way I thought a librarian should look.

"Oh, hi," I said.

"What did you choose?" she asked. She had a calm way of speaking, like she was carefully considering every word before she said it.

Before I could hold the *Valley of the Dolls* behind my back, she reached for my hand. "Oh, my goodness," she said.

"I was returning it," I said. "It wasn't so good."

"Oh, I liked it."

My heart surged, how easily she'd seen through me.

"But it's not really meant for a smart person like you. I've got something I think you'll really like." And shortly she was pressing *Pride and Prejudice* into my hands.

"It's about love and marriage, with all its ups and downs," she said. "And while it's old, there is something very modern about it."

"Sounds good," I said. She was so nice, I almost wanted to confess and give her back the death book. I dropped *Valley of the Dolls* into the slot, checked out *Pride and Prejudice* and slipped it into my book bag.

Tracy!

Giddy with guilt and anticipation, I told Miss Wendy I had to go, clutched my bag, and rushed for the door.

Tracy was glaring. "Took you long enough!" she cried. "Another two seconds and I was *out of here*."

I pulled *Death and Dying* out of my satchel and waved it in the air. Tracy's eyes widened.

"Cool, let me see." She snatched the book and flipped to the beginning. I sat down next to her, under the tree. Reading over her shoulder, we went back and forth, mumbling the words, "Epidemics have taken a toll…The use of chemotherapy…"

"Boring!" I said. "I committed a mortal sin for this!"

"*Mortal sin?*"

"I stole it," I said, as if I did this all the time.

"No way," Tracy said, giving me a thumbs-up. "I've only stolen nail polish."

"Wait, listen to this," I said. "In our unconscious mind," I read, "we cannot distinguish between a wish and a deed. Between the wish to kill somebody in anger and the act of having done so, the child is unable to make that distinction."

"Ca c'est bizarre! I don't get it."

I continued reading, "The child will always say, 'I did it, I am responsible, I was bad, therefore Mommy left me.'"

"You don't feel responsible" said Tracy. "That's stupid. It was an accident."

11

At home, I rummaged through the cabinets looking for a snack. I missed the sweet aroma of Mom's chocolate-dipped shortbread cookies, the way she'd lay them out on a plate and get me a glass of milk. No longer hungry, I slumped upstairs to my bedroom but pulled up short when I noticed Dad's bedroom door ajar. I gave it a kick so it opened more, made sure he hadn't come home early, slipped in. The bedroom was unchanged.

The shades were drawn tight. I sank down onto Mom's side of the bed, a tangled heap of blankets, not the neat, tight-cornered sheets Mom would have left behind that morning. On her dresser a crystal trophy sat next to Claire's and my bronzed baby shoes. The other kids hadn't rated, I guessed. When I was little, I would trail behind Mom room to room as she cleaned. While she dusted, I'd run my fingers over the smooth crystal trophy that read Best Lindy Contest and ask her to tell me the story of the night she and Dad won.

"Oh, honey, I've told you that story so many times."

But then she'd dust it off and tell it again: "It was at a dance at Schuetzen Park, before Dad and I were married. I wore a black long-sleeve turtleneck—"

"It was blue," I said.

Mom laughed. "See you know it better."

"More."

"I wore a blue turtleneck and a beige pleated skirt that made a twirl when Dad spun me. Your dad, well, he smelled so good, woodsy and pine." She smiled to herself. "We weren't yet engaged, but we had really fallen in love."

Then she'd shake her head, wave her hand as if shooing a fly. "Oh, what am I talking about? I have work to do."

The dresser was still next to the closet. Mom's vanity still opposite the bed. I arranged myself in front of the mirror. Mom had sat in this same spot. She had finished crafting the makeup table just months before. She loved that vanity. I did too. Dad had built the wooden base, while Mom sewed a skirt for it out of the same flowered fabric as the bedspread and drapes. She lined the edges with gold-scalloped trim and hung a gold tassel from each corner. I told her I wanted one exactly like hers.

"I'll make you one for your sweet sixteen."

"Mom, that's *three years*."

Mom, that's never. I opened the drawer in her small bedside table and started snooping, not a single thing I hadn't pawed before: reading glasses, coins, empty licorice wrappers, several pens, a triangular Campfire girl pin, a compact, an old address book, a sewing thimble, and a half a pack of Raleigh cigarettes. I opened the box, inspecting the cigarettes, lined up like crayons. Each pack of cigarettes came with one coupon. Mom had been saving up for a Tiffany-style lamp that called for over 3,000 coupons. On rainy afternoons, she'd pull down her coupon-filled shoeboxes and we'd sort them into groups of ten, count them, and then staple them together. Sitting close, our arms touching.

Could I still get the lamp?

Dad hated that Mom smoked. He said cancer sticks could kill her. It drove her crazy when he nagged her to stop, and he got us kids in on the nagging. He'd tell us to throw them away or hide them from her. Once I snuck into her purse, filched the whole pack, and tossed them in the trash. Another time Claire took one right out of her hand, snapping it in two before she could even light it. That got her steaming.

"Smoking is my only moment of peace," she said.

We should have let her smoke all she wanted.

I flipped through the address book, noticing the names of relatives and friends and a bunch of names I didn't recognize. It was like seeing Mom's diary, that curvy, neat handwriting, her detailed notes, like what Christmas gifts she'd bought and relative's birthdays. I laid it on the bed along with the pin and compact.

In Mom's closet, I ran my fingers over the fabrics, the ribbing of corduroys, an itchy blue oversized wool sweater, and blouses she'd sewn herself. Mostly there were straight-legged stirrup-pants in brown, black, and blue, along with floral housedresses. Clothes she'd never wear again.

Rummaging through the pockets of her flannel robe, I found a rumpled Kleenex and slipped it into my pocket. I rifled through her pants, the black ones, then the brown. I only found a tiny hole and a penny.

There was Mom's white cardigan with pills on the sleeves. I buried my face in the sweater, taking in a faint whiff of licorice and cigarette smoke. Pulling my bare arms through the armholes, I felt the softness of the cashmere against my skin. I buttoned up the tiny pearl buttons.

At the back of the closet I found her black wool dress, the one she called her "Jackie O," and the fancy green one she made. Last New Year's Eve, our living mom wore that green dress, her hair teased and stiff as a bird's nest. Sitting at the top of the basement steps, I spied on Mom and Dad and their neighbor friends. A cigarette caught gracefully between Mom's fingertips, her skin pink from drinking champagne, her lips lollipop red, a strand of pearls at her neck catching the glow of the Christmas tree lights. Nat King Cole sang through the smoky haze, "Unforgettable."

My face pressed between the banister railings, I watched as Mom, her head thrown back, laughed at something Tracy's mother, Amelie, told her. I wanted to hear what they were saying. It made me excited and uneasy: for in that moment, she wasn't my mother but a glamorous movie star.

From the overhead shelf, I pulled down the hatbox where Mom's fox stole, complete with beady glass eyes, still lived. I helped myself to one of Mom's old empty shoeboxes and flipped in the Campfire pin, compact, the thimble, and address book. Then I remembered the tissue in my pocket and dropped it in there too.

I wrapped Mom's fur around my neck and posed in front of her vanity's three-way mirror. My fingers lingered on the glass tabletop, where she'd kept her makeup and jars. A few stray pieces of her favorite black licorice hid behind the Ponds face cream. I picked up her tortoiseshell hairbrush, surprised to find strands of hair threaded throughout. I swiveled the tube of lipstick, put some on, blotted my lips with the Kleenex. I spritzed my wrists with her perfume, sweetest vanilla, rubbed it behind my ears the way Mom did. What happened to her amber ashtray that always rested here?

Adjusting the fox across my shoulders in the mirror, I searched for something I couldn't see. I stood on the bed so my head wasn't visible—yes, it was Mom standing there. Kübler-Ross said we can't imagine our own death. She missed it—we can't imagine anyone being dead.

Worn out, I flopped down on the bed and closed my eyes. My head throbbed. I drifted off. In my sleep I saw Mom. She was in a wheelchair, coming down a wide hallway, at a school or maybe a hospital. She wasn't really dead. She rolled closer and closer towards me, a baby swaddled in her arms.

The front door slammed. Claire. Phew. I heaved myself up, stripped out of the sweater, tossed the fox back up on the closet shelf, straightened the bed covers, and jumped into the hallway.

Claire was on the phone. Probably James. I turned back, found the pack of cigarettes and tossed them in with the pin, compact, Kleenex, and address book. My heart thumped wildly in my chest. I'd already stolen a library book that day. I was a thief and I was thrilled.

Back in my bedroom, I decided that the tiny gift boxes Grandma had given me were the perfect space for my new treasures—the pin and compact—each placed lovingly in a box of its own. The rest of the things I chucked back in the shoebox and shoved under my bed. I stuck the sweater and belt in my drawer.

"Jo-dee!"

Just in time!

᷽

That evening, Dad sliced the onions as I molded the hamburger meat into patties. Then outside, in our cement backyard, we barbecued burgers. It had been Mom's idea to cover the yard with cement. Dad would never have to mow the lawn, she said, and the kids could roller skate and jump rope, and the little ones could ride their trikes without going in the street. Mom had pressed marbles into the border, letting us kids each stamp our handprints into the wet cement.

Dad stepped back from the hot grill. "So, how'd your first day go, kiddo?" he asked, waving his spatula.

"Good."

"Not too warm?"

"Dad, no!"

But we laughed.

"I'm sure you looked very beautiful."

"I glowed," I said: that was Mom's joke. Dad flipped the burgers.

"Dad?"

"Yes, stringbean."

"You never gave me an answer."

"Oh, jeez. This isn't about the earrings again, is it?"

"Claire wants them too! And Tracy's Mom let her get them. The store at the mall does the piercing."

"The store at the mall, huh?"

Dad pointed to a burger and I topped it with a slice of American cheese.

Dad said, "When should we go?"

"*Everyone* got them this summer. I'm, like, the only one who doesn't have pierced ears." I reared back. "Wait, did you just say yes?"

"To be honest, I never understood your mom's objection. How about it's for your fourteenth birthday?" I wanted to run and tell Mom that Dad was on my side. I won! But suddenly it didn't feel as good as I expected.

"Why look glum, stringbean? Aren't you psyched."

"Yeah," I said. Happy-sad.

§

The moment the string beans hit Billy's plate, he tossed them on the floor.

"Damn it, Billy!" Dad cried. "When are you going to stop this nonsense? Do *not* throw your beans. Do you want to stay at the table with the big kids?"

"I'm big!"

"Well, kids who throw food sit in high chairs."

Billy nodded and shuffled his remaining green beans onto the floor even as Dad cut his burger into little bits.

"Is this cow?" Annie asked, pointing at her burger.

"Duh," Mae told her.

The rest of us stacked our hamburgers onto buns with favored condiments, wildly diverse, gobbled obliviously, splashing ketchup, sword-fighting with beans.

"I won't eat cow," Annie said.

"Just eat tots, then," Dad said kindly, taking her meat for himself.

"Tots are made from babies," Claire said.

And we all laughed cruelly. But Annie knew that wasn't true.

"Claire, guess what!" I said.

"Just tell me."

"Dad said…" I checked with him, he nodded: the news could come from me. "We can get our ears pierced," I said.

Her eyes went big, like a cartoon character. "Really?" she looked over at Dad.

"Yep."

She shrieked. And off we went, negotiating a closer date than birthdays with Dad, and quietening Billy, who wanted earrings, too, and Annie, who wanted her hamburger back and Mae, who kept tinking her glass the way Mom would do before making an announcement.

Dad made the rest of us shut up.

Mae held the floor. She cleared her throat. "Guess what," she said. She sat up straight, her voice strong. "This year we're going to do *Alice in Wonderland*. And I'm going to try out to be Alice."

"Alice!" Dad cried. "You'll be the star! We'll all go see you!"

For a moment everyone fell quiet. Were they thinking what I was thinking? We wouldn't all be there. There were so many things Mom would never see.

That night, in bed, I returned to *Death and Dying*. Kübler-Ross said that a kid whose parent died will unconsciously believe they are still alive. I grabbed my OED and notebook: *Unconscious: part of the mind not accessible.*

Then I read, *The child who angrily wishes his mother to drop dead for not having gratified his needs will be traumatized greatly by the actual death of the mother.* My hands went clammy. Traumatized? What happens to someone who is traumatized? It was as if the author were reading my heart.

Kübler-Ross went on about how, after a death, kids feel guilty and responsible, that they've done something bad and were being punished. My eyes widened. There it was, right there in black and white, what I had been feeling all this time. My anger, my wishing Mom dead—that's what had made it all happen. Now I knew for sure. It was my fault. I was to blame. Even worse, I had the proof in my hands, written clear as day, in a book I had stolen—while I was wearing a sweater I'd stolen too.

I was the nikkin' wickedest kid ever.

I read a bit longer, then stopped, realizing Dad hadn't come in to say goodnight. I hid the book back under my bed. This book was meant for me, not the kids in the library. Was that the trauma they're talking about—that I would turn bad, into a thief. Was more punishment coming?

I took off my sweater, ripped the page from the book, and stuffed it in the shoebox under my bed.

Dad was slumped over the dining room table, not moving. My heart stopped. I never should have stolen that book. I moved closer. "Dad," I said softly. "Dad," a bit louder.

Surrounding him were crumpled napkins, a half-eaten chocolate donut, and a mug of coffee. His head rested on a pile of order forms and bills splayed out across the dining table.

He'd written notes all over them in red marker.

"Dad, wake up," I said, panic in my voice. I lightly touched his shoulder. He popped up so quickly I screamed.

"What?" Dad yelled, also startled. Taking a long breath, he slowly unraveled himself from the chair, groaning as if every part of his body hurt. "I was just resting my eyes," he said, his face pale and drawn.

I glanced over at one of the papers on top—a bill with a long, itemized list from Memorial Hospital with lots of zeroes, stamped LATE. Dad caught me looking.

"My little girl, the grown-up's world isn't always simple."

Neither are a kids!

Back in my room I put Mom's sweater on over my pajamas, climbed into bed next to Claire, already asleep, and kissed her goodnight. We slept like that, all sweaty and tangled.

In the morning Claire said, nudging me off, "Get out of my bed," but she smiled so I knew she liked it too.

12

The harder Tracy and I pushed and pulled, the faster the Whirly-bird spun. We were little kids again, without a care in the world. Then the Whirly-bird suddenly stopped. Tracy's mouth opened in a yell. "Sacre bleu!" The center pole had snapped and the jagged end flew through the air, swiftly slicing my hand. Bright drops of red blood dripped down my finger and landed on the white cement, spreading slowly outward.

Lightheaded, without a word to Tracy, I ran inside for help, stopped short when I reached the basement stairs. "Mom," I cried.

But Mom wasn't there. She wasn't there at all. And there was no one else, either, no one to help, no one home. I held my hand up, blood trickling down my arm. What should I do? I tried not to look at my own blood. Splotches covered my white shirt. Mom would have washed my cut and doused it with peroxide.

Tracy rushed in, stunned, all the blood on the floor. "I'll go get my mom!" she cried and raced away.

"Your mom's not home!" I called after her. Tracy freaked out at the sight of blood. Reluctantly she stopped.

"A neighbor?"

Suddenly I remembered the new neighbor, Mrs. Landau, the lady who'd seen me barf.

"The nurse lady," I said. Tracy darted across the street and rapped on her door. I followed, blood trailing behind me.

"I can't watch," Tracy said.

"Go home then," I said. "I'm okay."

"Oh my!" the neighbor cried when she saw the blood. She drew me inside, quickly wrapped my hand in a paper towel. Her face was round and warm as Mom's. She said, "What happened, you poor thing?"

I told her and she listened closely. She smelled like babies. She was still in her uniform from work. At the kitchen table behind her a little boy stared, another, even smaller, in a highchair. She brought me to the kitchen sink, rinsed my wound, and put gentle pressure on my still-bleeding hand with the paper towel. The bleeding slowed. The little kids were silent. Tears pinched at my eyes. Something about her fingers as she worked, the way she held my hand, eyes blue as Mom's. Didn't matter her hair was dark, almost black. I stumbled, felt faint.

Mrs. Landau fixed me with her worried eyes and said, "You know, my nurse opinion is that we should get you to the hospital for a few stitches."

I thought of my brother's three-year-old body near death, the tubes sprouting out of his arms and chest, his cries coming down that long hall. "Sorry, Mrs. Landau, I can't," I said.

"I understand, sweetie. Call me Juliette," she said warmly, patting my back. "I heard what happened. I was in the hospital that day. Word flew around. So terrible." She shook her head like she was trying to shake away the image. "Why would you want to go back there? And I do believe that a butterfly bandage will hold things together nicely." She fixed up my cut expertly.

"I was going to give the kids a snack. Stick around if you like. This is John, who we call Bird," she said, picking up the little one. With his tiny face, mostly bald head, and huge forehead he looked like a light bulb! "And this is Ben."

"Apple," said Ben.

"How come you call him Bird?" I asked, covering my eyes to play peek-a-boo with Bird, as Juliette sliced apples. Ben hurried off to the living room to play cars.

"His first word was *bird*, and he said it so often we just started calling him that," she said, in an easy-going way I liked.

"My sister Mae called me Moe when she was little," I told her. "She couldn't say Jody. I don't know where she got Moe from. I kinda liked it. Back then I hated my name."

"Why? Jody's such a pretty name," Juliette said over her shoulder as she brought Ben a couple apple slices on a napkin.

"I couldn't find it anywhere. Like, at those highway rest

stops, they never had my name on the keychains or mini license plates. They always had Claire. It drove me crazy."

"I had that same problem. There was never a Juliette anywhere. Too old fashioned," she said sitting down across from me and taking a bite of Bird's apple.

"Too Shakespearean," I said.

"You *are* a smart one," she said with a smile.

"When I was a kid I watched *Romper Room*." I felt my cheeks redden. "It's silly, but at the end of the show Miss Louise would hold up her Magic Mirror and say goodbye to all the good Do-Bee's she saw at home. She never saw a Jody. I thought it meant I wasn't a good Do-Bee. I *really* believed it!"

"That doesn't sound silly at all," said Juliette. "I'd have wanted her to see me too."

"Sometimes I waved at the TV, like this." I waved my arms high above my head. "Miss Louise, Miss Louise! I'm here. Over here. See me. See me."

She laughed at my playacting. It was thrilling to spark that much laughter.

"Oops," she said, jumping up. "Forgot to take the meat out of the freezer. Mother's work is never done," Juliette said.

"You're a good mom," I said.

"I don't know about that," she said, nodding toward the countertops, stacked with dishes. "It's hard working and taking care of everything else. My husband is off reporting from some war zone. Important things," she said, doing air quotes. "Well, soon to be ex-husband. We're separated." I never expected that.

Unsure, what to say, I asked, "Do you miss him?"

"It had to be. But sometimes it's lonely."

"I bet," I said, feeling very grown-up. Bird banged his tray for another apple slice. I handed him one.

"And how has it been for you?" she asked.

No one had ever asked that—not so directly. Juliette just waited. I heard Ben in the other room: *Vroom. Vroom.*

"It's kind of weird. Sometimes I come home and expect to find my mom there. And when she's not there, I feel so angry at her." I looked away, making a funny face for Bird.

Juliette laid her hand on mine. "It's not weird," she said.

"I got this book from the library. It's called *Death and Dying*. And it said how kids can worry their anger caused the death."

Juliette leaned back in her chair. "I'd like to read that book."

"Then they feel guilty." She nodded. Seeing she understood, I surprised myself, adding, "A few times I told my mom I wished she was dead."

"Oh, sweetie. I'm sure she knew you didn't mean it," Juliette said. "People say all sorts of things when they're really mad. I once told my mother she ruined my life. And you don't even want to know the kinds of things Seth and I have said to each other when we're mad!"

"Sure, I do."

She chuckled and said, "Next time."

Bird put his hands out to me. Pleased, I reached for him, and careful of my injury, I lifted him out of the highchair and rested him on my lap. Ben came in, Matchbox car in each hand, and climbed into his mom's lap.

We were like two moms, two friends, getting together in the afternoon.

13

The musty stench of body odor and wet towels hit the second I entered the windowless gray-tiled room. Tracy took the gym locker next to mine. "How's your finger?" Tracy asked. I held up my bandage for her inspection. Tracy grimaced. "Was the neighbor cool?" "Yeah, she was nice." I wasn't going to tell her *how* cool. I was keeping Juliette for myself.

Isabel Farrow got her head stuck in the neck of her T-shirt, exposing her ginormous breasts. Rumor said that she'd go into the woods with older high school boys and let them touch her. What did it feel like to have breasts like that, to be the one that the boys all liked? I wish.

Like a contortionist, I slipped my arms out of my shirt, squeezed my blue gym T-shirt under the shirt, then pulled my arms through the sleeves of my gym shirt, before removing my school top.

I avoided the gaze of devious Debbie Doidge, who could take a girl down with just a sidelong glance. All six Doidge kids were mean, except Jake. Maybe that's because their dad died. Maybe they were traumatized too.

Hurriedly, I threw the rest of my clothes into my locker, slipped the combination lock through the loop and gave the tumbler a spin. I tapped Tracy's arm—signaling we should get out of there. Tracy slunk with me into the gymnasium as if she were the one with no boobs.

"You're so lucky," I said.

Tracy knew just what I meant. "You're not the ironing board. Maryann Kowalski is. You have *great* boobs." She poked my chest. I shrieked. She laughed so hard. "It's just when you look down that your boobs look small. Straight ahead, they look bigger."

"Really?"

"Maybe you should get a bra. Yeah, definitely. You need one."

Miss Costello marched in—Debbie Doidge close behind her—blew her whistle, blew it again. "No lollygagging!" she shouted. A bra.

Home that afternoon, I figured I'd try on one of Mom's bras. No way would I fill it. I opened her top dresser drawer. Empty! I leapt to Mom's closet—everything was gone, everything but a pair of old black pumps hidden in the dark corner, the leather cracked and worn, and a whiff of vanilla and cigarettes. Under the shoes were a few Raleigh coupons. The hollow of the closet felt like it was inside me. At least Mom and Dad's Best Lindy crystal trophy was still on her bureau. I thought I'd put it on my desk but decided it should be on the stereo cabinet in the living room, where everyone could see it.

Claire was in the living room. "You saw?"

"Everything's gone," I said, my voice cracking.

"Aunt Sheila will *never* fit in Mom's clothes," said Claire.

"Wait, what?"

"Dad had Aunt Sheila come and empty things out."

"Claire, what?"

"I know. How could she?"

I said, "What if Mom needs her stuff?"

"I know, I know," Claire said. Suddenly her voice got soft. "When Dad made noise about Aunt Sheila sorting through Mom's stuff, I thought, No way. She'd be mad if we gave them away. Come on," she said, pulling my arm.

Wow, Claire had some of those same thoughts as me and Juliette. She took me to the rickety ladder, and we climbed up to the roasting attic.

Claire pulled down two large cardboard boxes, stashed in the back, opened the first, and started tossing Mom's clothes into my arms.

"Oh my God! You took so many."

"Damn right," said Claire. "I should get them. *Not* Aunt Sheila!"

"We should get them! Wait a sec," I said, tossing the clothes back at Claire. I carefully made my way down the narrow ladder and returned out of breath. "*Voilà*," I said, and held up Mom's cashmere sweater.

"You rat!" Claire said with a laugh. "I was looking for that sweater."

"I got it first." I swept it behind my back.

"Mom hid that sweater from Dad for months. It was way expensive," said Claire.

"Hey," I held up the green sateen dress with a huge full skirt. "Remember New Year's Eve? She looked so pretty."

"She sewed the best dresses," said Claire. Turning her back to me, she peeled off her shirt and slipped on the dress. "What do you think?" she asked.

The sight took my breath away. "You look just like Mom in it. Spin around," I said. "I want to hear it swish."

Claire twirled. "That night Mom let me sneak downstairs for a little bit after you all went to bed. I got to try champagne."

"She always let you sneak down," I said, still resentful. "Like that time I woke up scared, and went to wake you and found just pillows stuffed under your blanket. I ran downstairs and found you and Mom cuddled up on the couch. Watching TV."

"We weren't cuddled up!"

"I saw you!"

"God no. I got in trouble. Mom was *talking* to me."

"You were in trouble? What happened?"

"It's too embarrassing, but it had nothing to do with you." Claire pulled off the dress. "So that's why you screamed at her, said *that*."

I didn't need to be reminded of another time I said: *I wish you were dead.* How could I have ever said that? And she hadn't even done anything wrong.

We were quiet, rifling through the box.

"Claire?" I hesitated. "I'm reading a book that says when

someone dies we can think our angry thoughts caused it." I looked her in the eye. "I worry about that. It's like Dad says, 'If you can think it you can do it.'"

"Where did you get a book like that? You didn't cause it, JoJobrain!"

Somewhat relieved, I folded back the flaps of the second box. At least Claire didn't think it was my fault. "I love this skirt." I held up the skirt Mom had made out of Dad's old ties.

"Me too," said Claire and nabbed it from me. "I'm going to take in the waist and wear it to school. It would be super cool. No one else has anything like this."

"Remember when Mom was trying to finish Mrs. Geiger's sister's wedding gown? We were driving her crazy! She said that if we didn't stop fighting, she just might walk out that door and never come back. Maybe she did that?" I said. "When the car crashed, she didn't die. She climbed out and walked off. They told us she was in the casket, but we never saw her. Maybe that's why Dad didn't let us go to the wake."

"No way would Mom do that," said Claire. "She loved us!"

Maybe she didn't love us—love me—enough and left.

"I took some of Mom's nail polish and lipsticks. They're in my closet," said Claire.

Suddenly Claire took hold of my hand. "Mom wouldn't have left on purpose. And do you think Dad didn't look in the casket? At the wake?"

"I don't know," I said. "Maybe, not on purpose. Like in that movie, the woman gets in a car accident and has amnesia. She can't remember who she is or who her kids are. And when she gets her memory back, she shows up at Christmas."

"No," Claire shook her head so hard, her ponytail hit the side of my face.

"But you saved her clothes," I said.

"That's just a wish, Jody. I wish it too." She pulled Mom's fox from under a pile and wrapped it around her neck. "We're not babies, dahling," she said.

I tugged the fox's tail and it slid off her neck, then I tossed it back at Claire, pointy nose first.

"Ha! I used to chase you with him and you'd scream your head off."

"Those nikkin' eyes were creepy."

Claire lunged the fox at me, laughing so hard I could see the fillings in her molars. "You're still a baby," she said pushing on my arm.

"You are so annoying," I said and fluffed her hair.

"I know I'm such a bitch," she said, tossing another shirt at me.

A horn honked. "James is here. I'm going, Dad," called Claire who was standing at the front door waiting.

"Come right home after the movie," Dad called back from the kitchen.

"I will," she replied, all sweet.

From my bedroom window, I watched Claire open the car door, lean over the gear shift, and give James a long kiss. I tried to imagine what that would feel like. When they pulled away, I pinched the latest issue of *Seventeen* from Claire's bed and settled down on my own side. The cover offered articles, *Smile! Sparkle! Be Yourself!* How could I sparkle if I was being myself? I wasn't sure which to look at first *New Hairdos to Try this Minute!* or *Quiz: What's Your Type of Guy?* All these exclamation points on the cover made everything seem Amazing! I decided to try the quiz.

Q: If the guy wrote you a poem, confessing his deep love for you, what would you think?

    a. This is so romantic, much better than a gift!

    b. He calls this a gift!

    c. Okay, not the best idea, but still sweet.

Definite A.

Q: Which would impress you most in a guy?

    a. He spends most of his money on you.

    b. He can really ride a wave! (surf)

    c. He writes songs for his band and dedicates them to you!

I picked C.

The quiz revealed that I would like the smart, shy, romantic type, getting it exactly right. Charlie. We were meant to be together. *Kismet: destiny, fate.*

Laying the magazine down, I picked up Mom's nail polish from Claire's dresser—*Celestial*, a shimmery shade of white, figures that was Mom's favorite–and painted my toenails. I thought about Claire out with James. What did they talk about? Were they making out?

In my head I saw Charlie in his basement, leaning over the *Trouble* board, leaning a little further. I couldn't stop myself, I kissed him. His lips were soft and warm and tasted like Lays potato chips. After that we were awkward, no longer friends playing. Had I scared him away?

I wiggled my toes. They sparkled!

Picking up *Pride and Prejudice*, I hunkered down on my bed, turned to page one, and began reading:

It is a truth universally acknowledged, that a single man in possession of a good fortune must be in want of a wife.

In want of a wife! How could Miss Wendy love this twaddle? I went back to *Seventeen*, flipped through the pages, and read about what bra works best under what shirt.

14

On Monday I woke early for school. It was still mostly dark, a new sun beginning to fill the room. I lay in bed planning my outfit. What goes well with a nikkin' bandage?

Claire, her pillow over her head, was still sound asleep.

Rolling over, I turned on my side and noticed something white lying on my lime-green shag rug. Without my glasses on I couldn't make it out—maybe one of Billy's toys? Climbing out of bed, I leaned over to get a closer look. Mom's sunglasses! I picked them up and ran my fingers over the white frame and brown-tinted lenses.

My chest seized. I could barely breathe.

"Mom, are you here?" I whispered.

A sudden breeze rattled the blinds.

She had come back! How else could her sunglasses have gotten here? Of course, she was wearing them, driving that car on *that day*. It was sunny. Nothing had ever felt truer. She'd left them for *me*. I was the only one who wore glasses. When I was seven, Mom had taken me to get my first pair—little pink cat-eyes with sparkly rhinestones at the tips that I swore were real diamonds. Because they were! I twirled the sunglasses in my hand. What was she trying to tell me? I put them on. Looking through the lenses made everything blurrier. Maybe they held a secret message. Who could I tell?

Claire was snoring. I didn't want to share them with her. Mom left them for me.

I tucked them inside my book bag.

After lunch with the usual gaggle of friends—Tracy, Jennifer, Bettina, Meg, and Kate—we were out on the blacktop, Mom's sunglasses resting atop my head like a halo. Bettina sat on the brick wall, holding court, while the rest of us stood around her in a circle. Most of the boys had a crush on her. She had that confidence that goes along with being the prettiest girl in the class.

Further down the wall leaned Debbie Doidge and her younger brother Jake. Why'd they have to stand so close to us? "You guys, these were my mom's." I touched the glasses dramatically. "I found them on the rug in my bedroom. This morning. She must have left them."

Tracy's eyes widened. "You saw Maggie, your mom?" She looked as excited as me. She loved Mom—she told me she wished she were her mother.

"Well, either she was here or her ghost," I said. I thrilled seeing my friends' eyes grow wide in fear and fascination—a dead mother returning to life.

"But, Jody. Come on. You saw her?" Meg said.

"Well, it was still a little dark. I'm not *sure* I saw her. She was fuzzy, just a presence. But, yeah, I think it was her. I mean— these glasses." I snatched them off my head for all to see. "Where else would they have come from?"

"Did she say anything?" asked Bettina, eyes wide.

"You must have been terrified! I would have been," said Kate.

I could see Debbie Doidge was listening, so I both turned up the volume and ignored her as best I could. "Of course, ghosts can't talk," I said.

"What happened then?" asked Tracy.

"Nothing. She just, sort of, well, melted away. And then when I got out of bed, her sunglasses were lying there." I paused, making sure they were all still with me. "I'm certain they weren't there when I went to bed. I had cleaned up my side of the room."

"Oh *my God*. What did Claire say?" asked Bettina, her perfect button nose wrinkling.

"Claire slept through the whole thing! But the glasses were for me."

"Maybe Maggie will come back for them," said Tracy. "Do you think she will? Could you touch her?"

It felt good to talk about her, but not in a sad, boo-hoo kind of way. For the first time in six months I felt special.

Debbie Doidge stood up from the wall, her brother at her side. They swept in close, and she said, "What's this about sunglasses?"

"Her mom!" Tracy said. "She came back."

"A ghost," Kate said.

"You're such a liar, Jody," Debbie hissed. "Dead people don't come back!"

I froze. Looking to my friends to back me up, I said, "I *did* see her."

"Or maybe you just *wanted* to believe it," Bettina said.

Jake gave me the saddest look. He wasn't like his sister, but he wasn't going to say anything in my defense either, even if he missed his dad.

"Well, yeah, when you think about it," Meg said, "there's no such thing as ghosts." Why were they taking Doidge's side?

"No, it's true," I cried. "Look, see, I have her sunglasses." I gripped the glasses tight in my hand, tweaking my bandage, but willing away the pain, then waved them in Debbie's face, in Jake's too. "She was!"

"Well, maybe it was a dream," said Jennifer, kindly. "Dreams can seem real."

"She had to have had them when she died. They're prescription! She needed them to drive."

"That's true. Your mom always wore glasses," said Tracy.

The others nodded, but uncertainly. Doidge crossed her arms and shook her head in triumph. But her brother. Well, Jake had sympathy in his eyes—fake or not, I couldn't tell.

"Come on, Tracy," I said. "I don't care what they think."

"We think you're lying," Doidge said.

And just like that, I lost Mom again.

Tracy and I stormed off together, best friends to the end.

I was tossing my pink Spalding ball at the side of the house, sunglasses resting on top of my head, challenging myself to complete all the levels in *Seven*. Level one, I threw the ball against the wall and had to catch it without dropping it. Level two was like level one, except the ball had to bounce off the ground and hit the wall, then I had to catch it without letting it hit the ground again. The maneuvers got tougher and tougher. If I made a mistake at any level I had to go back to the start. The nikkin' bandage was messing me up.

I had been at it since arriving home from school, but in truth I was waiting for Juliette. Ever since she fixed my finger, I'd been keeping an eye out for her. I was spinning around quickly, clapping my hands behind my back—level four—when Juliette pulled her blue Oldsmobile into her driveway. I hoped she'd seen how coordinated I was.

I watched as she gathered some things from the back seat.

"How's that finger doing?" she called across the street. "Come in and let me have a look at it." I crossed over and followed her inside.

Juliette barely had a chance to put her pocketbook down when Ben came charging at her. "Mommy," he yelled as he leapt up into her arms.

"Hi there, slugger. I missed you. Let me give you a big smooch," she said, then covered his face with kisses. He squealed with delight, then pushed her away.

From the kitchen I heard Bird excitedly calling, "Ma, Ma, Ma," his voice growing more urgent with each word.

"I'm coming, Bird," Juliette said as she lowered Ben to the ground. "Hi, Martina. This is my friend and neighbor, Jody." Friend!

Martina flipped her long blond braid over her shoulder. "Hi," I said gruffly. I wanted Juliette to myself.

"Is Bird feeling better. Diarrhea stop?" Juliette asked as she pulled off her jacket.

"Yes, much better," Martina said. "He ate a good lunch." While Juliette accompanied Martina to the door, I distracted Bird with funny faces.

"Okay, now your turn," said Juliette returning to the kitchen. For a moment I thought she meant me. She leaned down, whisked Bird up into the air, and gave another round of hugs and kisses. "Let me check that cut of yours," she said. She led me to the living room and held my hand under the lamp. Her touch was soft. "It's healing fine," she said. "Still hurt?"

"No, it's good," I lied.

"Where's Martina from?" I asked, curious at her accent. I sat down on the big blue chair. As soon as Juliette plopped down on the cushy sofa, Bird climbed on top of her. Besides the chair and sofa, the only other stuff in the room were toys.

"Germany. Seth and I lived there before Ben was born. He was on assignment with the *Tribune*. We got to know Martina, and I told her if she came to the US, we'd give her a job until she got settled. She's been a lifesaver."

"Mama, help me do my puzzle," said Ben.

"I'll help," I said, sitting on the floor next to him. "Oh, look. A farm!"

"And how was your day?" asked Juliette.

"Awful," I said. "Good job, Ben. Where does the cow go?" I asked.

"What happened?"

"I found these when I woke up this morning," I said. I lifted the sunglasses off my head and held them up for her to see. "They were my mom's. They weren't in my room last night. I told my friends at school that my mom must have come during the night because how else could they get there? Then Debbie Doidge told everyone I was lying." This was harder than bouncing and turning and clapping with my stupid ball. I hadn't *really* seen Mom, so I didn't say that. I said, "Only Tracy stood up for me."

"That's not nice. I'm sure you'd want to see your mom. Sometimes when you want something so much it can even seem real," said Juliette. I handed Ben another piece of the puzzle.

"I keep looking for a sign that she's come back." Bird climbed off Juliette's lap and brought me a stuffed bear. "Grrr," I said, growling like a bear as I waggled it at his belly.

"You must miss her." Juliette brushed her hand over Ben's hair, patting down his cowlick.

"Big time. But I can go a whole afternoon without thinking about her at all." It was alarming to realize I could get used to almost anything.

"And then you feel bad." Juliette pulled off her sweater.

"Yep. I'm not sure if it's worse remembering or forgetting her," I said.

"I know what you mean. My dad died right after Ben was born. Some days I'd pick up the phone, to tell him about something cute Ben did, and then the shock would hit me—he was gone, and I'd have to sit down."

"That's it!" I said. I wasn't the only crazy person thinking my mother could still be alive. "A couple times I thought I saw her walking on the street." My voice cracked a bit.

Juliette tilted her head, giving me a sad smile. She said, "That's not stupid. The way I see it, a death doesn't happen just once. It's like we have to keep being reminded that someone's gone. Remember her and miss her a little more, until one day we can remember her without all the sad feelings."

I took a deep breath and said, "I thought she loved my sisters more than me."

Juliette burrowed in closer. "Why did you think that? I'm sure it's not true."

"Mae is so sweet and cuddly. Claire is older and more interesting. And Annie and Billy, well, are cute babies."

"Well, I didn't know your mom. But it's hard to imagine her not loving you just as much."

"Not when I was in the hospital," I said. I looked down at my finger. A scar was starting to form on the tip.

"What do you mean?"

"When I was eight, I went to the hospital."

"What happened?"

"I was over at Tracy's house. Playing a game when my head started pounding. And when I got home, no one was there. I yelled for Mom, and then colors started flashing before my eyes."

"That's awful. What happened?"

"I don't know. I was in pain and then woke up in the hospital. It was scary. They kept me there for days."

"That must have been very scary," said Juliette.

"Dad came to see me every day. Bringing me candy, a set of paper dolls, a coloring book. Mom didn't. She never came. Dad said she had to take care of the other kids." Juliette was nodding.

"They took blood and stuck needles in my head. Which wasn't as terrible as it sounds."

"Yes, electromyography."

"I pretended to be brave. It's kind of silly, but I remember imagining there was a rocket ship on the wall next to my hospital bed, just like the one I have next to my bed at home. It's really just some chipped paint," I said, with a chuckle. "I wanted to feel as courageous as an astronaut, alone, taking off into outer space."

"You wanted to feel like you were back at home," said Juliette, nodding.

"I tried to act like I didn't care, that I wasn't going to miss her if she didn't miss me. Now I know she was pregnant with Annie."

"Did they figure out what was wrong?" asked Juliette.

"They thought I had a tumor but all I had was migraines."

"And as a nurse I can tell you. I'm sure her doctor said she needed to rest. And hospitals can be dangerous for pregnant women." Mom hadn't told me either of those things. It helped to hear it from Juliette.

"I'm really glad you told me," she said, smoothing down my hair, her eyes welling up. "And, Jody, I'm certain she loved you so, so, much."

"I guess."

"How couldn't she? You're smart, funny, kind, and beautiful." Juliette thinks I'm beautiful! Glasses and all.

Bird, a gleeful smile on his face, was making a beeline for the puzzle. Quickly I pounded on the colorful peg board laying nearby. Bird tackled me for the hammer.

"I hate that Debbie Doidge."

Juliette patted my arm. "It's good you stood your ground. With girls like that you have to. Deep down, bullies are afraid. If they see you aren't afraid, they give up and go look for someone else to pick on." I'm never gonna let her push me around. Juliette got up from the couch. "I'm going to get some ice tea, want some?"

"Sure," I said. "I saw a man in a red car yesterday. Was that Seth?"

"No, that's my brother Duncan. He stopped by," she called from the kitchen.

"Is Seth away?"

"He's off in Kenya. Or is it Nigeria? Who knows." She returned with two glasses of tea.

"Will you really get divorced?" I asked. I remembered a few years back, when two couples in the neighborhood divorced. It shook me up—parents were supposed to stay together. When I asked Dad about it, he said, "It's like a virus."

"A virus? It's contagious?"

"Kind of," he'd said. "When people start divorcing, it seems an easy answer. Others start thinking, well so and so did it—maybe I should too. It spreads and others can catch it. It becomes more acceptable. It's like it becomes a *possibility* when people are having trouble." Then he told me. "Jody, it's like intention, you don't want to put your intention toward divorce you want to put it toward making things better. Marriages all go through hard times, but you work at it." I didn't tell Juliette the virus idea, it might make her feel bad. But maybe I wouldn't mind her catching this virus.

Juliette went on, "Not that I'd notice either way. Even when we were together he was always traipsing here and there, some other country. I'd had it." Then she paused. "I'm sorry. You don't need to hear all that."

Yes, I did. *A man in want of a wife.* Maybe Jane Austen knew what she was talking about.

15

Outside the leaves were scattered across the lawn in bright oranges, reds, and yellows. Dad was packed, his black suitcase propped up by the front door.

"Okay, gang, take a seat," said Dad, pens in one hand, business cards in the other. "Before I go, listen up." Not another talk about how we are supposed to mind Miss June, do our homework, blah, blah, blah. He plopped down on the living room couch. "There's a famous fountain in Rome—the Trevi Fountain. Everyone who visits throws a penny in and makes a wish. I'm doubling your odds. You give me a penny to toss *and* an intention card for me to read with your wish."

On my card, I wanted to write *Charlie*, or even *boobs*. Dad would read them, though, so I just wrote: *new boots*. I asked him for an extra business card and jotted down my own secret intention: *Dad doesn't die on the plane*. The five of us would be orphans. I tucked the intention card in a white bracelet box that Tracy had given me. A box she was just going to throw away, so I said I'd keep it. Laying the card on the cotton, it fit perfectly. I stashed it away in my drawer.

This was Dad's week away in Rome:

Day one: All fine.

Day two: Annie wakes with a bad dream. June-the-Loon, our wacko babysitter, whose loud snores I could hear from down the hall, didn't budge.

"It's okay Annie, I'm here," I said softly. And even softer, "Are you scared something will happen to Daddy?"

Me too, I didn't say. Instead, I scoured through the cubby of books and pulled one out and began to read, "In the great green room—" By the time I got to, "Goodnight, nobody," Annie was calm and sleeping.

Day three: Miss June called, "Wake up, children. Wake up!" as she barreled into my and Claire's room. "It's time for school, sleepy heads. Get up!" The smell of bacon filled the house. At least she was making us breakfast.

"Go away," Claire said.

"Guess what?" asked Miss June.

"It's still dark," I said. No sun trickled in through the blinds. I shook my head, trying to rouse myself.

"That's what I'm trying to tell you," she said. "It snowed!" And then she flitted out of the room and into Mae and Annie's. I heard her singing, "It's beginning to look a lot like Christmas."

Annie, perky at any hour of the day, began to shout: "Snow! Yippee! Yippee!"

"Claire, did she say it was snowing? It's October!"

"She's a lunatic," Claire said, rolling back over.

I yawned, stretched, put on my glasses, climbed out of bed and threw my clothes on—green corduroy pants, plaid top.

Mae, dressed for school, was rubbing her eyes as we crossed paths in the hall.

Annie, clad in her school uniform, was already standing at the living room window, next to Miss June. No longer so perky.

"Jody, Mae, come see the snow," said Miss June, dreamily.

I drew the curtain back. The moon, just a sliver, didn't offer much light. Trying to focus, I blinked several times. "Where's the snow?" I asked.

"Look. Right there. Under the tree," said Miss June.

I groaned. "Those are pebbles, Miss June! White pebbles."

"I wanted snow," said Annie, pouting. "I wanted to go sledding."

"I'm going to eat," I said, flinging the curtain closed.

Pouring myself some orange juice, I looked up at the clock: 2:15 a.m.

Day Four: Claire called from the living room, "Hey, Jody, we're playing Beatle Baseball! Round everyone up." When I stepped into the living room, she was brandishing Dad's enormous red-and-white umbrella. James and Claire had moved all the living room furniture out of the way. Dad would kill us! James was tossing a nerf ball in the air, and Billy was at his side in a matching baseball hat. Since Dad had left for Rome, James was practically living at our house. Miss June was perfectly oblivious. Yesterday, I'd burst into the garage looking for a broom and found James and Claire, his shirt all the way off, her blouse open, bra like a beacon, his back a ripple of muscles. My breathing got faster, my insides all squirrely.

I yelled out in surprise and closed the door.

Anyway, Beatle Baseball. "Mae, Annie," I called. Mae's flute playing stopped, and in minutes she and Annie appeared.

"Hi, James," said Mae, crushing hard. James tousled her hair. Mae smiled so broad her face was going to crack.

"Look how strong I am," Billy said, showing James his muscle. "It got bigger." Claire and James shared a look. James squeezed Billy's bicep. "Wow, that's quite a muscle."

"What's Beatle Baseball?" I asked.

James said, "You'll see. Claire and I made it up."

Claire waved three record covers in the air. "Okay, Annie, you take *The White Album*," she said, and pulled the record out. "That's first base."

"I'm first. I'm first," yipped Annie.

"It's my ball! I'm first," said Billy.

"You're the second baseman, Billy. Just like me," James said as he plopped down *Yellow Submarine* where the big brown chair usually sat. "Second base is the best base."

I sidled up to Claire and whispered in her ear. "Yeah, that's what I heard." Sometimes I cracked myself up.

Claire swatted at my arm but laughed too. "Third," she said. I was shocked: Claire always knew how to shut me up.

Billy, thrilled to be playing, centered his bare feet on the second base cover and didn't budge.

"Mae, you're third base," James said. "Claire, toss me the *Sgt. Peppers* cover."

"Will Miss June let us play baseball inside?" asked Mae. "With an umbrella!"

"Pff. She won't even notice," I said. "She's too busy keeping her eye out for snow and boiled cabbage."

Sounding like a Major League manager, James called out, "Okay, Jody Moran, you're pitching. Claire is top of the lineup, batting first. I'll catch. I like the view from behind." He gave Claire's butt a slap.

My face warmed.

Then in a gravelly radio-announcer voice James said, "Right hander, Claire Moran is approaching the batter's box! Looks like she'll be swinging for the fences! Pitching, the Wild Sister of Randolph Road, Jo-Jo Jody! On deck, after Jumpin' Jody, Mae Moran!"

We all imitated a roaring crowd, hissing and muttering.

I tossed the ball. Claire swung the umbrella, missed.

"Whiff," I yelled.

"Go Claire," Billy cried from second base.

"Strike one," James cried.

"Ump is blind," said Claire. "Anyway, I was just loosening up." She waved the umbrella around a few times.

"Wait," I said. "New rule! After you hit it, *if* you hit it, you have to sing a song from the album you're running to."

"Stellar," said James. I bowed.

"I don't know the words," said Mae. "Can I just hum?"

"That rule is only for twelve and older," said Sweet Baby James.

This time Claire made contact. The ball took to the air. Claire dropped the umbrella, ran to *White Album*, started singing, "Ob-La-Di, Ob-La-Da".

"Go, Annie! Go!" we yelled. Annie, chasing the ball, was falling over herself laughing, with each step kicking the ball further away.

"Get it, Annie. Get it!"

"Safe!" James shouted. Then, "Batter up, Jody."

The infield rotated, Claire to the mound. I hefted the umbrella. "Still like the view, Jimbo?" I said, giving a little wiggle.

"The ump must be impartial," he cried.

The pitch. Swing. Miss. "Whiff," Claire yelled.

"Bad throw," I said. "Another."

Claire wound up for the pitch. I leaned in, ready. Claire tossed. With all my might, I threw my body forward, sending the umbrella flying out of my hands, sailing across the room. *Whack!* The tip pierced the living room wall, the umbrella quivered, momentarily suspended in the air, then I watched it hit the cabinet below, sending Mom and Dad's Best Lindy crystal trophy crashing to the floor.

"Oh, NO!" I yelled. The crystal trophy Mom loved. Tears welled up in my eyes.

"You're going to be in big trouble," said Mae.

"Shut up!" I said.

I started picking up the pieces of glass that covered the floor. If I got every one of them, I could put it back together.

"Wait, Jody. Let me get a broom. You'll cut yourself," said James as he reached down to pull me up.

"Don't throw them away!" I cried. Looking at the shards in my hand, I knew there was no putting the pieces back together.

"I'll go get it," said Mae. She dashed back with the broom and dust bin. James started sweeping.

Just then, we heard Dad's keys jangling in the lock. The front door swung open.

"Dad!" yelled Claire. "You scared us." What was he doing home? He had three more days in Italy.

"Hi, Dad," I said, my voice shaky. Mae was picking up the album covers. James froze, mid-sweep. Dad didn't seem to be taking it all in, not the furniture out of place, the hole in the wall, or the broken glass.

"Daddy!" Annie and Billy shouted, running to him, each grabbing onto a leg. Dad set down his luggage and lowered himself on to the coffee table. He pulled the two of them up on his lap, giving them each a hug. He was blinking his eyes. Was he trying not to cry? Strands of gray peppered his hair, more than I had recalled. Pulling a hankie out of his pocket, he blew his nose.

My insides churned. I looked at the shattered glass. It was all my fault.

"James give you this, Billy-boy?" Dad asked, tapping the brim of Billy's Edgehaven Bulldog baseball cap.

"I'm a bulldog," said Billy, lifting his cap off his head and wiping his brow, the same way James did.

"Nice of you, James," said Dad, as if it took all his energy to get the words out.

"Sure thing, Mr. Moran," said James. "Welcome home."

"Dad," I said softly.

Miss June appeared in the kitchen doorway. She looked at Dad as if she were unsure who he was.

"Hi, June," said Dad. He was trying to sound upbeat. "I decided to fly home a few days early."

"Oh, that's nice," June said. "I hope you didn't have any trouble landing with all that snow."

Dad shook his head, like he was clearing water out of his ears. "Repeat what she just said." I was relieved for the distraction. "She just said snow, right?" Dad asked, completely befuddled.

"Miss June woke us up in the middle of the night. She thought it was snowing!" said Mae.

"What are you doing home?" asked Claire.

Dad rubbed his chin, covered in dark stubble. "I just wasn't having much fun." He tugged off his wool suit coat, no easy feat. "I guess I didn't like being there without your mom." Pain filled every crease of his face. "So after a few days I threw in the towel."

It hurt my heart to hear him say he missed Mom.

Taking in our stunned faces, he quickly added, "And I missed all of you." At that, he gathered up Mae, pulling her in with Annie and Billy and giving her a deep hug. From behind I leaned in, hugging him. "And maybe it was a good idea, hearing this snow business."

"Daddy, remember Mrs. O'Donnell, my teacher?" Annie said, hopping off his lap. "She helped me make you a card. I'll get it." Off she ran.

"What's going on here? Why is the furniture all over the place? There's a hole in the wall! Wait, what broke?"

"I'm so sorry, Daddy," I said and started to cry. I never thought about how lonesome he must be. He had already lost so much—his wife, the woman he loved—and now, because of me, he lost the crystal trophy. A symbol of their love. I was the worst kid in the world. "I'm really, really sorry. We were playing Beatle Baseball. The umbrella went flying and knocked over your trophy. I didn't mean to."

Dad seemed too tired to care. He pulled me into the hug. "It's all right, stringbean. It was an accident."

16

"Where to?" Dad asked Billy, who was perched atop his shoulders. Billy was wearing his peaked military hat. A tug on Dad's left earlobe meant a left turn and a tug on the right one meant a right turn. A tug on both ears together were the brakes. Dad had big ears, perfect for steering. He could wiggle them, just by thinking about it. Billy, giggling, pulled at each ear making Dad turn in crazy directions.

The five of us, Dad in the lead, strolled the couple city blocks from where we parked to my grandparents' apartment. I noticed his pants hung loose around his waist. "This is where I played stickball," he said, for the millionth time, pointing to the sewer covers. "Those manholes were the bases. The Beatles didn't yet exist," he said giving me and Claire a side-smile.

"Dad, I can picture another guy walking on the moon easier than seeing you as a boy," I said.

As soon as we turned the corner, I looked up. Over the electrical wire that crossed Turner Place still hung a pair of white sneakers, joined by the laces. They dangled at dead center of that wire, day in and day out. And like every month before, Dad said, "Pete, the boy who lived on the floor below, tossed them up." Through the rain and snow, they remained, their abidingness like the refrigerator's hum, the ducks, comforted me. Abidingness was last night's word. *Abidingness: permanence, capacity for enduring.*

As we neared the building, I heard Grandma Moran calling, "Yoo-Hoo!" from her fourth-floor window. We hadn't seen my grandparents since school started.

"Going to Grandma's is the pits. It's worse than even church," said Claire. "At least church is only an hour."

"It could be *worse*. You could be going to church *with* Grandma," said Dad.

"You should have let me bring James then."

"Then Grandma could show him all those pictures of you in the highchair, with smushed peas all over your face."

The lobby was bleaker than usual. The bulb that hung from the stairwell was out, the wallpaper peeling, the linoleum chipped. I counted the steps as we climbed each level, just like when I was little and learning to count. When we reached the top, Dad asked with a sly grin, "Has the number changed?"

"Still eighty," I said.

Grandma greeted us in her crisply ironed brown-and-cream floral dress, smelling like Ivory soap, her lipstick perfectly lined, her snow-white hair in neat pin curls. "A lack of disposable income is no excuse to look slovenly," she liked to say. I breathed in deeply, loving that sweet smell of Johnson's Jubilee Kitchen Wax, like coconut candy.

"I like your hat, Captain," said Grandma, tapping the brim of Billy's military hat. When her eyes landed on Mae, Annie, and me, she gasped, "Joe, did you cut their hair?"

Dad, reached for her shoulder and steered her towards the living room. "Mother, not a word…" I didn't need to hear the rest, I knew he didn't want us getting upset again about our haircuts.

"That's my girl," Grandpa said and gave me a kiss. His eyes a milky blue. He had more hair in his ears than on the top of his head. He smelled of peppermint, a roll of Lifesavers always in the left pocket of his trousers. Claire came in next and he said, "There's my girl." We were all his girls.

Grandma lined us up, one at a time, against the living room door jamb to mark our height. Mae, eager to be taller, jumped in front of the door frame. "No tippy toes," she chided.

"Measure me. Me, Grandma," said Billy.

"Youngest to oldest," Grandma said, lifting the hat off his head. "You probably grew the most, young man," said Grandma. "Annie, you next." Annie and Mae had each grown almost an inch.

"Now stand tall," she told me as she ran the pencil across

the top of my head. I was trying to shrink. Even though Claire was two years older, I stood about the same height. Watching my line creep up a little higher, with the date and my name marked alongside, felt good when I was little, but now it made me feel gawky and skinny.

"I stopped growing," said Claire. "I don't need to be measured."

"Make Grandma happy," said Dad.

But she was right, she hadn't grown a smidge.

"Girls, it's important to have good posture," said Grandma. "I'm only five feet four inches, but I appear five-seven. That's because I stand so straight."

Claire whispered in my ear, "And I'm six-two, but appear five-two because I slouch."

I pretend-coughed to hide my laughing.

I heard Grandma say softly to Dad, "Joseph, dear, you are doing a wonderful job. I know it's a lot without Margaret."

The living room was crowded with a couch, Grandpa's chair, a dropleaf table, and a corner china cabinet that was crammed with dishes and miniature teapots. In another corner was a magazine rack with several ancient issues of *Ring,* the boxing magazine Dad collected as a boy. The drop-leaf table was open, in the center of the room, a name card at each seat, probably just like the Kennedy's used at their house. I liked to think we were like the Kennedys—Catholic, lots of kids, just without the cash.

Grandpa slowly lowered himself into the recliner, a whiskey on the table next to him. Grandma allowed one drink, one ice cube.

Seeing I was placed between Grandma and Mae, I waited for the right moment, snatched up my name and swapped it with Annie's who was on Dad's right.

"You're not allowed to move them," said Mae.

Ignoring her, Claire followed my lead, waiting for Grandma to look away and shifting her place card from Dad's left to my right. That made me happy.

Mae said louder, "You're not allowed!"

"Quit trying for sainthood," I hissed.

"Tut-tut, now. Let's have no fussing," said Grandma from across the room, getting a platter from the cabinet.

With a sly grin Dad turned Grandma's card upside down.

I tossed Mae's card to the middle of the table.

Claire licked Grandma's spoon.

"Joe, tell me about Rome," said Grandma. She said *Rome* in the same way she said *pizza*, like it was a booger on her finger. "You said on the phone it was difficult."

My ears perked up.

"Don't go making him cry again," Claire whispered to me, not a joke.

"I'm fine now. I just got too lonely and came home. I missed Maggie. I missed the kids." Dad looked up, noticed us listening, even Annie. He crossed the room and stood next to Grandpa.

Tapping his shoulder, Dad said, "Grandpa, did you ever tell Roo the one about Spotty?"

"I'm not sure that I have, son," he said, his eyes twinkling. We all chuckled—he always told us about Spotty. "Annie, you and Billy climb up here," he said patting his lap. "You each get a knee. Let's see. Where were we? Well, you remember Spotty had run off from his mommy and got lost." I flinched. I wished he'd made it a daddy. "And New York City is no place to get lost. No, *sireee*."

"Now, Joe, don't forget to get their hands washed before dinner. I'll go finish up," said Grandma. It was four p.m.!

"Yes, dear, right after the story," Grandpa, continued, his voice throaty and warm.

Grandma said, "Jody dear, come give me a hand with dinner." Grandma chose me. "You can mash the potatoes." I signaled to Claire to come with me.

She mouthed, *No way.*

The sun streamed in through the white sheer curtains of the tiny kitchen. The appliances—even the icebox, as Grandma called it—were old and miniature.

"I'm having a nice cup of tea. Want one?"

Grandma poured a golden-brown tea into delicate cups,

placed her pointer finger through the loop of the handle, securing the cup with her thumb. I did the same. When I stuck my pinkie out like I'd seen in the movies, she said, "Never raise the three fingers. Let them follow the curve of your other fingers," as she guided mine into place.

Her hands were brown-spotted and wrinkled. The makeup on her face, like the coats of yellow paint on the walls, was getting thicker.

Grandma handed me the masher. "You're such a good helper," she said.

Feeling special, I decided to ask, "How old are you, Grandma?"

"A lady never tells her age." Grandma added a splash of milk to the pot.

"You can tell me. I won't tell anyone. Grandma Cupcake's sixty-three."

"Doubtless that's true. But never you mind about me."

I wasn't going to be thrown off. "When you go to the doctors, what do you put on the form where it asks your age?"

"*A*," she said, her lips firmly set.

"*A* for age?"

"*A* for adult."

"You are so enigmatic," I said. "That means difficult to understand; inscrutable."

"You know so many big words. And, so do I—a woman should be *mysterious*." I didn't tell her that mysterious was not such a big word and meant the same thing.

"Do you even go to the doctor?"

"Gracious, so many questions!" she said. She put her hand to her throat like I had asked her where she buried the bodies. "Why do you ask so many questions? Are you writing a book?"

Two could play at this game: "Don't answer a question with a question!"

"Now you sound like Grandpa."

Why wouldn't anyone answer my questions? Like, what happens when we die if there is no heaven? Like, can someone come back from the dead? Like, where could I find those kinds of answers? Maybe when you died, you get to know what happens, find out all of the answers—but I didn't want to wait.

Shortly, we all sat down to plates of mashed potatoes, overcooked canned green beans, and pork chops as dry as leather. Definitely where Dad learned to cook. Grandma used fancy things, like a gravy boat, matching table cloth and napkins. The food seemed a kind of afterthought. We had to sit up straight, pass the platters to the right, not grab for them, and wait for everyone to finish before asking permission to leave the table.

"Dad," Mae whispered. "I can't chew the meat." She slipped it on to Billy's plate.

"Yummy," cried Billy. If you served him a plate of dog-doo, he'd probably eat it.

"Billy, no hats at the table," said Grandma. Dad pulled it off Billy's head before he could grab for it.

"Annie, I can't believe you started school. How old are you now, thirteen?" asked Grandpa.

"*Grandpa*, I'm almost five," said Annie, giggling.

"My, my, I would have thought you were thirteen."

"Mrs. O'Donnell is my teacher. I *love* her! And I wear a uniform," said Annie. Grandma's head shot up. Dad mustn't have told her.

"St. Paul's?" Grandma asked. Dad explained how Annie, with a November birthday, was too young for public school. St. Paul's had an end-of-year cut off. "That will be five kids at five different schools! Won't that be a nightmare."

"I know, Mother. But it's okay for a year or two, and then Annie can switch to public school. I need a place for her *now*."

"I don't want to switch schools," said Annie, scrunching up her face, pouting. "I'm staying with Mrs. O'Donnell!"

"Pork chop, you aren't switching. You will be with Mrs. O'Donnell all year." Dad closed his eyes and sighed.

"Lillian, dear, I'm sure Joe is making the best decision," said Grandpa. "And speaking of birthdays. Jody, I believe you're the next one up. A big one. Is it twenty-one?" joked Grandpa.

"It's more like fourteen," I said.

"And what are you hoping to get?"

"A VW Beetle."

Grandpa laughed and laughed. "That's my girl," he said.

"Well, in fact," I said, with a quick grin for Dad, "I'm getting my ears pierced."

Grandma pursed her lips. Claire kicked me under the table. What an idiot I was!

"Joe, why would you have a lovely young girl do that to her ears?"

Dad clinked his glass and said, "Mother, did we tell you? Mae is trying out for the role of Alice in *Alice in Wonderland.* Mae, tell Grandma and Grandpa some of your lines."

I had run lines with Mae so often, I could be trying out for the play.

Mae cleared her throat. "Just a moment ago I was sitting by the riverbank with my sister. She was reading a book…and…I can't remember," she said, her voice all trembly.

"Mae, remember what I taught you. Close your eyes and envision yourself onstage. Imagine yourself as Alice. Can you see it?" She nodded. Dad said, "Now, the rest will fall into place. Try again." Mae gave the rest of the line perfectly.

After dinner, our usual treat awaited us: a half a bag of M&M's. Grandma cut the bags down the middle, with us kids watching over her slice as if it were brain surgery, assuring a perfect dissection. *Dissection: the act of cutting a body to study its internal parts.*

She was big on self-discipline, or maybe she was just cheap.

Out on the street Dad reminded us to wave to Grandma, who hovered at the window.

"Gang, it's getting late," he said as we meandered to the car. "Annie and Billy, as soon as we're home it's baths and pajamas. Claire, Jody, Mae, finish up your homework."

"Shoot," I groaned. "I forgot to study for my nikkin' metric test. I hate metric!"

"Oh, and Mae. Mae Moran!"

"Yes, Daddy. What?"

"You have a dentist appointment tomorrow."

"I just went!"

"Then it's Claire." Dad chuckled. "I knew that."

"Ugh, I hate Dr. Ganz," Claire complained. "He leans over and breathes all over you and you can see up his hairy nose."

"Miss Phyllis will watch Annie and Billy till I get home." Ever since Miss June left to "find another situation," as Dad called it, Miss Phyllis looked after Annie and Billy. When Mae had asked Dad what happened to Miss June, Dad said she got "a job at a nursing home." I laughed so hard, I blew milk out my nose.

"Billy, stop at the corner!" yelled Dad. He kept moving. "Sergeant, command halt!" Dad said firmly. Billy stopped and saluted, his hand tapping his cap.

"Oh no, I *forgot!* Tomorrow is Lisa's birthday party. After school. I didn't get a present for her. I have to get one," said Mae, as tears flowed down her cheeks. "Everyone at the party will have a gift. I'll be the only one without one."

"No problem," Dad said. He stopped walking, fished a five out of his wallet and handed it to Mae. She stared down at the bill and then back up at Dad. Her face scrunched up in disgust.

"This isn't a *present,*" Mae said. "I can't give her this!"

"Of course, you can, honey. It's a much better present," said Dad, pulling the keys out and unlocking the car door. "Lisa can pick out whatever she likes. When you get home make her a nice card, put the money inside. Believe me, she'll love it."

As Dad drove, he kept talking, mostly to himself. "And I'll make your lunches. Save me time in the morning." Then a few second later he hit his hand against the steering wheel. "Damn it!"

"What?" I said, startled.

"I didn't go to the grocery store today. We're out of cold cuts. And milk." He paused. "Okay, I'll run to the store while Claire's at the dentist." There were plenty of times Mom had run out of milk, cereal, or lunchmeat, but sometimes with Dad it felt like it might be the domino that would bring everything down. Someone needed to help the guy out. "I can go after school," I offered. "To the A&P. I've been there lots of times." I said it with a shrug, like it was the easiest thing in the world, stopping myself before I said, "With Mom."

His hesitation was obvious—probably he worried that I'd buy only candy and snacks—but so was his desperation.

"I can find everything," I assured him. "Meat, vegetables." It would be a cinch to food shop.

"Oh, okay. Great...sure...sure. Just this time." His face brightened. "I'll make a list and leave it with some money on the counter for when you get home. You shop and I'll come pick you up after my five o'clock tile appointment. It shouldn't be long. That's my girl."

I liked being his girl. "That's my dad," I said.

Claire liked that. We laughed and laughed all the way home.

That night in bed I read more of *Pride and Prejudice*. Even though I could tell it was going to be one of those happily-ever-after books, I was liking it more and more. *When breakfast was over they were joined by the sisters; and Elizabeth began to like them herself, when she saw how much affection and solicitude they showed for Jane.* Solicitude. That was a new word.

I leaned over and reached for my *OED*. Too heavy. Laying down the novel, I lifted the book up with two hands. I remembered Dad bringing it home from a job and joking, "I think it weighs as much as you do, stringbean."

I leafed through, looking for long ones, till finally I came across the word *solicitude: care or concern for someone or something*. A good one. I jotted down the date, the word, and its meaning in my word notebook.

Dad said he'd spied the dictionary on top of a pile the woman was throwing out, and he told the customer lady, "I have a daughter at home who would love this book."

Dad was solicitous like that.

17

"Jody, slow down. Slow down." There was Mr. D'Agostino, the school counselor, standing in the office doorway. God, he was cute, with his dark curls and sweet gravelly voice. I slowed my pace. I didn't want him to see me huffing and puffing.

"Morning, Jody. Running late?"

My words tumbled out: "Sorry, Mr. Dag. I can't stop and talk. I left my house early to study at the library. The one on Jessup, not the school one. I have a test in science, third period, the metric system. My house is way noisy in the morning and the light is so much better at the library. My house is getting darker by the day. No one remembers to change the burned-out bulbs, and I really needed to study. Miss Vitter says everything is going to change in a year, no more inches and feet. This metric business is infuriating!"

The hall was now empty. Mr. Dag waited, so on I went: "What, I mean, like in gym class we won't be running miles, we'll be running kilometers. I don't know kilometers. I won't know when to stop running. What next? Are they going to spring Celsius on me when I finally got the hang of Fahrenheit? I can't deal with all this change."

"How are things at home, Jody?" he asked, his brown eyes warm and sympathetic.

"What?" I finally took a breath. "Fine…fine…I guess. Super. Except, I mean, the light bulbs."

"Jody. Jody, listen. You know, if you're feeling sad or stressed, showing your feelings isn't a weakness."

"I'm just upset they're changing the whole American number thing when I spent years learning inches, feet, yards, and miles!"

"Jody, come on in my office. Give yourself five minutes."

"And that was just for distance," I continued heatedly. "Then there's measuring. I don't know liters or grams! And my dad needs to measure his tile jobs and he only knows inches and feet. He won't be able to work."

"I'll give you a late note to homeroom."

He pulled me along into his office. I flopped into the big student armchair. Mr. Dag, leaning on the desk, said, "You know, Jody, I've been thinking about you."

"Me? Don't think about me. I mean..."

"You've been through a rough time. It's okay to be upset. You have to talk. If you don't, it can wear on you and come out in other ways."

Mr. Dag folded his arms. On the shelf behind his desk was a collection of mugs: Edgehaven Bulldogs, Yankees, Best Guidance Counselor EVER.

That sounded right.

After school, I stopped at home, dropped off my book bag, and picked up the money Dad left for food shopping. Thirty dollars.

I grabbed my blue pullover, then swapped it for Mom's cashmere sweater. It was big and cozy, and I felt like someone who could stay organized while shopping. On my way to the front door, Billy blocked my path.

"Jody, Jody. I want to come."

"Billy, Billy. No. I'll be back soon."

"Please," he pleaded, his eyes welling up. None of us could say no to him.

"Okay, okay," I said. "Go get your sneakers."

"Mrs. Phyllis," I called out. Mrs. Phyllis was parked, as always, at the kitchen table, feet up on a chair, sipping a soda, watching Mom's tiny TV. "I'm taking Billy with me."

She wasn't hearing a word I said.

I stood over her. "Mrs. Phyllis!" I shouted. Yikes, she was nikkin' bald on top. "I'm taking *Billy* with me."

"That's nice," she said, never taking her eyes off the screen. Why bother?

"If Dad calls to check in," I said to Mae, who was working at the dining room table, "remind him I went food shopping with *Billy.*" I said his name loud enough for even Mrs. Phyllis to hear. "And tell him *not* to forget to pick me up. Wait, where's Annie?"

"Where else?" said Mae. "She stayed to help Mrs. O'Donnell clean up their classroom."

"She's obsessed," I said.

"I'm going to pick her up soon," said Mrs. Phyllis. So she *was* listening. But would she remember in five minutes?

"Mae, can you go get Annie?"

"No, I'm going to Lisa's birthday, and I have to make a card for my *stupid* present."

"It's not that bad to give money," I said, feeling sorry for her. "And your card looks good. She'll like it. Mrs. Phyllis, I'm *leaving*. Mrs. Phyllis!"

"Ah, Jody. Where are you going? Why don't you take Billy along?"

"I am! And I think you should go get Annie. Now!"

"All right already. I'm going." Mrs. Phyllis slapped her knees and stood up.

Billy, astronaut helmet on his head, came scampering along the hardwood floors.

"Hey, Billy," I said, tugging off his helmet, "that hat is great for going to space, but we are going out on an Earth adventure, so why don't you pick another hat." Surprisingly, without a fight, Billy agreed.

I packed up Mom's tote, with a juice cup and a baggie of crackers, and bumped the stroller down the front steps. Billy was now in a cowboy hat. I felt proud, liking the feeling of having my very own formerly injured but now healed toddler. But wait! I ran back in for Mom's sunglasses and placed them atop my head. They were like a movie prop. I couldn't actually see through them—our prescriptions didn't match—but wearing them on my head felt cool.

Seeing Mrs. Phyllis's soda glass, I picked it up and sniffed. It smelled like Grandpa's whiskey glass. *Dipsomaniac: a drunkard.*

I watched as Mrs. Phyllis staggered off, down the front steps to get Annie.

୬

My new boots rubbed against my heel, and I could feel a blister forming. Billy was out of crackers, we had at least six more blocks to go, and I had heard a replay of every *Superman* episode, word for word. I regretted not having gotten myself a snack.

"Billy, how about we get a slice of pizza to share?" I suggested.

"Pizza!" Billy shouted.

The bell jingled as I pushed open the door to the empty pizzeria, the room extra hot from the large pizza oven. Nico—with his sauce-stained white apron, dark eyes, and mane of black hair—was behind the counter. He was kind of cute for a guy in his thirties, more handsome than his father, Mario, who was old, grumpy, and bald.

In his Italian accent, Nico said, "Ah, there she is. My prettiest Moran girl, come to keep me company. How are you?" Pretty? Me? I felt a familiar flush rise up my face and down my neck.

"I'm good, thanks."

Nico cruised around from behind the counter, wiped his hands on his apron, and patted Billy on the head, saying, "Look, a cowboy. Billy the Kid."

Billy said, "Pizza!"

Nico petted the back of Mom's sweater, his fingers lingering. "So soft," he said, as his hand continued down my spine, rested on my bottom, and gave it a squeeze. My insides squirmed. I shifted out of his grasp and looked away, noticing the frames of the black-and-white photos of Italian actors, hanging on the wall, were slightly crooked.

Nico held me by the shoulders, kissed both of my cheeks and said, "That's how Italianos say hello." Then he circled back around the Formica countertop. He was only being friendly.

I put Billy on the stool closest to the window and ordered pizza and a Coke for us to share.

"Only one slice?" Nico asked, reaching into the case to slide a slice in the oven to warm.

"It's just a snack," I said.

"Like yourself, Bellissima!"

I attended to Billy, spinning him around and around in one direction, and when I could go no further, I let him go and spun back the other way.

"Again," Billy demanded. Nico patted Billy's head, sang, "Pitza, pitza, I likea veddy mucha." Or that was how it sounded to me. Billy giggled. I started to relax and giggled too, enjoying Nico's silliness. He came back around the counter when the pizza was ready. He put it on the counter and stood behind me.

"Let me see if they feed you enough," he said, and suddenly wrapped his arms around my waist, squeezing my middle. The smell of onions and garlic scratched at my nose. "No, they don't!" he cried. He nestled my neck, his breath warm against my skin, his lips brushing my cheek.

"Give Nico a kiss," he said.

Was it because I had Mom's sweater on, that I looked older? I wondered. Was I doing something to encourage him? Grandma Cupcakes always says girls shouldn't encourage boys, whatever that means. In my mind I saw Claire leaning over to kiss James. I let Nico hold me a moment too long, then pulled away as his whiskers brushed me again. Pressing myself up against the stroller, I pretended to be looking for something Billy needed. My heart raced. Nico laughed, leaned around the stroller, acting as if we were in the midst of a fun, friendly game, his hand again on my bottom. I maneuvered back and forth, avoiding his kiss, his busy hands. Thank goodness for Billy between us, gobbling pizza! I hadn't gotten a single bite!

"I...I have to go to the grocery store," I said, confused by the mix of feelings that vibrated through me.

Billy protested as I handed him the last piece of crust, stuffed him in the stroller, and rolled him toward the door.

Remembering I hadn't paid, I turned back. "How much?"

"How much? My girl doesn't need to pay!"

I rushed out the door, down the street, my heart beating fast against my ribs. I hadn't realized I wasn't breathing until I exhaled. What had Nico seen in me? What made him try to kiss me? Was I pretty? Or was there just something wrong? I wished every answer in life could be as simple as finding a word in my OED. I recalled a word from several months ago. *Consternation: a sudden alarming amazement that results in utter confusion and dread.* I'd never wear that sweater again!

At the A&P I left the stroller, collected a cart, parked Billy in it, and wheeled down the first aisle, slowly regaining my composure. Nico was a creep, I decided.

We took our time, checking prices and adding things up to make sure I could get everything we needed, reciting my choices to Billy. It surprised me how much things cost. A gallon of milk was $1.19 and I needed *two*. The dozen eggs were almost half the milk at sixty-four cents.

Gliding my cart in and out of the aisles, Nico's wandering hands and kissy pout kept popping in my head. I pushed the images away. Was it weird to feel excited? Did I do something wrong?

The more I added to the cart, the harder it was to keep track of the total. And Billy's chattering did not help. "Jody. When I get big I'm going to push you in the cart."

I started planning dinners for the week: chicken two nights, pork chops, fish sticks, and hamburgers for the other three. Annie popped into my head. Had Mrs. Phyllis remembered to get her?

And Nico's hand on my backside! What an oinker!

In the next aisle, I stocked up on Green Giant peas, corn niblets, and green beans.

"Get spinach," Billy said. "Popeye eats spinach and gets muscles."

I picked up a can of spinach to show Billy. He asked to hold it. "I'm Popeye the sailor man," he sang.

I passed the shelves bursting with pastas and sauces. I gave our cart a shove past them. "Vroom," Billy yelled with glee.

When we hit the snack aisle, Billy dropped the can of spinach, pulled himself up to standing and started pulling potato chips and Doritos off the shelves.

"Billy!" I cried. "Sit down, you're going to fall." Taking a package of Cheese Doodles from him, I said, "You can't get that"—words I kept repeating. "You can't get everything you want."

But gradually, I couldn't resist and I picked up extra Oreos, chips, and Doritos, tossing in some of Mom's favorite black Twizzlers.

"Pow, pow, pow. I shoot you, Jody," said Billy. I turned back to see he had an orange water gun. Where had he pulled that one from?

"Billy, give me that," I said.

"No, it's mine," he shrieked.

When I went to take it out of his hand, he started howling. A woman gave me an annoyed look.

"Okay, hold on to it till the register," I said, through gritted teeth. "Then we have to put it back. We can't buy it. You hear me?" He shook his head yes. The tears immediately stopped. Crocodile tears, Grandma Moran would call them. Why did they put toys in a supermarket anyway? Now I knew how Mom felt. Was it the sweater or had I truly grown older?

From the corner of my eye, I caught sight of her. I squinted. It couldn't be Mom. Could it? Then I noticed her green poncho. It was! It was her! The floor dipped beneath my feet. My eyes followed her as she leaned down for some sugar: the same golden-red hair, the same hand on her hip as she read the label. I froze, barely breathing. She's alive! I was right. I scooted my cart up behind her.

"Mom?" She turned and I saw dark eyes and a flat nose, nothing like Mom's blue eyes and thin, straight nose.

She gazed at me, then she noticed Billy in the cart, our hodge-podge of groceries, and something else—she saw it. Something was wrong with us. But she didn't say anything, just patted my arm.

"Sorry, wrong number," she said.

I felt gut-punched, unable to speak.

Mom was there and then she was gone. She wasn't coming back.

I turned around to find Billy digging into a Hershey bar he'd swiped from the shelf. His face and hands were already covered in chocolate, and there was even some in his hair. A trail of torn-up candy wrappers surrounded his seat and littered the floor.

"Give me that!" I said and snatched the chocolate out of his hand, a little roughly. "I told you stop taking the food. You hear me?"

The shame of my mistake stung. How stupid could I be? I knew Mom was dead. Juliette knew. Even Kübler-Ross knew. Dead people don't come back.

Quickly, I went to the meat aisle, choosing at random from all the confusing packages, the cheapest chicken and beef I could find.

As we waited to pay and bag our groceries, I caught the woman in line ahead of us staring at Billy's chocolate-covered mouth. Or was it his scar? She winced and recoiled and then tried to hide it, as if nothing was wrong, but I'd seen her flinch.

After the lady took her change, she asked, "Oh my, what happened to him?"

"A car accident," I said, not looking at her. Stop talking! I was trying to watch the check-out lady punch in the numbers to see if I could add the total in my head before she got to the end. I was worried I didn't have enough money. I continued adding food to the conveyor belt.

"Who was driving?"

"My mother."

"Is she okay?"

"Hush now," said the cashier to the lady.

I clenched my fists, held them back. "No, she's not okay. She's *dead*." The nosey lady winced. I didn't care what she thought.

Billy started shooting at her. "Pow, pow, pow."

"I'll take the gun," I said to the pink-smocked cashier as I tossed the cardboard packaging from the gun onto the belt. I watched as her fingers pressed down on the register numbers, then on the large black button on the side. A total appeared. "That will be thirty-two-twenty-two, dear." I was two dollars and twenty-two cents short. I bit my lip, fearing I might break down and start crying.

"How much are these?" I asked, holding up the Oreos. I wasn't giving back the gun.

"Fifty-eight cents."

"And this?" I handed her a jar of peanut butter.

"Two oh two."

She handed me the change.

Parking the cart, along with Billy, by the large plate-glass window, I opened the package of napkins and wiped Billy's dirty face and hands, licking my finger to moisten the chocolate around his mouth.

I glanced at the large wall clock. Twenty-five minutes past five. Where was Dad?

At five forty-five the cashier asked, "Is your dad coming to get you, buttercup?" I gave a surly shrug. "We're closing soon."

Five fifty-five. "He's not here yet?" Joining me at the window, she leaned in closer and whispered, "He hasn't forgotten you." There was something about her voice and the way she looked at me, that made me want to crawl under the cart. I shifted from one foot to the other, pulling on the sleeves of Mom's sweater. I didn't want her feeling sorry for me.

"We're fine. My dad will be here soon."

I turned away, watching for Dad's red van. Before Mom died, no one had ever looked at me with pity. Like I was missing an arm or a leg. I wanted to get out of there. Jane Austen was way wrong on the pity business—people who don't complain are definitely still pitied.

As the time ticked by I flipped back and forth between anger and fear. What if something had happened to him? What if he'd gotten in an accident? Or had a heart attack? Who would take care of us?

Finally, Dad pulled up in front and parked. It was five past six. I pushed the cart out the automatic door. Dad threw his arms open—his long-lost children. So not funny.

"Daddy," Billy squealed.

"Sorry, I'm so late, Jody," Dad said, striding toward us. "Things got so busy. I had to go check on the new guy, see how he's working out." Dad gave Billy a kiss as he lifted him out of the cart and put him in the back seat.

I wanted to say something, something angry, but all that came out was hysterical weeping, then hyperventilating.

"Jody," Dad said, worried. "Sweetie, what's happened?"

I couldn't catch my breath for sobbing, couldn't stop. Dad reached to put his arm around me. I pushed him off hard and shouted right in his ear: "I can't do this anymore! I can't do it all. I can't be the mother."

"Okay, calm down. Jody, I hear you. Calm down. You're right. It's not your job," Dad said.

"Don't be nice!" I shouted.

Mr. Dag had seen this coming. I couldn't hold it all in. I said, "And stupid Mrs. Phyllis watches TV all day. And drinks alcohol!"

"Drinks?" said Dad. He stepped back like he'd been socked in the nose.

"Yeah, her soda has *whiskey* in it."

I tossed the grocery bag into the van. Splat! The sound of eggs breaking. The shells, yolks, and goo oozing into the floor mats was satisfying.

Dad threw his arms up into the air. "Dammit, Jody, those eggs are all over the van floor! Who's going to clean that up?"

"Not me!"

Dad said, "Bloody hell you won't."

Now we were both angry, which was better than pretending that everything was going to be all right.

18

Finally it was Friday, and Mae's show. Dad made us dress up, saying it was a special occasion, so I added Mom's heart necklace to my outfit and told Billy, "No hats allowed."

The four of us—Dad, Annie, Billy, and me—ambled across the school parking lot. Dad had driven Mae there earlier and Claire was coming with James. As we made our way in to the school auditorium, Dad nudged me and nodded across the room. It was Charlie. Softly he sang, "Some enchanted evening, you may see a stranger." How did Dad know about Charlie?

"*Dad!*"

Charlie gave me a half nod and about a quarter of a smile. A good sign. I checked the program—yup, Charlie's younger sister Cynthia was in the show—Tweedledee. Dad took hold of my hand, leading me to a row of chairs. I shrugged his hand off, embarrassed.

"Jody, look," said Annie, pulling on my sleeve. "Mrs. O'Donnell is here! I knew she would come." She climbed over my lap, then over Dad and Billy into the aisle, and raced across the room to Mrs. O'Donnell.

Mrs. O'Donnell was younger than I expected, with a dark flip and a crisp shirtdress, like the teacher in a kid's book. I wasn't sure what the fuss was all about. She didn't even wear lipstick. But I guess she was nice to show up.

Dad stood and introduced himself. "So you're the famous Mrs. O'Donnell," he said with a chuckle. "I've heard so much about you."

"And me, about you." They laughed.

"This here is Billy and my second oldest, Jody," said Dad. I waved. "And Claire should be here somewhere."

"And this is my daughter Patty. When Annie told me about her sister's starring role," she said, and mouthing the words:

many, many times. "I thought Patty would enjoy it. She's a year ahead of Annie in school." She pointed to the flowers Dad held under his arm. "So thoughtful, you brought flowers."

"I picked them up on my way home from work." Dad smiled at her "Well, very nice to meet you."

"Sit with us," said Annie.

And the agreeable Mrs. O'Donnell and a slightly pudgy Patty, with her bobbed blond hair and party dress, found a seat in the row behind us, with Annie plunking herself right in between the two of them.

Shortly Mrs. Porter, mother of Lisa, the Queen of Hearts, spotted Dad. She touched his shoulder, said, "You all seem to be managing *so* well. Thank God."

Dad gave a wry smile. "No, don't thank God, thank Joe Moran."

She lingered, asked a dozen nosey questions, though Dad had nothing much to say.

"Everyone's checking up on me," Dad whispered, when she finally got the hint.

That made an opening for Tommy Marshall's mom, who hurried over with her wild jungle of hair and tight shirt. I nudged Dad. Mrs. Marshall was one of those moms on our street that had caught the "divorce virus."

"Watch out, Dad," I said under my breath.

"Be nice." Dad stood.

"Hi, Joe," the former Mrs. Marshall said, all sultry.

"Hi, Jackie. Good to see you. How are the boys doing?"

"We are all just *dandy*," she said, drawing out the last word.

"Glad to hear," said Dad. I thought his face was going to fall into her shirt.

She didn't seem to mind. "You know, Joe, a few of my bathroom tiles have come loose. Would you mind coming by and taking a look-see?" I rolled my eyes at Dad. There was an *OED* word on the tip of my tongue, from months ago, but I couldn't find it.

The auditorium lights blinked, and everyone hustled to find their seats.

Dad said, "Why sure. Happy to help out."

I did a quick search for Claire. She was parked in the rear of the auditorium, James's arm draped over her shoulder. As I turned my head back around, I blinked. Double blinked. I'd nearly missed her. Debbie Doidge. Sitting three rows back with her mom, Jake, and a bunch of little Doidges. No eye make-up. No slouching. Wearing a skirt and her hair in a ponytail! Our eyes met for a second, and her cheeks reddened. Just like any old dorky kid, hoping no one would notice her with her family. Hand close to her chest, she actually lifted her pointer finger and waved, and I gave her a little nod.

Suddenly, the auditorium went dark. A spotlight shone on the curtain, the rustle of actor's footsteps quieted slowly, and Mae's teacher, Miss Fredianni, stepped into its glow; her voice weaved a world of wonder as she described the scene of Alice, terribly bored, sitting at the edge of a pond watching her sister read a book without pictures.

The stage lights came up and there stood our own beautiful Mae in her blue Alice dress, with its white apron. Her strawberry hair was pulled back with a blue headband. She looked out on the audience.

Billy yelled, "Mae. Mae!"

Our sister gave a tiny Alice smile and recited her lines for all to hear. Mae had turned into Alice! She pretended to fall down the rabbit hole, projecting well as she cried: "Well, after such a fall as this, I shall think nothing of tumbling downstairs!"

Everyone laughed!

Dad gave me a look, and we couldn't help our grins. She was good!

Afterward, Mae came out, still in her stage make-up, beaming. Dad gave a big bow. "For Alice," he said, handing her the flowers.

"Thank you," Mae said with a curtsy unlike her, but very like Alice.

Mrs. Marshall appeared, leaned down to shake Mae's hand.

"Quite a little actor you've got there," she said to Dad.

Mrs. Marshall's blouse looked like she'd tried to get two

pillows into one pillowcase, I swear. The *OED* word I was looking for popped back in my head—*subterfuge: deceit used in order to get what you want.*

I looked for Annie. She was enthusiastically telling Mrs. O'Donnell something, who was leaning down, carefully listening. It was nice to see Annie's teacher loving Annie as much as Annie loved her.

She brushed Annie's hair out of her eyes.

ം

The five of us Morans, plus James, piled into the Friendly's booth. Dad let Mae get a sundae, the rest of us cones. She ate it like a princess at a banquet.

When we all had ice cream in front of us, Dad said, "Jody, I asked Claire first, but she's got after-school plans. Please do me a favor, just this once. Tomorrow, before dinner, pick up Annie from her friend Lilly's house. I have a very promising estimate that can't be moved."

"Dad," I groaned.

"I'm sorry, stringbean. Just this once, I promise. Mrs. Phyllis got another job.

"What kind of job?" asked Claire with a smirk.

"A cocktail waitress," Dad said with a chuckle. "But I'm working on another babysitter, I promise."

"What's a cocktail waitress?" Billy asked.

James said, "It's like a babysitter without kids." Claire and I cracked up.

Dad said, "You could stop at Nico's first and get a slice. Annie's friend is just down the street."

"No pizza," I said.

"What? You're the pizza queen!"

"No pizza. Nico makes me feel nikkin' weird."

Dad was suddenly serious. "What do you mean?"

"He just does. He tried to kiss me."

Dad's voice rose. "Kiss you!" he demanded.

"You didn't tell me?" Claire said, insulted. "When was *this*?"

"Billy and I got a slice before I went food shopping. I was

wearing Mom's sweater and he kept petting it, then he patted my butt and tried to kiss me. Are you mad? You're mad." My ice cream was almost completely melted.

"Mad? No, no. Absolutely not!" Dad said, his voice angry. "At Nico. Not you."

"Excuse me," said James. "I need to go to the restroom."

"You're freakin' him out," said Claire with a laugh.

Mae was reciting some of her lines for the little kids. Billy was staring at her like she was a movie star.

"He's, like, almost dad's age!" said Claire.

"That's right, Claire. Jody, sweetie. You did nothing wrong."

"He is kinda cute," Claire said

"Claire, that's not helpful," Dad said. "Jody, he should have *never* touched you. Never tried to kiss you! No grown man should ever do that." He took my hand. "Stringbean, I don't want you thinking this was your fault."

"Off with his head," said Mae. I laughed. She'd been listening.

"It's one rabbit hole after another these days," said Dad, with a sigh.

19

The next Friday I was flipping through grease-stained cards in Mom's recipe file, from appetizers, meats, grains, to the dessert section. And there it was—the one for her yellow cake with chocolate icing. She'd cut it out of a magazine, but there were some notes in Mom's swirly handwriting—*add tsp. baking powder, less salt, and half-packet vanilla pudding mix, richer.* It felt like she was off visiting a friend, or maybe out shopping with Claire.

I found the sifter in the junk drawer, poured in the flour and squeezed the handle, making that awful squeaking sound. I measured and added each of the other ingredients and stirred. After coating the two tins with Crisco, I poured in the batter, then lightly tapped the pans on the countertops, the way Mom used to do. Using a mitt, I placed the tins on the top rack of the wall oven and set the timer for twenty minutes.

I dug into *Pride and Prejudice*, eager to see if Elizabeth and Darcy finally realize they belong together. I read until the timer brought me back to 1970.

As I pulled the golden cake out of the oven, Annie, puzzle in hand, came sliding down the hallway, her socks slipping along the hardwood floor, almost crashing into me.

"Ow," I yelped, burning my arm on the edge of the baking sheet. "Be careful, Annie. Don't touch. This is hot."

"Look, Jody, I've grown. I can see right in the oven." I placed the tins on the cooling racks.

"What? Wow! You sure have, pork chop!" I brushed myself off, flour flying everywhere.

"Can I have some?" asked Annie. She was holding my old wooden Map of the United States puzzle, each state a different color. I hadn't seen it in years

"No, it's for my birthday tonight. You *may* have some then and an Oreo now." One for Annie, two for me.

"What do you say?"

"Thank *you*!" said Annie. "Jody, do the puzzle with me."

"Sure. Go on in the living room. I'll be right there." I flipped the tins and left them to cool.

I sat cross-legged, novel in hand, next to Annie on the gold carpet. "Mrs. O'Donnell said I can bring Roo to school."

"Roo? School? I don't think so, Annie."

"Yes!" Annie said, thrusting out her lower lip. "She said she needed a class ascot."

"I think you mean mascot," I said. "Okay, I guess."

Claire and Michelle slipped in the front door. There was a hint of Mom's Fiery Evening lipstick on Claire's lips. Funny, because Mom would never have let her wear that to school.

"Cookies!" Claire bellowed, sniffing the air, as the two of them scooted into the kitchen.

"Don't touch my birthday cake," I called.

I heard the cabinet open and the rustling of the Oreo packaging. A Coke can popped and hissed. "Bring Annie another Oreo," I called. "And a soda for your loving sister," but before I could finish, she was already in the living room, tossing me a Coke and Annie a cookie.

"You will now paint my toes for me, pissant," Claire said as she stretched out on the couch next to me, giving the nail polish bottle a good shake.

"You got that word from me," I said, sticking my tongue out at her. *Pissant: a worthless or contemptable person.* Jody Moran was no pissant!

Michelle parked herself on the brown velvet side chair across from us and began flipping through Claire's latest issue of *Seventeen.*

The polish, like the lipstick, was another one of Mom's–Wild Rose–a shimmery shade of pink. I got on my knees, positioning myself near Claire's feet. At this rate I was never going to find out what happens to Elizabeth Bennet.

"You're doing the puzzle with me," Annie protested with a pout.

"I am. I can do both. I'm watching you." I opened the bottle and took hold of Claire's right foot.

"Where's Billy-boy and Mae?" asked Claire.

"Dad took Billy to check on some jobs," I said. "And Mae went home with Lisa. She's sleeping over—not butting in on my birthday party."

Holding my hand steady, I painted a line down the center of Claire's pinky toenail. Her middle toe slightly overlapped the second, exactly like Mom's, making it difficult to paint.

"No!" Claire barked. I jumped, making my hand slide, smearing the polish along Claire's skin.

"Hey, dorko! You made me mess up," I said, grabbing a tissue and wiping the polish off Claire's foot.

"You're not doing it right," said Claire reaching for the polish. "Mom said you always paint nails from left to…" Claire stopped mid-sentence, pursing her lips. Mom always said? What else didn't I know?

"Let me show you," said Claire. "You want to make three even strokes. So start on the left and go straight down the toenail. Like this."

"Your mom was the nail *expert*," said Michelle.

"She was," said Claire. "But now I assume the mantle: the fantabulous nail polisher of Randolph Road."

"Is Mommy done being gone?" asked Annie.

Claire picked up the mitten-shaped puzzle piece. "Where does this one go, Annie?" She studied the piece, the tip of her tongue peeking out between her lips.

"That's Maine." She fit the state in place. "Mrs. O'Donnell was born in Maine."

Claire said, "Hey, Michelle, get this, Jody thinks Alaska is an island."

"I was five!" I said. "How could I know? Look, it's got Alaska floating out in the water. Next to nikkin' Hawaii!"

Annie said, "Alaska's next to Canada but too far away to fit on the puzzle, that's all."

"Some of us are pretty bright," Claire said.

"Claire, cross your feet," I said, smacking her leg.

"I'm next," said Michelle. "You need all the practice you can get!"

"Michelle, it's five o'clock!" Claire jumped up and waved at us. "James got his dad's car for the night. We're not missing that!"

I called after them. "I thought you'd come to my bowling party? It's at seven."

"Sorry!" Michelle popped her head back inside. "We'll stop by after."

"I'll come," said Annie, so sweetly that I could not help but smile.

℘

Home from the bowling alley, Dad brought Billy and Annie up to bed after birthday hugs for me. Tracy and I set up our sleeping bags in the living room, then raided the kitchen for chips, Doritos, and M&M's.

Michelle and Claire swept into the room. Claire's red hair glistened under one of James's Edgehaven baseball caps. Michelle's jet-black hair was slicked back in a ponytail. Claire whispered something to Michelle.

"Hey, foxes," said Claire.

"Come pig out with us," said Tracy.

"Get any good loot?" asked Michelle.

"Jennifer gave me this great necklace. And Bettina, Katie, and Meg all gave me earrings. And look what Tracy gave me." I held up the Ouija board.

"Only the best from moi," Tracy said.

"Cool," said Michelle. "I'm the Queen of Ouija."

"She is," Claire said. "Even her dead dog Biff talks to us."

We all laughed.

"Claire, sleep here with us. You and Michelle. *Please*. We have tons of snacks, and we can Ouija."

"This is your lucky day," said Claire, all queenly. "For your birthday, *you* have the honor of *our* presence." Two stairs at a time, they flew upstairs, quickly returning in their pajamas, with stacks of pillows and blankets under their arms. Claire brought a wrapped box, too small for a shirt, but bigger than a jewelry box. "Here you go," she said, tossing me the present.

"Nikkin'!" I said, amazed that Claire had bought me something.

Michelle gracefully lowered herself onto the blanket, years of ballet evident in her every move. "And we need these for proper Ouija juju," she said, tossing two candles onto my sleeping bag, along with a pack of Mom's old matches.

Dad startled me, clapping his hands together. "There's my birthday girl," he said. "Settled in for the night?"

Claire lay across the contraband candles and matches. And what was this? Dad had on a clean shirt and smelled of Old Spice. "Listen, ladies, you don't need me around for this little shindig. I'm going to excuse myself and just march up the street and give Mrs. Marshall a hand with her tiles. The little ones are tucked in. I'll be back soon."

Dad bowed and, in a British accent, said, "I will be serving breakfast for my ladies at your leisure in the morning." He whistled on his way out.

"Mrs. Marshall?" Claire asked.

"Skank," Michelle said.

"It's just tiles," I said, not liking Dad leaving on my birthday.

"Give her a *hand*," Claire said, and she and Michelle nudged each other.

I ripped off the wrapping paper, popped open the box, and held up a pink lacy bra. "Audacious! You bought me a bra!"

"You can grow into it," said Tracy. "Just kidding."

"Claire, thank you, thank you!" I turned my back, tore off my shirt, and struggled to hook the clasp in front the way Claire did. Then, spinning the bra around, I hoisted up the straps. "It fits!" I cried, twirling around.

Flash. Click. Churr.

"Claire!" I squealed as my image slowly appeared from her Polaroid camera. She let out a wicked laugh. "Gimme that picture. You can't show it to anyone! I mean it." Claire could not stop laughing. "Let me see," I said, finally grabbing it. "Wow. The bra makes my boobs look bigger!"

"For your scrapbook," said Claire. 'You'll thank me later."

"Love the little heart in the center," said Tracy.

"For your eighteenth birthday maybe I'll find a guy to take it off you," Claire said, swatting me with a pillow. Tracy jumped right in, swinging hers, and soon feathers were flying.

"Enough! Let the Ouija begin," said Michelle, her voice all serious and deep.

I positioned the Ouija on our blanket. Across the top of the board were the words *yes* and *no*, and in the center below was the alphabet.

"The spirits are restless tonight," said Michelle, holding her hands together as if in prayer. "Light the Ouija candles, Madame Claire."

Claire struck the match and lit the wick, as the four of us huddled over the board.

"Ask a question," Tracy said.

"You three hold hands," Michelle said, lightly placing her fingers on the wooden heart. She asked, "How far did Claire go with James last night?" The disc glided across the board, spelling out S-E-C-O-N-D.

"Oh my god, it's true!" said Claire. "We went to second base."

"Well, he is a second baseman," I said, cracking myself up.

"I went to second base once," said Tracy.

"What! When?" How did I not know this?

"In the basement of my old house."

"You were five!"

"He was older…six!" She burst out laughing.

"How did it feel?" I asked. Tracy started to speak. "Not you, doofus! Claire!" My insides felt squirmy thinking about it.

"Awkward," Claire said. "But, also, good. I like kissing him better."

"Is he a good kisser?" I asked.

"Better than Nico I bet," said Claire, smirking.

"Very funny," I said.

"Eric was the worst kisser," said Michelle. "It was like this," she leaned over, pretending to lick Claire's entire face.

Claire squealed. I rolled onto my back, laughing.

"Under bra or over bra?" asked Tracy.

"Over. He kept trying to unhook it and got his hand stuck."

"Super-awk," I said. We giggled. What if Charlie tried to unhook my new bra?

"My turn," said Claire.

"No. It's my birthday."

Claire shrugged. "Ask away."

I placed my fingers on the heart-shaped wood. "Ouija, will Charlie ever kiss me again?"

We watched as it glided over to the word, *YES!* Fantabulous.

"Mom told me how awkward her first kiss was with Tony," said Claire. "She said he was shy."

"Tony! Wait! What? I never heard of any Tony," I said.

"He was her first boyfriend. A year older, like James. He went into the navy and they broke up."

I would have done anything to go back in time, sit with Mom, have her tell me about Tony. "Do you think they were, like, serious?"

"She said he couldn't dance, that Dad was a way better dancer. And if you must know, James is a *very* good dancer."

Michelle said, "Let's ask if you'll marry James."

"It's my turn, my question," said Claire. "Mom, are you here with us?" The candles flickered. I bit my lip. Claire's fingers pressed the wooden disc as the Ouija board slowly spelled out the spirit's message, *I-t-s-M-o-m.*

We screamed. The hairs on my arm quivered. I wasn't sure if I was thrilled or terrified.

Tracy looked like she'd seen a ghost.

"One more," said Claire, looking at me. "Ouija, should Dad date?" This time Claire's hands moved more quickly: W-h-e-r-e-s-D-a-d?

"Oh my God, she knows Dad is at Mrs. Marshall's!" I said.

"The door to the spirit world has opened," said Michelle.

※

Spooked, I was wide awake. How were the three of them

sleeping? Every sound made me jump. Was Mom angry that Dad was out? He wasn't even home yet. Broken tiles! Yeah, right.

"Arrgaaaaah." A scream came from upstairs. My heart nearly leapt out of my chest. "Claire," I said. "Claire!" I nudged her arm. Mom always said, waking Claire was like trying to wake the dead.

"Arrgaaaaah." It was Annie. Clock: one-thirty in the morning.

I tugged a T-shirt on over my bra, put on my glasses, rushed upstairs and into her room, and threw on the light. Annie was sitting straight up in bed, shaking and moaning in her princess sheets.

"Annie, you had a bad dream." She continued thrashing.

"Annie!" She moaned louder. Her flailing arms wouldn't let me near her.

"Annie, are you okay? Answer me!"

Wide-eyed, her tiny freckled face was seeing something horrible that only she could see. She kept shaking, screaming, over and over again.

"Wake up, Annie. Please, please wake up!" This was nothing like her other bad dreams. What if she was having some kind of seizure like that girl had had at school?

I ran down the hall to find Dad. His bed was empty. How could he not be home? Quickly, I tore back to Annie. Lying by her side, I gently put my arms around her, trying to hug away whatever was terrifying her and said, "Shh, it's okay, pork chop. I'm here, I'm here." Gradually her shaking and flailing stopped, her warm little body nestled in next to mine. "You're safe."

When I looked over at the side table, I was surprised to see Mom's amber ashtray, filled with Annie's barrettes.

When I finally slept, I dreamt about Mom, about the van crossing the lane, the crashed car with Mom slumped over the steering wheel and Billy crushed inside. I shuddered awake, and I remembered what Juliette had told me: a death doesn't happen only once. The hit comes over and over.

The smell of pancakes reached me all the way in Annie's bed—had the girls started without me? I hurried downstairs.

"Good morning, teenager!" Dad whispered, full of energy. The clock on the stove said 6:20 a.m. "Girls still asleep?"

"Where were you?" I demanded.

"What? Where was I?" He waved the spatula, an innocent accused. "I'm right here, making pancakes, as promised, for the birthday girl."

"I see that!" I said. "Last night you *weren't* here. When did you get home?"

Dad stopped clowning around. "About twelve-thirty or so. Looks like Claire and Michelle joined the sleepover. I'll bet that was fun."

"At one-thirty Annie was going ape. And you weren't home!"

"I wondered why you were sleeping in her bed. What kind of ape?"

My hands shaking, I put the milk down so it wouldn't spill. "She was screaming! It was like she was awake, her eyes wide open, but she couldn't hear or see me. I thought it was some kind of seizure!"

He couldn't hold my gaze. "Oh, stringbean, I'm so sorry. That must have been scary." He flipped some pancakes onto a plate and handed them to me like a peace offering.

"Why were you so late? It doesn't take four hours to fix some tiles! You act like there is some kind of secret."

"Don't be silly, Jody. I fixed those tiles. Took forever. Then I had some coffee with Jackie. We talked and talked. Then I came home. End of story. You know sometimes I need some grown-up time."

"If you want to date, date someone nice. Someone like Juliette."

"Mrs. Marshall and I are not dating," he said. "And Juliette's separated, which means, sweetie, that she's married. I'm not gonna date married ladies. Though I'm sure she's lovely."

Dad gave me a big hug. The way he talked about Juliette made me think he'd given her some thought, and I didn't feel as angry.

"Dad, can we get my ears pierced today?"

"It's a date. Maybe while we're at the big store, let's think about getting you some other things, now that you're fourteen. Some dressy shoes? A couple of what, bras?"

"Claire gave me one for my birthday," I said, not looking at Dad.

"From what I've seen, a woman needs a few. Now, should we feed those girls?"

"Dad! It's six in the morning."

"Well then, it's you and me, kid." And we sat and ate pancakes. After, Dad pretended he needed to check on Annie, but I knew he was going up to his room to sleep. I slipped into the living room, slithered into my sleeping bag between Tracy and Claire on the couch pillows, and slept too. Slept till noon, still in my new lace bra.

As we roamed JC Penney's that afternoon, Dad asked a clerk where to find the bras. He just said it out loud, like that—"the bras."

"How can I help you?" The saleswoman asked Dad with a flirtatious smile. She had dark hair, high heels, a tightly buttoned shirt, and, of course, gigantic breasts squeezed into bra cups like rockets.

"My daughter needs a bra," Dad said.

She glanced down, as if just noticing I was there, and with a horrifying little laugh said, "Oh no, I don't believe she does. It's much too soon."

I reached for his hand to pull him away. "Let's go," I whispered.

He patted my arm, his words firm, commanding. "I'm sorry, you're mistaken. My daughter *is* in need of a bra. Please help her find one."

She waved her hand, signaling for me to follow her into the fitting room, and once inside she tossed the curtain closed and told me to take off my shirt. The room felt barely big enough for one of us.

"If you want a bra, we need to get you measured," she said, clutching a floppy tape measure between her outstretched, manicured fingers. I pulled my top over my head, relieved I had my new bra on. I stared up at the ceiling, not wanting to see my reflection.

"Move your arms away for me to measure." Reluctantly I raised them enough for her to slide the tape around my chest. She looked like Dad when he was measuring a bathroom. "28AA. That would be a training bra."

Training bra. I hated that word. I hated her. I could just hear Debbie Doidge—"You need training wheels on your bra!"

The saleswoman returned with four bras, and I chose two. Dad paid and asked, "Where do we go for ear piercing?"

She barely looked up from the register. "Jewelry, first floor."

"I wouldn't want to be her husband," Dad said as we left lingerie. I burst out laughing.

The saleslady in jewelry was friendlier. "How nice to see a father and daughter out shopping," she said.

"Yes, nice for me," said Dad. "We're here for an ear piercing."

"It will be over in a pinch," he whispered to me. "Won't hurt at all."

"It won't hurt *you* at all! You've never had your ears pierced."

"Well, I guess you're right on both counts."

The woman pointed to a stool, signaling me to sit. She wiped my earlobes with rubbing alcohol, leaned over, and eyed my ears. With a red pen she drew a dot on each lobe.

"Your earlobes are a bit asymmetrical," she said. What was with these nikkin' salesladies? I didn't come to hear I had defective earlobes and too-small boobies.

"Does that look level?" she asked Dad.

"They look good to me, but I'm no expert," he said.

The woman handed me a mirror. "Does that look okay?" she asked. I wished Claire or Tracy had come with me. They would know.

"Yeah, I guess," I said, glancing at the mirror. They weren't so asymmetrical! Then the woman turned and picked up a silver gun. Now I didn't feel so brave. I was finally getting what I had wished for, begged for, but now I wasn't so sure. Ear piercings were permanent. Forever.

Dad took hold of my hand, squeezing tight. His fingers were strong and thick against mine. Mom always said you could tell a lot about a man by his hands.

Turning my throbbing head from side to side, I stared at my reflection. I looked like a grown woman—with another cool white jewelry box. And two bras.

20

Ever since Miss June and Mrs. Phyllis left, I couldn't find any of my clean clothes. I kicked the dresser, stubbing my toe, and yanked another drawer open. I found Mae's shirts. Nothing was in the right place. Couldn't Dad tell our sizes apart? My pants turned up in Mae's dresser, and Claire's in mine. I wore the same underwear two days in a row, and none of my socks matched.

I stormed off to Mae and Annie's room and rooted through their dresser, hurling clothes to the floor. To add to the laundry fiasco, Mae had started stealing my shirts. The more I searched, the angrier I got. Still no blue shirt and all I had to show for this was a big mess. I scooped up the clothes and stuffed them back into Mae's stupid drawers.

Ignoring Dad's calls, I headed back to my room to hunt some more. After a few more minutes, Dad stomped in, clearly frustrated. "We *have* to get going, Jody. We can't be late again for school. Take off that pajama top and put something on."

"No, I need my nikkin' blue shirt. It matches my new earrings!"

"Okay, calm down, Sputnik. Let me have a look."

"The blue one with the gold polka dots," I said. "I already looked in there!"

"Fresh eyes," he said. "It doesn't hurt to look again."

As he moved aside my pajamas, he noticed my stash of white boxes. "Whoa, wow! Maybe that's why your clothes are missing. You don't have any room for them!" Then he picked up my red shirt. "Here wear this for today. It looks terrific on you."

"Fine," I said, fuming, and swiped the shirt from his hand.

In the kitchen there was Claire in my blue shirt. Was Dad blind?

"Da-ad, she's wearing my shirt. My polka-dot shirt!" I yelled. "Claire, gimme that." I lunged at her.

"Hey!" Claire shouted.

"Well, you're wearing MY shirt!" Mae hissed. "Give it back."

It shocked me. Sweet, sensitive Mae. We were all a-changing.

"Jody, Claire, Mae. Stop it!" Dad said, then made a gong sound, like calling the end of a boxing match. "It's a draw. Jody, wear what you have on for today. It looks fine. Everyone will be looking at your ears, not your shirt." I touched my ear and spun the post. He went back to clearing the bowls off the table. "All of you, no more taking each other's clothes without asking. You hear me?"

Mae scowled. Claire heaved a sigh and looked off into the distance, like she couldn't be bothered with us.

Dad said, "Gang, this is probably a good time as any to tell you."

We looked back and forth at each other and at him, trying to gauge what was coming. Something good or bad? Not another trip, I hoped.

He said, "I've come around, and Grandma and I have been talking. Discussing her coming to stay."

My head shot up. "Live with us? Like forever?"

Dad's eyebrows were raised, like a hypnotized cartoon character. "Yep."

"Yes!" I had done it. Annie and Mae cheered.

Billy stopped shoveling cereal in his mouth. "What? Tell me!"

"*Dad?*" Claire said.

Dad poured boiling water into his mug. "Grandma said she'll stop work at the end of the month, and she could be here after New Year's."

"Cupcakes!" Annie shouted.

Dad stood by the door, handing off our lunch bags as if they were footballs. I didn't need to look inside.

"Dad?" Claire said again. What was she up to?

Annie reached for her bag.

Claire said, "Not so fast, Annie."

"We gotta get a move on," said Dad.

"Dad, Annie has no school today. It says right here," Claire said, pointing to one of five calendars taped to the refrigerator. "Says there's a nun sleepover."

"A retreat," I said, laughing.

Dad looked stricken. "What? What am I supposed to do with her?" Dad's eyes fell on me. I shrugged.

"I want to see Mrs. O'Donnell," Annie cried.

"Send her on the retreat," Mae said.

"I got it," he said. "No problem. Let's go, troops."

As the little yellow bus pulled up to the curb, lights flashing, door opening, Dad gave Billy a kiss goodbye and steered him up the three steps. But then to our astonishment, he kissed Annie and hurried her—St. Paul's uniform neat as a pin—right up the stairs behind Billy.

I don't think the bus driver even noticed.

Mae spoke for us all: "Dad, Annie can't go to school with Billy!" Dad waved his hand behind his back at us.

The bus drove off.

"Oh my god," I said. Claire laughed.

Mae was dumbstruck.

Dad threw his arm around Claire, clearly an ally. "Oh, it's fine girls. It will be great. Annie can play with the kids at Billy's school. She'll have lots of fun. That's what school is for, right!"

It wasn't a question.

❧

Walking up the school path, past the flagpole, I brushed my hair behind my ears so the earrings would show. My fingers kept being drawn to the posts to see if they still hurt, the way my tongue returned to a sore in my mouth.

I reached the fourth step when I stopped, frozen. There was Debbie Doidge, leaning against the railing, her eyes fixed on me. My mind flashed on one of those nature shows I'd had to watch for science, the ones where you see the lion spot his prey and you know what's coming. And it's going to be bloody. I willed myself to take the next step.

I adjusted the strap of my new bra as it slipped off my

shoulder, letting it peek out a smidge. It was a bit awkward, but felt wonderful.

"Well. It's Jody Moran," Debbie said.

Slowly she prowled over, blocking my way. She looked down at my shirt, then back up at my face, and with a sneer said, "YOU STUFF!" loud enough for anyone nearby to hear.

"I. Do. Not." I said. My eyes locked on her razor-sharp fang teeth, a zit on her chin. I dug my hand into the side pocket of my bookbag, felt for Mom's sunglasses. "I don't know what your problem is, but it ain't me." I said, stepping past her.

Debbie's eyebrows shot up to the middle of her forehead, then she grinned, which was different from her smirk. "Earrings," she said. "Cool."

"Poetry is about language and meaning," said Miss Hart.

Miss Hart was the youngest and coolest teacher at Edgehaven Middle School. Even her name sparkled. She had long straight frosted hair, pointy-rimmed glasses, musky perfume. She was curvy and dressed in tight skirts, with little jackets and black high heel pumps. Her lipstick was a shade of peach. And she always wore big fancy earrings, dangly ones with glittery stars at the bottom.

"When we read a poem, we want to notice all the sounds and images," she said. "The way the poem is structured on the page. Listen as I read this poem called "Little Boy Blue" by Eugene Field. And just note what feelings it arouses in you."

> The little toy dog is covered with dust,
> But sturdy and stanch he stands;
> The little toy soldier is red with rust,
> And his musket molds in his hands.
> Time was when the little toy dog was new,
> And the soldier was passing fair;
> And that was the time when our Little Boy Blue
> Kissed them and put them there.
> "Now, don't you go till I come," he said,
> "And don't you make any noise!"

So, toddling off to his trundle-bed,
He dreamt of the pretty toys;
And, as he was dreaming, an angel song
Awakened our Little Boy Blue—
Oh! the years are many, the years are long,
But the little toy friends are true!
Ay, faithful to Little Boy Blue they stand,
Each in the same old place—
Awaiting the touch of a little hand,
The smile of a little face;
And they wonder, as waiting the long years through
In the dust of that little chair,
What has become of our Little Boy Blue,
Since he kissed them and put them there.

"So what images do you respond to?" asked Miss Hart.

"The musket," said Rob.

"I like how it starts with the dust on the dog and later the dust on the chair. We know they've been there a long time," said MaryAnn.

"The boy stopped playing with them. He grew up," said Rhys Finley.

I read the poem again and stopped on the sentence with the angel song awakening the boy. It hit me. The lines clicked. The boy was dead. Like Billy almost was, like Mom was. The poem had meaning, not just some fuzzy feelings. I felt myself start to well up, thinking of Billy and how he'd almost died. Annie was like the toys, she couldn't understand Mom was gone forever.

"I like the line how *faithful to Little Boy Blue they stand,* and *Awaiting the touch of a little hand"* said Jennifer. "The toys are loyal to the boy, and we know they've waited a long time because the soldiers are rusty."

"The boy is *dead,*" I said. I glanced at Debbie Doidge. She nodded.

Rob said, "Yeah, shot. With the musket."

Finally, Miss Hart said, "That's not usually the first thing people say. But, yes, you're right, Jody."

Just then, the bell rang.

"Okay," Miss Hart said. "Just one more minute. Here is a poem by Edgar Alan Poe." She passed out copies of "Annabel Lee." "Your homework assignment is to read it and make a Venn Diagram comparing it with 'Little Boy Blue.' You've all made Venn Diagrams before. Want a hint? Make one circle for 'Annabel Lee' and another for 'Little Boy Blue.' Similarities between the two poems will be in the overlapping circles and differences in the outer circles, looking at content, structure, and poetic elements. All the things we've been covering."

I went to my locker to swap books and peeked at Mom's sunglasses. They were my secret amulet, like one of Billy's hats, making me strong.

Amulet: an ornament or item that gives protection.

Charlie passed, giving me a small wave.

"Hey, Moran," said Debbie Doidge. Friendly!

Tracy came up from behind and took my arm, "Lunch!" she said, and off we went.

21

That afternoon, as promised, I brought a slice of birthday cake over to Juliette. But it seemed I'd surprised her. There were dark circles under her eyes. An ashtray with several cigarette butts rested on the kitchen table. An open bottle of wine sat on the counter top, almost empty.

"Happy birthday," she exclaimed, giving me a big hug. She smelled like cigarettes and old socks. "You are now officially a teen!" Smiling, she handed me a glittery wrapped present. Inside was a small white box with the most perfect daisy earrings.

"I love them!" I squealed. "I've wanted dangly earrings. The box too! I collect them."

"You do? That's interesting. Why boxes?"

"When I have something special, I have a place to keep it. Like my mom's campfire girl pin and her sewing thimble."

Juliette nodded. "So they hold things with lots of meaning?"

"Yeah, I guess," I said. "I like to take them out sometimes, look at them, then put them away. The boxes keep them safe."

"What a great way to save special things," said Juliette, taking two forks out of the cabinet drawer. "And the feelings that go with them." She opened her mouth wide, taking a big forkful of cake. "Mmm, this is delicious. You made it?"

"Yep. My mom's recipe from her little card thing."

"It calls for milk," Juliette said, pouring a glass. "We better finish before Ben and Bird get home. We don't want to have to share."

"Home? Where are they?"

"My mom had them overnight. I got a night off!" she said. "She'll be bringing them home soon. But for now, I'm all yours. Tell me something juicy."

With a big grin, I pulled my shirt down, off my shoulder, to give Juliette a peak at my new bra. "Claire gave it to me."

"Nice! Fancy, with lace!" she said.

Juliette fed me a bite of cake. It was still surprisingly moist. I took a big gulp of milk, passed the glass back to Juliette, who took her own gulp.

"You know the night of my birthday? When Tracy slept over? Annie had a nightmare. Sometimes she does, but this was different. Really scary. She was sitting up, looking wide awake, shaking and moaning. But she couldn't see me or hear me. I thought she was seeing a ghost. I was *freaked.*"

"Oh, Jody, that's called a night terror. Ben had them a couple of times. It does look scary, but they're okay. Best not to wake them, just let them go back to sleep."

"You kind of know everything, don't you?"

"I know nothing except what I know."

"Something else weird?" I said. "Tracy got me a Ouija board. It sounds stupid. It is stupid. But, Juliette we tried to summon my mom. I mean her spirit, and it seemed like she came. Did she? Or were we were just spooking each other?"

Juliette sat up straighter, ran her hand through her mussy hair. "Oh, sweetie. At my parties we had séances. I couldn't sleep for days."

"Do you think the dead really come back?"

"You know, it's kind of like your boxes. I mean, we want to keep people we love with us, not lose them."

"Yeah, like the *Death and Dying* lady says, we want to imagine the person is still with us." I put my glass into the sink. "But, Juliette, maybe Annie *was* seeing Mom. Maybe we really did summon her back. Annie really looked like she saw a ghost."

"Maybe," she said. "Or I wonder if Annie could have heard you girls."

"Oh no!" I lightly hit the side of my head. "You're probably right."

"Or not. I'm sure you all wish your mom could return."

What I was really wishing was that Juliette could be my mom. We would be so close, talk like this all of the time. I'd be her *only* daughter.

"Did your dad help with Annie?" No way was I telling her about Mrs. Marshall.

"I didn't want to wake him. He's been working so hard."

"I'm sure he's exhausted," she said.

"I think he's lonely," I said. "Do you ever feel that way?"

"Sure," said Juliette. "But most of the time I'm so busy with those two munchkins that I don't have time to be lonely."

"That's why Dad came home early from Rome." My throat tightened. "He was too sad."

Juliette touched my arm. "Rome is a romantic place. It would be hard to go alone. Seth and I spent some time there when he worked for UPI. Before we had kids. We were happy then." She laughed. "We even took tarantella lessons!"

"What's that?"

"A traditional Italian dance. A bit like the hokey-pokey."

"Mom always said my dad was the best dancer."

"Oh, wouldn't I love to go dancing again one day. Raising kids, Jody, can be lonely. I wouldn't trade them for anything, but some days are tough." Juliette poured herself some coffee, then lit a cigarette.

"You smoke?" I asked.

"Bad example, right? A nurse, smoking. I quit before Ben was born, but since Seth and I separated I sometimes get the urge. Last night, with the kids gone, I indulged myself. Don't you ever start."

"I won't. Don't worry about that." Juliette leaned back in her chair, cigarette smoke trailing from her lips.

"In English class we're reading 'Little Boy Blue' and 'Annabel Lee.'"

"Oh, I remember that one: 'And this maiden she lived with no other thought than to love and be loved by me.'"

"Wow. You know it!"

"In school I loved Edgar Allan Poe. I had to memorize a poem to recite for English class and chose 'The Raven.' Nevermore!"

"Why is every nikkin' poem about death?" I asked.

"Right? How about this one: 'Bury me when I die. Beneath a

wine barrel in a tavern. With luck the cask will leak.'" I cracked up.

"For school I have to make a Venn diagram comparing 'Annabelle Lee' and 'Little Boy Blue.' Do you know that one?"

"No, what's it about?"

"*Death.*" Juliette laughed. "It's really sad because it's a little boy that dies. It doesn't say it outright, but his toys gather dust on the shelf, waiting for him to return."

"It does sound sad. I hate to read anything about kids dying." Juliette put the plate and glass into the dishwasher. "There's an old Clark Gable movie on at five, *It Happened One Night.* Want to watch?"

"Def," I said. "I'll just call home and tell them."

Hanging up the phone, I joined Juliette in the living room. "Mom, Claire, and I loved watching old movies. Our favorites were Rock Hudson and Doris Day. You know, the ones where they act like they hate each other while getting into all sorts of messes, then suddenly realize they've been in love all along. The three of us would cry buckets, laughing at the same time. At the end, one of us always said, 'Well, I never saw that coming.'"

We watched, Juliette nestled in next to me. But instead of getting wrapped up in the story all I could think about was how all of the actors were probably dead. Clark Gable, dead. How had he died? Was he sick, an accident? Claudette Colbert. She must be dead too. As each person appeared on the screen, I realized it was the image of a dead person. There was no way to stop it. We were all here, living our lives, then one day we were gone.

I would be gone. Dad would be gone. My sisters and brother, gone.

"Look, that guy kicked the bucket," I said. Juliette smiled quizzically. A moment later, I said, "See her there, she's probably pushing up daisies."

Catching on, Juliette countered with, "That guy there, he bought the farm." We went on and on, laughing, back and forth. "Gone to Davey Jones Locker." "Food for worms." "Six feet under."

With those last two, I saw Mom's box at the bottom of a hole, dirt falling on top of the casket. My throat tightened, strangling my laugh.

"You know," I said. "One day we're going to school, playing with friends, eating breakfast, acting in movies, picking up kids from nursery school, and the next day we could be dead. Bit the dust."

"Yes. It's sad," she sighed. "Everyone dies."

No matter the power of our intention.

"But not at thirty-six," I said softly.

Poof. Empty space. Gone forever.

The front door opened. In came Ben, running and leaping onto Juliette's lap, followed by a lady—an older Juliette—carrying Bird, surprised to see me, waving his hand at invisible smoke.

22

Dad stood by as we picked up dollhouse furniture and tiny Barbie clothes, many of them dirty and rumpled. We sorted through red, blue, and yellow Sorry pieces, the Trouble board, Monopoly tokens—the hat, the cat, and the car—and the deeds for Park Place, Ventnor, Reading Railroad. The basement was a mess.

Pacing back and forth, Dad barked orders. "I can't believe this disregard for your stuff." If we slowed down, he shouted, "Get moving. You hear me?" For the first time I was able to picture him as a soldier. "If your mother were here, this place would never look like this."

He didn't have to remind me—I really, truly knew.

Dad was furious. "The men are coming Monday to work on Grandma's bathroom and the downstairs is a wreck. Do you girls even see this mess? It's an absolute disgrace."

After we finished cleaning and organizing the closet, and not wanting to wait for Dad to find another mess, I packed my bag to sleep over at Tracy's, as we'd planned. I left a note on the kitchen table: *Went to Tracy's for sleepover. Bye.*

I slipped out the side door, hurried away under cover of the bushes and crossed the street.

≈

Amelie, Tracy's elegant mom, opened the door. "Jody, ma petite," she said, kissing me on both cheeks. "So wonderful to see you, cherie!" She always sprinkled her sentences with French.

Stepping into Tracy's house was like being beamed out of New nikkin' Jersey and reappearing in Alsace, France, where Amelie was from. All the furniture and mirrors were curvy, with lots of gold and tassels. Everything was elegant, yet at the same time it looked like it had taken no effort at all. And Amelie, dressed in crisp black pants, a silky white blouse, and scarf, was just as perfectly put together.

I found Tracy splayed out on her bedroom floor. When we first met, I was super jealous that she had her own room, the bedroom I'd always dreamed of, with a canopy bed, fancy white sheets, and ruffled pillows. A princess's bedroom. Her shelves were filled with beautiful dolls that looked perfect. All of my dolls had their hair chopped off and one eye open and one shut. Maybe now I was only a little jealous.

"Took you long enough," she said. "I was so bored I was making cootie catchers!" Spread out all around her were squares of white paper and markers. I hadn't made one of these finger-fitted paper fortune-tellers in years.

"Oh, cherie," I said. "My dad was going *crazy* this morning about the house being a mess." I planted myself on the white shag rug next to her.

"*Your* dad? He never gets angry," said Tracy. "He just makes pancakes and looks like he's going to cry." Tracy finished folding her paper into precision triangles.

"I think he can't handle it all," I told her seriously. "It's starting to get to him."

"My mom says she can't figure out how your dad does everything."

"At least Grandma Cupcakes is moving in soon," I said. "That'll help."

"That old Twinkie? She hates me. She always calls me Stacy."

"She's just playing with you," I said. "Really she thinks you're very glamorous and bold."

"Well, that's obvious," Tracy said, wiggling her shoulders all cat-like. "She called my mom hoity-toity!" Tracy was madly scribbling fortunes on her cootie catcher.

Tracy, holding her catcher poised on her fingers, said, "How old will Jody be when she first has sex? Give me a letter, *A* to *F*."

"*F*," I said.

She flexed the origami, opened and closed it six times, intoned: "You won't have sex until—" and turned over the flap. "Never!" We burst out laughing.

"Never would be fine!" I shouted, and snatched the fortune-teller away from her. "What's your letter?"

"*D*," Tracy said.

I flexed the origami, opened her flap, shouted with laughter: "Tomorrow! You picked that letter on purpose."

"I better get busy," she cried.

"I wish I could get busy with Charlie. I don't know if he hates me or if he's just shy."

"Shy. He likes you. No doubt," said Tracy.

"I should make a cootie catcher fortune and ask if Dad will marry Juliette."

"Marry her? That nurse across the street?" said Tracy.

"Yeah, she's the best." I lay back on the soft rug. "You know how in English we had to do that Venn diagram assignment?" Tracy nodded. "Well, I've been thinking it might be a good way to help find the best person for Dad. Figure out what makes for a good wife and marriage, then see which woman has the most overlap with Dad." Tracy's mouth hung open, looking at me like I was from another planet. "Nothing wrong with a little accuracy and precision," I said, annoyed.

"Okay, okay. Could be fun, I guess," said Tracy. "Here take my extra notebook." I was jazzed. "Write this down," she said, bossy as ever. "They have to be pretty, like me," she said pushing my leg.

"Give me a sec," I said. On two separate pages, I made two large intersecting circles. On one page, I wrote *Dad* above one circle and *Juliette* above the other. On the second page I jotted down *Dad* and *Miss Wendy*. When I last saw Miss Wendy at the library, she didn't have a ring on her finger, so I assumed she was still in the running.

"That's it? No other options?" asked Tracy. "What about Tommy Marshall's mom? She's got the hots for your dad."

"No way," I said. "She's a skank. We need to think of things that matter in choosing a wife, like age, looks, if they have kids, what they like to do for fun, what they like to eat."

"Big boobs," said Tracy, smirking the way she always did when she said something shocking.

"You're a pervert," I said. "And maybe where they grew up. My dad always says: Life is simpler if you marry someone from a similar background. Let's start with Juliette," I said. "She's my first choice."

"Good location," said Tracy. "And she has kids and seems the right age."

"Slow down," I said. "This will be my mom not yours! Juliette is pretty and smart. And always positive, never cranky. Dad definitely needs someone upbeat."

"What does she like to do?" asked Tracy.

"She's wild for dancing, like Mom." Even Jane Austen said: *To be fond of dancing was a certain step towards falling in love.* "Plus, she loves old movies."

"How about a great butt?" said Tracy.

"I'm ignoring you!" I cried. "Juliette has a lot of Venn positive overlaps."

"What's outside the circle?" Tracy asked. "You can't only put the positives."

"Well, she loves spicy food," I said, shaking my head. "Dad doesn't eat anything different. I don't know where she grew up. And he's not keen on divorce, that whole virus thing, so that's a negative. And, well, there's religion. She's Jewish."

"Your dad's always singing *Fiddler on the Roof.* 'Matchmaker, Matchmaker,'" Tracy sang.

I finished, "'Make me a match!'"

"And he almost never takes us to church. Plus his good friend, Dr. Katz, is Jewish. And anyway, Juliette isn't into Jewish stuff, so maybe that won't matter to either of them."

I flipped the page.

"I don't know this librarian lady," said Tracy.

"Me either, but her hair is curly, kind of strawberry blonde, not all orangey," I said. "Dad likes redheads. And I once heard him say he's a leg man. Whatever that means! I'd guess she has pretty nice legs."

"Maggie had the prettiest red hair," said Tracy.

"Yeah, like Claire and Mae's. I wish mine was that color."

"How old is the librarian? Aren't they always old?" she asked.

"I can't tell, but I'm worried she might be too young for Dad." I put *Age* outside the center circle along with *No kids*. In the center, I jotted down *Loves books*.

"Pff, I've never seen your dad read a book."

"That's for me," I said. "I'm doing all the work, so I should get a few things I like."

The next morning, I woke earlier than Tracy and found Amelie in the kitchen, sipping coffee in a tiny, frilly lace nightie with high-heeled slippers trimmed in fur. She looked like a film star from one of those old black-and-white movies. Even when Mr. Bernard was away on a business trip, she looked dazzling. When he was home, they were like two teenagers, always kissing—way different than all the other parents I knew.

"Did you and Tracy have fun? Stay up late? I'm afraid she will sleep all day." Amelie sighed. Even sighing she did beautifully.

"I won't let her," I said.

"Would you like an omelet?" she asked. "With cheese?"

"Yes, thanks."

Wanting to find out what she'd think of Dad marrying, I said, "We made Venn diagrams, trying to figure out the best woman for my dad to date."

"What is this, Venn diagram?" she asked, cracking two eggs into a bowl. I explained how they work.

"Yes, I understand. Everyone needs love. He misses Maggie. Moi aussi. Your mother could do anything she set her mind to and still have five children!" She waved her fork in the air. "Jody," she said—and I loved how my name sounded on her lips—"the other day, I remembered when you were in the hospital and your poor mother was so big with the bébé Annie. Do you remember? I asked her how you were, and she broke down in tears."

"Really? She cried?" I'd always thought she didn't care.

"She was so worried." Amelie sprinkled cheese on the omelet, then flipped it over. "Have you been for a visit?" A visit?

"The hospital?" I asked, stupefied. Why would I go back there?

Amelie lightly laughed. "Oh no, no. The cemetery. It's nice. I can drive you if you like. Tracy can go." She meant a visit with Mom. I shook my head. I hadn't done that, but I didn't want to either. I was a terrible daughter.

Amelie said, "Oh, and, cherie, Venn diagrams are for school, not love. Only the heart, the moon, and the stars can dictate love."

❧

Amelie pulled up to the gate of Our Lady of Victories Cemetery. The statue of the Virgin Mary loomed large, looking down and smiling as if she were pleased to see us.

"Mon amours, it's one o'clock. I am going to the grocery. Take your time. I'll pick you up at two-fifteen."

The place was deserted, except for one man, off in the distance, riding on a mower.

Making our way through the graveyard, roaming up and down the line of markers, we were on the lookout for flowers. There were lots to choose from on the graves that stretched out before us.

We dawdled, looking for names we recognized and scanned the dates on the stones to see if any of the dead were kids. Most of the headstones were cracked and moss-covered, making them difficult to read.

"Let's see who can find the year we were born," I said.

"This one says 1956," said Tracy, pointing to a gravestone. "A year before us."

"Died in 1961," I said. "He was five!" I tried to imagine what illness or accident might have befallen him—a drowning, a choking, a murder?

"I brought two of my mom's cigarettes," said Tracy. She could still shock me. "Let's try them over there." We planted ourselves on the grass beneath the shade of the tree.

I lay down the flowers I'd swiped along the way and held the cigarette between my two fingers. Inhaling deeply, I started coughing. Tracy laughed. My lungs burned and my eyes teared. Why would anyone keep smoking these things? I pictured Debbie Doidge, a cigarette hanging out of her mouth. She did kinda look cool. Charlie might think it was gross.

There was something upside-down about smoking my first cigarette at Mom's grave.

"Light mine," said Tracy. I leaned over and struck the match. It took several strikes to get it lit. When Tracy breathed in she coughed too.

"Do I look like Rose Voss?" asked Tracy as she waved the cigarette between her fingers.

"Definitely. Don't I look like Ali McGraw?" I tipped my head to the side and blew smoke dramatically into the air. Tracy laughed, and the sound echoed through the trees.

Looking at my hand, I could so imagine Mom's fingers holding her lipstick-stained filter. Then Dad's voice popped into my head. "Those will kill you, Maggie."

I stood up so fast I felt dizzy. I stomped on the cigarette. "We need to find my mom."

"You don't know?" Tracy said.

"I'll figure it out. Follow me."

But I grew more and more confused. Mom wasn't in the place I remembered. The longer we searched, the worse I felt. Shouldn't I know where she was?

"I've gotten all turned around," I said.

In the distance I saw a sign that looked familiar. "There it is," I said. But it wasn't. With each false sighting, I was sinking further down into a deep hole. I wanted to go home, but I took a deep breath and continued walking, until there it was, right near a big oak tree. Tracy stood with me, staring down at the rounded headstone. Mom's birth was chiseled into the stone—born March 15, 1934, died April 20, 1970. I laid the wilted bunch of flowers next to her name.

I felt something was expected of me, something dramatic or meaningful, but I didn't have a clue. All I could think about was her body lying under that earth, maggots eating her flesh. *Food for worms.*

I brushed the fallen leaves off the marker. "I don't know what to say."

"Me either," said Tracy. "Tell her we had a smoke." I gave her a dirty look. "Sorry." And then seriously: "Hi, Maggie."

I traced my pointer finger over the *M*, for *Margaret*. For Mom.

"Hi, Mom." I said. "Billy is better," I said finally. "He's doing really good. So are Annie and Mae. And Claire and me, we're like friends again, like you wanted us to be."

Maybe she saw that I hadn't known where she was buried. Maybe she'd seen me awake in the night. Maybe she saw my earrings—not good. "Dad said I could get my ears pierced. You'd be happy with him. He's been taking care of everything."

Tracy blurted, "Maggie? You were the best mother."

"Yeah, Mom, the best. Sorry we were smoking." I didn't say out loud: *And sorry I didn't know you worried when I was in the hospital. And most, most sorry, that I said, I wished you were dead.*

Maybe she couldn't see us, so I told her, "I went grocery shopping, and I talked Dad into having Grandma stay with us, and Claire and I read Billy and Annie to sleep most nights."

Though a crisp breeze sent leaves spinning around us, I felt a warmth in my chest, the way I did after drinking hot cocoa. I wanted to tell Mom every single thing I'd been doing to help Dad and my sisters and brother, everything we were doing to help each other. I could see her in her cashmere sweater and the heart necklace she liked, lighting her own cigarette, nodding her head in approval. I knew it was Tracy's arm around my shoulder and not Mom's, but I heard her say, *You've done a fantabulous job.*

23

Not having been on skates in a year, I started off slowly, but soon I was gliding along, backward and doing turns, the chilly wind biting my face. Tracy and I competed for number of spins, and then pushed off together. We kept a close eye on the older boys who were wielding hockey sticks, my ears alert for the sound of scraping blades coming too close.

Claire and James arrived, like king and queen of the prom. I watched them lace up their skates, link hands, and glide onto the ice. Claire's spins were straighter, her turns more confident than any other girl on the rink. On one turn, she lifted her back leg up high, then skidded to a stop, creating a flurry of ice dust.

I picked up speed, my skates shimmering above the ice. My bra—one of the clunky ones I'd gotten with Dad—kept digging into my back. I stepped off the ice, at the dark end of the rink, squirming a little, as I slipped my hand under the elastic and wiggled it loose.

A tap on my shoulder. Yikes! It was Charlie, wearing a blue parka and a *Giants* wool cap.

My heart leapt, hoping he didn't see me with my hand up my shirt. I shrugged my bra back into place, sort of.

"Hi," Charlie managed. His lashes were thicker and longer than I remembered. Black skates, tied together by long laces, hung from one hand, his hockey stick in the other. "You done skating?" He sat down on the wood benches, pulling off his sneakers.

"No, I was just taking a break. I'll wait, if you want."

"Okay, sure," said Charlie as he laced up his skates. From the side, his nose had the cutest bump from when he'd broken it playing ice hockey.

Charlie and I stepped onto the ice and took off together, in perfect sync. We passed Claire, who was laughing cozily at something James was saying. Hockey players were zipping by, almost knocking me over.

Claire came up on my left, tapped my hat, and said, "Hey, Jojo, having *fun?*" I tried not to smile.

As we did the next loop, I did a quick spin, hoping to impress Charlie. Tracy skated up alongside of me and whispered in my ear, "I dare you to hold his hand!" and skated away. She thought I wouldn't, but I'd show her. Oh geez, my nikkin' bra was going to be up at my neck soon!

Each time I thought of taking Charlie's hand, my stomach did a flip-flop. Finally, when we got to the darker end of the rink, I pretended to trip and grabbed hold of Charlie's hand. He looked startled but held on. Even through our gloves, a shot of electricity flashed through me.

"Yo, Charlie," called one of the hockey players. He zipped up next to Charlie, gave him a hip check, jamming Charlie up against me

Charlie dropped my hand. "Quit playing kissy face with the girls," the hockey player called as he sped away. "Your team needs you."

"Okay, I'm coming," Charlie called back. "Just gotta grab my stick. See ya, Jody." He blinked those long, dark eyelashes and power-skated after his boys.

The next Saturday I decided to take Billy in his stroller to Edgehaven Park, popping in at the library to drop off *Pride and Prejudice,* and with luck find a book on how to find the right wife.

First, I had to remove all the barrettes that Annie had attached to the tufts of Billy's wispy hair. I parked his stroller by the front door. Under his parka, Billy had on his Superman cape. "You can't fly around the library and make a lot of noise," I said. "You need to be extra quiet, people are reading. Okay?" He nodded, lifting his arms straight out in front of him. *Uh-oh.* He was ready to leap tall buildings in a single bound. "Billy, look at me," I turned his head to make eye contact. "You need to stay right with me. No flying. If you're good, I'll let you pick out a book." At least he appeared to agree with me.

Before I could reach the desk to ask for help, Billy noticed the shiny metal water fountain and made a beeline for it, yelling, "Sprinkler!" He loved trying to catch the water as it spouted up in the air.

Picking him up, I struggled with how to simultaneously hold down the foot pedal and hold him over the fountain to let him take a sip. Every time I put him back down, he yelled, "More!"

"Hi there, Jody. Who do we have here? Superman?" It was Miss Wendy.

I blushed at a recurring fantasy—my father kissing her as she cooked a yummy dinner for us all.

"My brother, Billy," I stammered.

"And how old are you, young man?"

Billy worked to hold down two fingers to show three.

She was taller than I remembered. Close to Dad's height. Mom was petite. Miss Wendy had the red hair Dad liked too, just a few shades darker than Mom's.

"You must love to dance," I said.

"Oh, dance? I'm a terrible dancer. But I'll tell you what I love, watching musicals, like *West Side Story*, with lots of dancing." Venn positive!

Billy wiggled in my arms, and I set him back down with a warning look. He stared up at Miss Wendy.

"Can I help you find something?" she asked.

"I have to do a report on marriage for health class," I said. Austen's Lady Catherine said that no one should run hastily into a marriage without the proper information and background on the suitor. "We're learning about being a good wife. Are there books on that?" I smiled, pleased with my quick thinking.

"Oh, gosh. Well, no doubt there's more to being a good wife than you'll find in a book! For one thing, it goes hand in hand with someone else…being a good husband! But follow me," she said. "We might have just what you're looking for in home economics."

In the stacks, Miss Wendy ran her finger along the spines, reading aloud some of the titles. She knew right where to look. A lot of information lived in her head. Dad would like that. He'd definitely like her long legs. Suddenly I noticed my brother was no longer standing next to me. But—*phew!*—there he was, sprinting back across the room and into the stacks on the other side.

"Sorry. Monkey trouble. I'll be right back!" I said and chased after Billy, just as he wanted.

I caught his shirt, yanking him to an abrupt halt. It was like stopping a bulldozer, with many of the same sounds. He squealed and sputtered with delight.

"Do I have to put you back in your stroller?" I demanded.

"NO!"

Miss Wendy approached. "Here, Billy. Let's go find you a book." She took hold of his hand. Dad might find her quite kissable.

"I bet you'd like one about Superman."

"Yes!" cried Billy.

There were other things besides dancing.

Once home, I stole to my bedroom to check out my new books. In *When You Marry*, I read that you are sure to have an unhappy marriage if the wife doesn't give in to her husband's wishes. Whoa! What about the wife's wishes? On another page, the author recommended that the wife avoid being argumentative. Who would want to be a wife with this idiotic stuff? Dad wouldn't want this kind of wife. Like Miss Wendy said, the man has to be worthy of her.

How to be a Good Wife was more of the same. This one said a wife should always have dinner ready when her husband walks in the door. *Plan ahead, even the night before, to have a delicious meal— on time. Most men are hungry when they come home, and the prospects of a good meal are part of the warm welcome needed.* On top of that, it recommended you take fifteen minutes to rest before your husband arrives home so you'll be refreshed when he arrives.

Touch up your makeup, put a ribbon in your hair, and be fresh-looking. His boring day may need a lift.

I could see Mom laughing at this advice. With five kids, somedays she was lucky to have her hair brushed. She would have killed for fifteen minutes of rest, at any time of day. I glanced up at the collage of Polaroid pics over Claire's bed—the one she took of us in the pond; the last photo of us; another of Mom, breaking every stupid *rule* in those books, with no makeup, hair like a lion, paint drips all over her sweatshirt with the shredded cuffs, and looking at Dad with such joy.

24

Dad made a sharp left turn. We were going to a Saturday estimate, my favorite Dad-activity. Today I was his assistant and would do the measuring and chat up the customer.

"Stringbean," he said, "it helps if you tell me *before* we get to the street. Maybe if you put that catalog down and instead look at the map, we won't miss the turn."

"Okay. But I'm trying to tell you. I can buy the Christmas presents this year. I mean, right out of the Sears catalogue. They just come in the mail. What do you think? Christmas is only weeks away!"

"Sure," he said, only half listening, scanning house numbers.

"Dad," I said, more firmly. "I can do the Christmas shopping for you. Christmas, coming right up!"

"Mmm," Dad said. His eyes rose up as he nodded his head in consideration of the offer. "I guess that could work. Yeah, sounds good, stringbean. Make sure you get all the kids what they want. And that it's equal. And keep a budget."

He'd found the house, and late as we were, we leapt out and ran to the double wooden doors. Dad juggled his clipboard, pen, and tape measure, as well as his hammer and chisel for checking subfloors.

❧

Later, at home, I rushed to find Claire. It wasn't hard—she was sprawled as usual on her bed, reading one of those stupid romance novels, the ones with the shirtless guy on the cover. She had her period, and it was well known not to bug her at that time of the month.

"Hey, stupid bear," I said, standing in the doorway, holding up the revered catalog. "Guess what Dad said?"

"It always seems impossible until it isn't?"

"He said I can order our Christmas presents this year!" This was power. "I'll be in the kitchen making a list. Even though you've been *very* bad."

"Oh, well, Christmas," Claire said. She dropped her book, rose, stretched, and followed me to the dining room.

Mae was already sitting at the table, doing her homework, pencil sharpened at the ready. "Give me," she said.

"Age before beauty," said Claire.

"What's all this?" Dad said.

"Christmas! Remember, I'm getting the gifts."

"10-4."

From the hall bathroom, Annie called, "Help! I need to wipe! There's no more paper."

"Just maybe wash?" Dad called back.

But Annie was adamant. "Mrs. O'Donnell says we have to wipe."

Dad always picked me. "Jody, old stringbean, go grab a roll of terlet paper from my room for your sister." He was making a hot dog for Billy. His second lunch.

Claire was flipping through the pages of the enormous catalog, stopping periodically, to say, "I want this."

"Let her perform her own ablutions," I growled. *Ablutions: the act of washing oneself.* One of last month's OED words. "Claire, don't pick stuff without me."

In Dad's bathroom there were only a few precious sheets left. I was definitely not handing them over. I checked in the cabinet below the sink. Nothing.

"We're all out!" I yelled to Dad.

"Did you look under the sink?" Dad asked.

"Zippo," I said, making my way back to the table. I grabbed for the catalog, but Claire held tight.

"You're going to rip it!" I shouted.

"Girls, if you are going to fight over it. No one will look at it."

Annie was yelling even louder, "Wipe!"

"Just hold tight, pork chop," Dad bellowed.

"Jody, look at this crankin' guitar," said Claire, circling the item and turning down the corner of the page.

"Here, Billy," Dad said, handing him some napkins. "Be a big helper and go give these to Annie." Billy protested. "When you get back your hot dog will be ready."

"We can't use napkins," said Claire.

"It's paper, isn't it?"

"Gross," said Claire.

"Well, I don't know what makes it gross," said Dad. "If Grandma Cupcakes were here already she'd make you use that catalog." He laughed. "Now that's gross!"

"Grandma loves to be gross," I said. "When I had a cut, she told me to pee on it! It disinfects, she said!"

"Ew, you're being gross," said Mae.

"Well, *I'm* not using napkins," said Claire.

"Don't go getting your knickers in a knot. After dinner I'll run out to the store and pick some up."

"It's Sunday. The stores are closed," Claire said, a snarky grin on her face. Another curve ball for Dad. He took a big breath and let it out slowly.

A few minutes later Dad, trying to make up for the lack of supplies, said, "Hey, troops, finish up what you're doing. I'm taking you to Friendly's for an ice cream. What do you all think of that?"

Whoops sounded all around. "Last one out is a rotten egg," yelled Mae. Grabbing our jackets, and me the Sears catalog, we bolted for the car.

"Dibs on the front seat," yelled Claire before I could.

With Claire up front by Dad, I let Mae choose her presents first. I wanted to pick with Claire. Flipping through the catalog, I put a pen mark next to each of Mae's choices—a charm bracelet, Hula Hoop, the game of Life, Twister, and lots more. When I saw the telescope, I double circled. It provides: *Exacting color definition even for stars of the eleventh magnitude!* This was for me. Mom had always talked about someday buying a telescope for me and her to look at the moon and stars. Wait! Two hundred dollars! Then again, all of us could use it, more like a family gift. If we divided it equally that would only be sixty dollars each. Not so bad.

Annie pouted in the car.

At Friendly's I jumped out almost before Dad put the car in park, clutching the catalog, now filled with creases and turned-down pages. I wanted to be first in line at the walk-up window. Mae did, too, and we jostled for position. Claire, in jeans and a blue sweater, made a show of not caring—her nose still buried in her romance novel.

Dad, holding Billy's hand, followed behind and said, "No, ladies, let's go inside, sit down, and enjoy our cones."

Mae, in the lead, raced inside, first to the hostess stand. I pointed to the catalog, and she made way. The hostess gave Dad a special smile—she was cute, but her teeth were way too big and she was only five feet tall. Claire sashayed in, leading Annie. And all of us scooted over into a booth, three to a side, the two little ones' feet dangling above the floor. The ordering took forever—fudge ripple, chocolate, strawberry, and Annie changing her mind three times. Dad a coffee, black.

The light fixture hanging above Dad was like a spotlight on him. His green shirt perfectly matched his eyes. The waitress seemed to notice too. I heard her say to the other waitress, "He's easy on the eyes."

When the last bite was done, and Billy's face well-wiped, Dad pressed a ten-dollar bill into my hand. "Beanster, you pay the bill. Claire, get these kiddies cleaned up. I'm going to run to the men's room."

As the hostess counted out our change, I spotted Dad hurrying out of the bathroom, his jacket draped over his shoulders in a way I'd never seen him wear it before. He barely slowed as he passed our table. "Kids, head for the car. Move it," he said. As we reached the car, a roll of terlet paper bounced behind him.

Claire scooped it up, cool as a jailbird, and tossed it in the car. We piled in after it, falling over each other laughing.

Dad peeled out.

Back in my bedroom, I pulled out my notebook, along with the catalog, and heaved myself onto my bed. "Hey," said Claire. "Give it here."

Together we picked out clothes. A maxi-length coat and fleece robes. Mom always gave us new pajamas to sleep in on Christmas eve, so I bought matching red and white flannel feety pajamas for all five of us. And then I ordered a pair for Mom, I could hardly say why.

For me, besides the clothes, I selected a wristwatch, a little ivory porcelain clock that played the theme song from *Love Story*. And, of course, the best present of all—the telescope!

I went in search of Annie and Billy. "You've been so good this year. We need to pick out what you want for Christmas and send Santa a letter." Looking Billy in the eye, I said, "And you need to be good till Christmas for Santa to bring the presents. You can't scream to get your way." Billy could really pitch a fit. He nodded and lunged for the catalog.

"Hold on a sec," I said. "Let me hold it and you show me what you want."

Quickly I gave up. There wasn't a single toy on the page that Annie and Billy didn't want. I'd figure out what was best for them. For Annie, an Easy Bake Oven, a Tubsy doll, a scooter, and lots of games. Billy loved *Sesame Street*, and especially Cookie Monster, so I picked out the hand puppets, a matchbox track, and all sorts of Nerf toys and guns. I was thrilled to find a white pith helmet, a hat he'd likely never seen before. And his best present—a new blue two-wheel bike with training wheels.

At the last minute I decided to surprise Mae with a pottery wheel.

My list completed, I called the number listed in the catalog. The woman on the phone didn't even know I was a kid. I just read her dad's revolving charge information from the back of the kitchen cabinet where Mom had pasted all the numbers and told her what we wanted. When she read the list back, I was thrilled but suddenly realized I'd forgotten Dad.

So I threw in a silk robe for him.

25

Today, like every day of the previous week, I watched for deliveries, grabbing any boxes, large and small, that arrived and whisking them off to the basement closet.

At four, when I saw the truck, I ran outside without my coat. I waved. "Hi, any packages?"

"Three today. It's always nice to have someone looking forward to seeing me," the driver said. "You should put a coat on. You'll freeze."

One box was Hasbro games, another Nerf balls, and the last Dad's silk robe. Dad would love it. I pictured him wearing it at Juliette's house and added it to their Venn.

I marked the gifts off my tally sheet, making sure things stayed equal, like Dad said.

I wanted Christmas morning to look like all the years before—except even better.

On the weekend, Dad dragged the decorations down from the attic. I'd asked him if Juliette and her kids could help with the tree, but Dad said, "Let's keep it just us this year, do it the way Mom would like it."

Claire and I plowed in, opening the cartons, pulling out all the Christmas memories, while Billy, more or less, helped Dad assemble the tree. It *almost* looked like a real tree.

"Mae, unknot the lights so we can string them on," I said.

"Annie, careful with the glass ornaments. They break easy," said Claire.

"Coffee break," said Dad. "I'll be back."

"Look, our stockings," I said. Mom had embroidered each of our names in gold. "I get to hang mine." I said. Each of my siblings did the same. The basement door still had seven nails in it from prior Christmases. Claire looped Mom's stocking over the hook. "Maybe we shouldn't," I whispered. "It will remind everyone she's gone."

"It will remind everyone she was here!" said Claire.

"Maybe she still is," I said. Claire smiled and draped her arm over my shoulder.

Dad returned, mug in hand. "The stockings look nice, girls." He said nothing about Mom's.

"Now the best part. I get to sit back and watch you kids decorate," said Dad.

Claire, Mae, Annie, and I draped the tree with silver tinsel, then added all the familiar decorations—the angel on top, the glass balls, and a lot of yarn and sparkly homemade ornaments.

"Dad, make Billy stop. He's taking off the ornaments as quickly as we put them on!" Mae yelled.

"Billy, come over here," said Dad.

"I'm helping," he said.

"No, you are only helping drive your sisters crazy," said Dad. "Here, I have a job for you. Place the Christmas blanket around the bottom of the tree."

When the tree was decorated, I taped Christmas cards onto the wooden handrail going down to the basement.

"Dad, we didn't send any Christmas cards this year," I said, mad at myself for forgetting this important task.

"Dammit, you're right." Then he waved his hand in the air and said, "It's okay. I think our friends will understand if we skip a year."

Days before Christmas, Dad called me into the kitchen. He was holding a piece of paper in his hand and waving it at me. His jaw clenched. *Uh-oh.*

"Jody, how could you buy all this?" His voice was pulled tight. "You spent over six hundred dollars!" He was waving the bill from Sears and Roebuck in the air.

"You *told* me to do the shopping. And you've been selling lots of jobs."

"Yes, business is good, but it doesn't mean you can buy the

whole damn catalog! Beaner, we have lots of bills. Didn't you think about the cost?"

I had. But only one item at a time.

Once again his eyes scanned the bill. "A pottery wheel!"

"Mae will love it. She can make cereal bowls. We're always breaking them. It could save us money. Plus, I don't know, maybe she can sell them."

"We'll have to return some of these things."

He kept staring at the bill, shaking his head and repeating, "I can't believe you bought all of this. Christ! A telescope! TWO HUNDRED DOLLARS! Who in this house needs a telescope?"

"It's for Mom," I said. "She wanted me to see the moon."

"Don't pull that on me."

But I wasn't pulling anything. He didn't tell me how much was too much. It was his fault. I was never doing his stupid shopping ever again.

Dad put an arm around my shoulder, which was shaking with sobs. "It's okay, stringbean. You're right, I asked you and you picked some great things. But we have to send some of them back, like the telescope. That's way too much money."

"You should have told me how much to spend! I thought about every single one of us and what everyone liked and what would make them happy and…and…why don't you just get yourself a *wife*," I said. "Some stupid lady with *nice* legs."

Dad stepped back and dropped the bill on to the table. He scrunched up his eyes and sighed. "You know, Jody, I wish it was that easy."

"You're right, it wasn't easy, it was hard. I worked so hard picking all those presents, making sure the kids would be happy on Christmas and all you care about is money."

"I want us to open great presents, stringie, but I want us to have food on the table too."

Dad was quiet then, as if talking to himself, he said, "How did your mother do it every year, come up with teepees and quilts and doll clothes? It's hard for all of us. She made it look so easy."

❧

Christmas morning, Annie, in her red and white Christmas pajamas, was the first one up. We were all in last year's matching pjs, hitched up in the legs. Dad had returned the new ones. Just in case, I took Mom's old pair from the attic and left them under the pillow on her side of the bed. The woman in the movie— the one in the car accident, who suffered from amnesia, gets her memory back and shows up at Christmas.

Running into my room, Annie jumped on to my bed, "Wake up. Come on, Jody. Wait till you see all the presents Santa brought! It's huge! We peeked. Mae and I peeked!"

"Okay, I'm coming," I said, putting on my glasses. This time it wasn't for the thrill of getting presents but to see the excitement on the little kids' faces. "I'll wake up Claire! You get Dad and Billy!"

After Dad had returned a bunch of gifts to Sears, he was happy to be Santa. Last night he stayed up late with Claire and me, wrapping, putting together Billy's new two-wheeler and piling the presents under the tree. And the presents were still pretty good. I was happy he let me keep the pottery wheel for Mae, even if I didn't get my telescope.

Annie ran back in. "And Santa ate the cookies we left him."

"You did peek!"

Once we were all assembled, Dad did his usual. "Ready, set, go!" And we were off, diving for boxes, a frenzy of wrapping paper flying, followed by squeals of delight, hollering for everyone to look at something they received. Billy was trying to ride his little bike over the mess of boxes and paper.

"Tubsy," cried Annie. "Santa brought me Tubsy!" I was barely opening my gifts. I knew what was inside. And it felt so good, watching them, seeing their smiles as they opened their presents.

Annie hugged me. "Thank you for telling Santa!" I remembered being little and asking Mom if she was sad that she didn't get all these presents. Now I understood what she meant when she said, "Watching all of you is my present."

"Here, Dad, open your present," I said, handing him a box.

"For me!" he said, acting all shocked.

"Wow, now look at this." He stood up, letting the maroon silk robe unfold and holding it up next to him. "I'll be the most handsome guy in town wearing this."

"Put it on," Annie said. Dad did. "So what do you all think?" he asked, turning around. He did look handsome.

"Oh my God!" Mae shouted. "A pottery wheel! A pottery wheel! A pottery wheel! I always wanted one! Mom! Mom! A pottery wheel!"

She froze. We all did. Then she ran over to Dad, who was sitting on the floor helping Billy assemble his Matchbox race track, and threw her head into his lap and started to cry.

"Me too," said Annie, also starting to cry as she hugged Dad's other side.

Billy jumped off his bike and dived on top of Dad's head.

"Ow," yelled Mae, crying harder. "You're hurting me."

"There's room for everyone," said Dad.

I jumped in too. I wanted to be part of the missing-Mom pile.

Dad held his arms wide and said, "Claire?"

"Aw, hell, whatever," she mumbled and threw her body on top of mine.

We were all laugh-crying.

Fantabulous," said Claire.

Then I noticed a large box in the corner. I knew every box size, color and shape. "What's that?" I asked.

"I don't know," said Dad. "You better take a look. Maybe Santa dropped off a present at the wrong house." One by one, we climbed off Dad. Annie pulled off the tag and read, "For Jody."

"It weighs a ton," said Claire.

I looked at Dad, my mouth wide open. Was this what I thought it was? All five of us tore at the wrapping. The telescope! It took my breath away.

"Now be careful with it," said Dad. "Remember, it's a real telescope, not a toy."

Billy returned to his bike.

"What's a telescope?" asked Annie.

"It's a really powerful eyeglasses, to make you see things clearly that are very far away."

"Like heaven?" asked Annie.

"Like the planets," said Dad. "We can look at the moon and see the craters. Jody will show you. Your mom always wanted to see past us. She wanted you to see it all."

26

It was a new year, 1971.

It seemed like overnight Mom's sewing room had been transformed into a bedroom. Claire, Mae, Annie, and I helped Grandma Cupcakes empty her cardboard boxes, each one stinking with a gross smell. Mothballs or Ben Gay?

Grandma Cupcakes handed me her Bible. "Put this on my nightstand. Or maybe take it with you. You always got your nose in a book, give the Good Book a go." She grinned, her blue eyes twinkly, and gave my bottom a swat. Maybe moving in would be good for her, put some color back in her cheeks.

Annie, reclining on the bed, hands behind her head, was rattling off facts about her teacher love. "Mrs. O'Donnell is the best teacher. And she has a daughter Patty, in second grade. She's my friend. She has pretty blond hair."

"Enough jibber-jabber about Mrs. O'Donnell. Come help," said Mae, who was standing on a stool, putting Grandma's shoes in the pockets of the gold shoe bag that hung from the closet door. She had lost her little bit of baby fat. "Annie, hand me those slippers."

Annie wiggled off the bed, a slipper on each hand. "Look, mittens!"

"Annie, that's gross," said Mae, pulling them off her hands.

Claire was emptying boxes, ripping tape, cracking flaps. "Yikes," she cried, grabbing hold of the porcelain doll Grandma's sister Margaret, the nun, had given her. "It's like a doll from a horror movie."

Grandma's sister was a Sister. We'd only met once because she lived in a convent far away. The doll had a different fancy velvety gown for each Catholic holiday, feasts I had never even heard of before—St Anthony of Padua, Our Lady of Guadalupe, and Feast of the Epiphany.

"Grandma, can I have it? It's so cool," I said.

"Be careful with that, you rascal. Aunt Doris gave it to me. You'll break it. You can visit her in my room any time you like." Claire hefted a tough old suitcase onto the bed.

"Criminy. Hand me that, Claire," Grandma said "It's got all my privates." The flesh on her arms hung a good four inches below her bones. Her skin was so light, I could almost see through it. I couldn't resist. I flicked at the hanging skin with my finger and watched it flap. Grandma Cupcakes was sixty-four and everything about her talcum-dusted body fascinated and kinda repulsed me.

"Now quit playing with the ole Bingo wings," she cried, slapping her thigh like it was the first time she ever said it.

Out from the box came several bras, each cup big enough to fit my entire head!

"Over the shoulder boulder holders!" Claire shouted and we all burst into giggles and snorts.

"Don't make fun of the girls," Grandma said, cupping her breasts and giving them a dramatic hoist. When I was little, I'd loved disappearing into their softness, but now they were horrifying. While I burned to grow breasts like Claire's, I didn't want those.

"Let me feel them!" Annie cried.

I fell on her chenille bedspread, laughing.

"Oh, Annie!" Mae said.

Carefully, I lifted Grandma's old box radio onto her dresser. Whenever I slept at Grandma's the voices of talk radio had drifted in and out of my sleep. One morning I had asked her, "Why do you sleep with the radio on? Doesn't it keep you awake?"

She'd shrugged and said, "I like the company."

"Put it over there," Grandma growled.

I placed it on the side table, plugged it in, turned it on, and started spinning the dial. "Good Lovin'" by the Rascals!

"Yes!" I cried, throwing my arms up and shimmying around Grandma, who sat in the chair folding hankies. Mae was shaking her bottom as Annie bounced on the bed.

Claire picked up Grandma's hairbrushes, tossing me one. She sang into the brush microphone: "Yeah, yeah, yeah!" She pointed at me and I bellowed, changing the words, "Yes, indeed, *all we* really need!" Then I signaled to Mae and Annie to join in: "Gimme that good lovin.'"

"Come on, Grandma, join in!" I shouted holding the hairbrush up to her mouth. Grandma stood up, shook her big bottom and sang off-key in a pretend-growly voice, "Good lovin', baby." I pressed on her Bingo arms, making them gyrate to the beat.

Just what I had dreamed of—we were a new family.

Grandma popped out her set of false teeth and clicked them like castanets on her fingers, "Mae, give-a-me a kiss goodnight," she said. Mae squealed as Grandma tried to touch Mae's lips with her false teeth.

Annie, jumping up and down, cried, "Kiss me, kiss me, Grandma!" Then she started one of her hyena-snorting laughs, which got Claire imitating Annie's snorts and me in hysterics.

"Oh no," I cried. "I'm peeing my pants!"

It was late. After rifling through the OED and finding a cool word of the day: *Abhorrent: inspiring disgust,* I stayed up to look at the waxing crescent moon with my new telescope. Another man would walk up there soon. Mom had told us that the waxing moon is close to the sun and mostly dark except for the right edge, which is brighter than usual. At that time everything is clearer, illuminated. So true.

Suddenly I heard a clatter of pots in the kitchen. I ran inside, found Grandma in her old blue robe putting a saucepan on the stove.

"Oh, it's the flap-napper," she said as she took the milk from the refrigerator.

I said, "Grandma, don't you ever sleep?" It worried me, for she looked older by the day, her hair thinner and grayer, the creases in her face deeper. We were already wearing her out.

Without looking up, Grandma said, "Oh, I sleep here and

there, chickadee." She made that familiar sucking noise between her lips. "In fact, I'm sleeping right now! What about you? Creeping around at all hours!"

"I was looking at the moon!"

Slowly, Grandma Cupcakes roused herself up from the kitchen chair, toddled over to the window, brushed the curtain aside, looked out into the darkness, and said, "Yep, it's still there." She smiled at me. "Your mom loved looking at the moon."

At the stove, she turned on the heat under the saucepan, the flame flickering below. The fuzz on her blue slippers was worn and bare in spots.

"I'll keep you company if you like," I said.

"That would be swell." She pulled her robe tighter. "I'll pour you some warm milk and we'll slurp it out of bowls like kittens!"

"Grandma?"

"Oh no, here it comes. Another question from the peanut gallery."

"Are you shrinking?"

"No, toots. You're growing."

"I can almost rest my chin on your head. You *are* shrinking."

"Well, stop putting me in the dryer then! And for Jake's sake, have a seat."

Grandma Cupcakes stirred the milk, poured us both a cup, and lowered herself back down in her chair beside me at the little table. Mom's chair. Mom's table. Grandma slid a biscuit towards me, ignoring the burn mark. But I loved to outline it with my finger.

Grandma sputtered. "Indoor barbeque!"

I said, "Mom built the grill herself. The legs are from an old metal lawn chair. She soldered an old frying pan to the chair legs to hold the charcoal, and an oven rack on the top of the pan to make the grill. And that cutoff piece of vacuum hose is to vent the smoke out the window."

"And who called the fire department?" Grandma said. Her daughter still amused her.

"Claire!" I said.

"Luckily it was a small fire," Grandma said, and we laughed fondly.

"My feet are killing me," Grandma said as she removed a slipper. I could see the bunion on the edge of her foot, swollen and red.

Usually Grandma Cupcakes was like a jack-in-the-box, rarely sitting still for more than a minute or two. But that middle of the night she rested quietly, the silence surrounding us, wrapping us comfortably.

"Tell me more about Mom." I wasn't sure she would. Grandma Cupcakes kept her feelings tucked deep inside. Sometimes a feeling peeked out but just as quickly she tucked it back in. "She was an inventor, wasn't she?"

"If you call taking things apart and not putting them back together inventing." Then Grandma shrunk another couple of inches, like a turtle going into its shell. "Oh, it's too hard to remember," she said, waving her hand at me. "We need to all of us move on."

The next morning, I came down to breakfast. Grandma Cupcakes was sitting right where I'd left her the night before, in the same worn blue terry cloth robe fixed up at the waist, her early morning burps tearing at the air. I held my breath. Her morning burps were *abhorrent*.

"Want some breakfast? I can fry you a *nikkin'* egg." Grandma said, taking a sip of coffee.

"Yes, please. I'll make the nikkin' toast."

Grandma gave me a long look, then pulled herself up and got a skillet from the cabinet.

I found the butter and handed it over.

The pan sizzling, Grandma cracked the shell with one hand. She said, "You know, I was thinking back. One time I was sound asleep. When I used to sleep." Grandma winked at me. "And oh, if I didn't hear a terrible racket. Someone was pounding on the front door. I looked at the clock. Three in the morning, it was! I said, 'Tom, Tom wake up. Someone's at the door.'"

"Grandpa's name was Charlie!"

"Was it? Oh, right," she said. She was always teasing. "He just growled and rolled over. That man was never much help. The banging kept on and on." Grandma paused and took another gulp of coffee. "I got myself out of bed, put on my robe, cussing, and grabbed the wooden spatula."

"A spatula! What would that do?"

"Never you mind. This is my story. I called, 'Who's there? Do you know what dag-nag time it is?' And you won't believe who it was." She paused, waited. Flipped the egg.

"Grandma! Who? Who?"

"Your mother! I about near had a heart attack. She had sleepwalked *right* out that front door. I was fit to be tied. She couldn't have been more than eight or nine. Never done anything like that before. Or, thank the Heavens, after. That girl always knew how to keep me hopping."

For a brief moment Mom was there. I could see her—her coffee cup in her right hand, her first cigarette of the day in her left. Grandma held my eye with the same crooked smile.

Dad had been talking about the *Apollo 14* launch all week, insisting we watch the historic event together—January 31, 1971. He made two enormous bowls of buttered popcorn, and we piled in on the basement couch, love seat, and floor, all smooshed around Grandma. To convince Claire to join in, Dad had said James could watch with us. I hadn't needed any persuading: two days of moon walks! My moon, Mom's moon, and a blue moon!

Grandma gave it barely ten minutes before she said, "Well, I've seen about enough of this. Why would anyone shoot themselves into the sky in that thing?" She took her finger and made circles at her temple, casting us off like puppies, and upstairs she went.

"Cranky," Claire muttered.

"Annoying," I said.

"Girls," Dad said.

"I like her. She's a hoot" said James, his baseball cap turned backward.

"She used to be nice," Claire told him, snuggling up next to him on the love seat. Perfect.

"Dad, make Billy move over. I can't see past his stupid space helmet," said Mae.

Dad, sitting on the carpet, leaning against the couch, scooched Billy over into the depression Grandma had left.

Seeing that rocket ship ready to launch, my stomach did a flip-flop. What if this time it really crashed? That same news guy, Caterpillar Face, said the rocket ship was the size of a football field. No wonder it had trouble taking off.

Then we waited and waited some more, popcorn flying, Claire giggling over something James was doing. Soon Billy, bored, became a rocket ship, blasting off the couch and flying around the room.

"I thought you were an astronaut," I said. "Not the rocket."

"I'm the astronaut going up to the moon," yelled Billy, making all sorts of sound effects.

"Billy," Dad said.

"There you are!" said Tracy arriving in a new plaid jacket and plopping down next to me. "So what are we watching?"

"*Apollo 14*," said Dad. "I have to give you a space lesson, Tracy." She glowed. She loved it when Dad treated her like one of his own.

The news people kept explaining that they were investigating trouble with the docking equipment. This was not making me feel any better about this launch—total dèjà vu.

Dèjà vu: a feeling you've already experienced something.

"Here's the lesson," said Claire. "A metal tube blasts off, goes up in the sky, flies around, stops at the moon. A guy in big shoes climbs out. Whoop-de-doo."

"James and Claire, sitting in a tree, k-i-s-s-i-n-g," Annie sang.

"Claire, let's see a little light of day between you two," said Dad. And my big smart-alecky sister moved over a couple inches. When Dad looked away, she was right back snuggled next to James.

"Why don't you sit on his lap?" I said, under my breath.

"No room," she said.

"Be nice to your little sister," James said.

"Why? 'Cause she's never had a boyfriend."

"Girls," Dad said, but he was absorbed by a report from Mission Control.

Tracy came to my defense. "Jody will have Charlie."

Claire squealed, suddenly, some secret thing.

"James, how about you join me over here on the floor," said Dad, patting the spot next to him.

"Gawd," Claire huffed.

James jumped up. "Oh, I nearly forgot, Mr. Moran, my dad needs me home to help with the yard."

"I'll help," said Claire.

"No, Claire. You have helped James quite enough for today," said Dad.

"Very funny," Claire said.

"This is history in the making. Just think about it," said Dad. "All the science that went into making this happen. You'll be telling your kids one day."

"Can I at least walk him out and get my nail polish, so I have *something* to do?"

"Yes, Ms. Bear, but come right back down. I don't want you to miss this. Neither would Mom."

Surprisingly, she returned quickly and started painting her nails a bright bubblegum pink, the polish letting off hellacious fumes.

"I feel sick," Annie said.

"Rocket fuel," Mae said.

The news guy was still talking about the delay.

Suddenly Dad snapped off the sound. "Hey, kids," he said. "How would it be, you think, if I got out and started dating?"

"Yeah, you should," I said. It was about time.

"Def!" said Tracy. "Who are you going out with? My mom says you could have your pick!"

"I don't mean right this minute!" said Dad.

"Better not be that weirdo woman at the A&P who's always

flirting with you," said Claire, carefully brushing on Mom's nail polish.

"What weirdo lady?" Dad said.

"Or Mrs. Marshall," I said.

"No Mrs. Marshall," Dad said.

Billy said, "Lois Lane." Did he understand? Sometimes he surprised me.

"I feel sick," Annie said.

Mae, still in her Alice role, said, "Curioser and curioser." I laughed.

Claire jammed the nail polish brush back into the bottle and stalked up the stairs.

"Claire, come back. Talk to me," Dad called after her. "Please."

"Fine," she said, reappearing and huffing back on to the love seat.

"Well, I know where Claire and Jody stand. How about you, Mae?"

"Mrs. O'Donnell," piped up Annie.

"Annie, Mrs. means she's already married," I informed her.

"No fair!" she pouted.

"What are you saying?" asked Billy, now playing with his Hess truck.

"Daddy's gonna get a girlfriend," I said.

Billy went back to his truck—I might as well have said that Dad was getting a bologna sandwich.

"Not so fast," Dad said.

"What will Grandma think?" I asked, suddenly worried she'd be upset.

"She'll understand," said Dad. "Well, I hope so."

Dad turned back to the TV, spun the volume up. "Hang on, gang. They've fixed the problem. Look, they're getting ready for lift off."

Claire examined her nails.

"Twenty-seconds and we are still a go," the commentator said, then counted with Houston down to zero. Then there was a huge plume of smoke. "We have lift-off!"

My heart jumped. I couldn't tell if the shuttle had made it or exploded. I held my breath and squeezed Dad's arm.

In a minute, a very long minute, the commentator announced that *Apollo 14* had safely launched out of the Earth's atmosphere.

"Are we done yet?" asked Claire. Maybe she was.

27

Weeks later, Dad went to his first "parents without partners" get-together and the next morning I was in the kitchen waiting for him. Before he could sit down, I asked, "So, how was it? Did you meet anyone?"

"Can I first get myself a cup of coffee?" He turned on the gas under the tea kettle. He seemed in good spirits.

"What was it like?" I sounded like the parent and he was the kid home from his first date.

"Well, like any dance, there was a three-piece band and people dancing."

"*Funny.* And. Did you meet anyone?"

"Gimme a little time," Dad said, chuckling.

After two more PWP gatherings, he finally made a date.

"Which tie do you like better, stringbean?" Dad asked, holding up two options. I chose one.

"Red it is, then," he said.

His barrel chest filled out his navy-blue suit, his hair smoothed down with Brylcreem.

"You look so handsome," I said.

When Dad bounced into the kitchen, my sisters and I were lying in wait. "Pizza," we yelled in unison. My father, imitating the guy playing the executioner on the commercial, asked, "What do you want on your Tombstone?"

We, the accused, replied, "Pepperoni and cheese." Grandma, happy not to have to cook, turned on the oven for the frozen pizza.

Dad was whistling show tunes as he left.

When the timer went off, Claire and I snagged the hot pizzas, Mae the bottle of soda, Annie the plates, and Billy, demanding a job of his own, got the napkins. Off we tromped to the basement to watch our Friday night favorite, *The Brady Bunch*. Well, we were the Moran bunch, just waiting for the other half. According to Grandma, pizza and Swanson's TV dinners were the only two meals acceptable to eat in front of the television.

Claire and I squeezed into a space on the supple brown leather couch, pushing the younger ones off to the matching love seat, a lesser view. When Dad remarried, our faces could fit in those same squares that appeared in the show's opening—Juliette in the mom square? Wendy the librarian? We even had a kind of housekeeper for the middle square: Grandma Cupcakes! Being the second oldest made me the Jan Brady of the group. Everyone thought Marsha was the popular, perfect sister, but I preferred Jan, with her long golden-blond hair.

At eight-thirty, when the show ended, Grandma, in her thick flannel nightgown, despite the warm weather, turned off the set.

"Let's play Twister," I shouted.

"But first pajamas and teeth brushed," our very own Hazel instructed.

౿

"So did you like her? What was she like? Will you go out with her again?" She wasn't Juliette, so I wasn't sure if I wanted a yes or a no.

Dad laughed. "Nope, I don't think so."

"Why not?" I asked.

"Well," he said, guffawing, "it was the strangest date ever. When I got there, the woman, Susan, asked me in, saying that we needed to say goodbye to Rob." He paused a moment, shaking his head.

"I thought it was her son, so I went along. She brings me in to an empty room, except for a candle and an urn. I was getting the heebie-jeebies. She tells me I needed to say goodnight to her husband!" Dad laughed harder. "Boy, did I want to get out of there quick. But I didn't want to hurt her feelings so we went to dinner."

I laughed and laughed, though nothing about it seemed so funny.

❧

Knocking first, I walked in—something Juliette told me I could do.

"Juliette, O Juliette, wherefore are thou, Juliette?" I called, pleased with my literary cleverness.

A man's voice said, "Who are you?" I jumped.

"Oh, sorry. Uh, I'm Jody. A friend. Is Juliette here?" I had my hand on the doorknob, ready to turn back.

"Jody! Jody!" Ben called. Do all little boys say people's names twice?

"Oh, they know you," said the man. This must be Seth.

"I live across the street," I said.

"Oh yes, Juliette mentioned you." That made me smile. "I'm Juliette's husband, Seth." His shiny shaved head, mustache, and goatee was not a look ever seen in our neighborhood. What was he doing here?

"She'll be back soon if you want to wait."

"No, that's okay," I said. "I'll come back later."

As I crossed the driveway Juliette pulled up and gave a wave. I stood, waiting for her to get out of the car. She was wearing her nurse's uniform, with a pretty blue scarf I'd never seen before.

"Come on in," she said.

"That's okay."

"You met Seth," she said.

"Yeah," I said unenthusiastically. After a moment I asked, "What's he doing here?" She gave me a sympathetic smile.

"Something to tell you," she said. "We're trying to work things out. I mean, things *are* working out. I wanted to tell you when we had time to talk. I didn't want you to hear it from someone else." She hesitated. "Seth was offered a spot at a Pennsylvania newspaper, more money. We're going to, well... we're going to move with him." She squeezed her lips tight. "At the end of the month."

"That's, like, next week!" Do I make people go away? I felt instantly stupid for having imagined us as a family. Juliette as my mother. It hit me in the gut—she didn't belong to me. She belonged to Ben, Bird, and Seth.

"I'm sorry to be going, Jody. I really am. I'll miss you."

I already understood. People disappear. *Poof.* I had wanted everything, now I wanted nothing. I thought of Grandma Cupcakes saying, "Don't go thinking you can get everything you want."

I had experience in how to lose people. I would try to not even notice she was gone.

"Well, okay," I said, and turned to leave.

"Jody," I heard her say.

But I was on my way.

❧

Opening the icebox, as Grandma Cupcakes insisted on calling it, she pulled out whatever wasn't eaten from last night's dinner— or gross, the night before that—and into one pot it all went. She seemed to think the more you glopped together the better it tasted. She never used a cookbook. I don't think she even knew what a measuring cup was.

Standing, dishtowel in hand, stockings rolled up to her knees, Grandma bent over the stove, stirring a concoction that she called, "Slumgullion stew." Her apron was cinched around her ever-thickening waist. When she went out for the day, she wore a girdle, but as soon as she returned home, off it came. With a loud exhale she'd say, "Aaaahhhh, now I can breathe!" Her stomach instantly expanded, like dropping one of those tablets into water and watching it become a spongy elephant within seconds.

Dad wasn't home yet.

Grandma called us to dinner—a meal that appeared to consist of boiled potatoes, roast beef, beets, peas, corn, and onions. Was that fish in there? An array of colors—green, yellow, brown, purple, all mashed together. The smells were just as varied and nasty, sour and vinegary.

"It's all mushed together," Claire said, a look of pure disgust crossing her face.

"I can't eat this," I said, gagging. Then whispered to Claire, "Send it over to James, he'll eat anything."

"Not this," Claire hissed.

"I heard that. And don't be so salty," Grandma Cupcakes said, giving me the stink eye, her lips drawn in a line.

"I like it," said Mae.

"Brown nose," I said.

"Am not. I do like it."

"Now that Dad's dating," I said, "maybe he'll meet someone who doesn't mush food together." Shocking myself with that spiteful barb, I picked up my fork and took a small bite. It really was gross.

"Sit up like a lady," said Grandma. Then she made that annoying sucking noise between her lips where teeth had once been.

I straightened myself in my chair, scooted some food around on my plate.

"Stop playing with your food and eat. There are children in China starving."

"Send it there then," Claire said.

Oh, I laughed.

Grandma snapped her dishtowel at Claire.

I stared above at the long coil of yellow sticky flypaper, twirling lightly, with old dead trapped flies that had never freed themselves. I filled my napkin with the partially chewed food and made for the bathroom to flush it down the toilet. On my second mission, Grandma grasped my shirt. "What do you think, you're too clever by half?"

"Grandma, nobody can eat this stuff. It's all mixed together!"

"Why does it matter? They all go down the same *pip.*" She said the word pipe as pip, another one of her favorite expressions. "When I was growing up, back home, we would have been thrilled to get this food."

"You used to be fun!" I shouted.

Dad arrived in the midst of this revolt. I ran to him, crying, "Don't make us eat this."

"Now, beanie," Dad said. But when he saw our plates, he

pulled up short. He liked his courses cleanly divided, preferably the same color, overcooked, for sure, but never mixed together. This made him a big fan of Swanson TV dinners.

"Ma, remember we talked about this. We can afford new food every day. We really can. I'm sorry, but the kids can't eat this."

Grandma pulled up her chin and harrumphed her way over to the stove. "Fine then, that leaves more for me." Grabbing a dish towel, she gave the pot another stir with her liver-spotted hand, staring absently at the pot, making tsk-tsk sounds and muttering under her breath, "That's not how I raised *my* daughter."

"I love it," said Mae.

"Me too," said Billy.

But Dad was on my side.

✎

A few days later, arriving home from school, I was hot and sweaty. March had definitely gone out like a lamb. I made my way to the kitchen, opened the refrigerator, and stood there deciding what to eat. But, mostly, it was to keep the cold air on me.

"Close that icebox door," said Grandma. "What do you think, we're the *Rockefellers*?" Was she in an even worse mood because of Dad going on dates?

With an eye roll, I snapped up a brownie and marched down to the basement to watch the latest vampire episode. That poor guy was forever battling his bloodthirsty nature, but in the end he always loses control and his fangs appear.

"Jody, you come back here this instant! I need you to walk to the A&P and get a can of beans."

"I'm watching my vampire show." If Mom hadn't died, Grandma Cupcakes would have been visiting, not standing here nagging me. We would have been laughing, her chasing me around the room, flicking me with a rubber band.

"That's just foolishness," Grandma said. My own fangs were starting to appear, but it was daytime, and I was powerless to defeat her. "I'm not *allowed* to use leftovers, so I need you to go." She stood, hands on her wide hips. So this was payback. A trip to A&P meant walking all the way back to school plus several blocks farther.

"Jesus," I mumbled anyway.

"What did you say?"

"I said, 'Thank you, Jesus.'"

"You did not. Apologize to Jesus this instant!"

I rolled my eyes and mumbled, "Jesus Christ...I'm sorry."

"You'll be sorry all right!"

"Oh, Grandma. Why don't you send Claire?"

"'Cause I'm sending you."

Claire would just refuse. I said, "I'm tired and hot. I just walked all the way home."

"Tired! You don't know what tired is," Grandma cried, yanking bills from her bra. "Here's some money!"

I took the cash with the tips of my fingers and said, "I'll go to Sam's Deli to get it."

"No, you won't, missy. The beans cost five cents more at Sam's. Do you think money grows on trees? You'll go to A&P. And don't give me any more guff."

Well, fine. But along the way I'd do what I wanted. I'd buy candy and go to the library. I'd been wanting to get a book on the telescope and see Miss Wendy. With Grandma moving in, I hadn't been going to the library as often. Hopefully Miss Wendy still worked there.

"Can I at least have money for candy?" I asked.

"No, you'll spoil your dinner."

No way was I listening to her. I thought of how when Dad arrived home from work he emptied his pockets, dropping the loose coins into a basket in the top drawer of his bedroom bureau.

My stomach bubbled and roiled as I snuck into his room, pulled open the drawer, and rummaged through. Alone in the silence, I found hankies and a mishmash of things Dad collected over the years—a subway token, some cuff links, a few old intention cards. One read: *Jody will get an A on her Viking project.* I smiled. I had gotten the A. There was a broken watch, a mini calendar with the name of an accountant at the top, a tiny magnifying glass in a red leather case, several loose keys, the white-and-black beaded bracelet I had made him in elementary school with the letters spelling out *I Love Dad,* some loose aspirin, pens, a money clip, and lots and lots of coins. I scooped some up and heard them jingle as they fell into the bottom of my pocket. There was a tiny package I didn't recognize at first.

I picked it up: *Durex Protectives.* Dad?

With the coins settled uneasily in my pocket, I clutched Mom's sunglasses, marched out to the strains of Grandma's parting shout of, "No dawdling!"

I couldn't help myself, I looked across the street. No Juliette. Now I wish I had said goodbye. After buying the beans, I stopped at the Sweete Shoppe and bought a Three Musketeers bar, a bag of M&M's, a Nestlé's Crunch, a handful of Atomic Fireballs, and a week's worth of gum: sixty pink blocks of Bazooka.

When older kids passed, I adjusted my bra, took off my glasses, lowered the sunglasses to the bridge of my nose to look more grown-up, and dawdled on to the library. I popped a Fireball in my mouth. My tongue tingled and burned. I challenged myself to see how long I could keep it in before the sizzling cinnamon pain was unbearable. Tears leaked from my eyes until I yanked the candy from my mouth and breathed hard. I moved on to the other candy, but none satisfied the burn in the pit of my stomach. Then I went on to eat the two candy bars. I felt full. I felt empty. I was a bottomless pit.

Once inside that familiar glass and red-brick building, taking in the shelves chock-full of books and the brown wooden card catalog, a wave of energy overtook me. Under subjects, I looked up telescope and saw the title *Galileo's Telescope.* This looked promising, so I went to the books numbered 522 in the Dewey decimal system and pulled it off the shelf. The back cover read: *Galileo's Telescope tells how this ingenious device transcended the limits of human vision and transformed humanity's view of its place in the cosmos.*

Miss Wendy was sitting behind the checkout desk. I smiled and handed her my book.

"Well, hello there, Jody. We've missed you," she said. I beamed at her. "This looks interesting. Is it Galileo that caught your eye or the telescope?"

"Both, I guess. I got a telescope for Christmas and wanted to learn about them."

"You'll have to teach me when you finish. I'm not very familiar with telescopes," said Miss Wendy. "I bet you're looking forward to when school lets out."

"Yeah, I can't wait," I said.

"Any big plans?" she asked. *Getting you to meet Dad*, I thought. "Edgehaven pool," I said. "I hang out there all summer."

"Oh, I joined too. Maybe I'll see you there."

"Yes. Definitely. The pool. I can tell you about the telescope." I laughed. Here was my chance. "Do you have a boyfriend?"

"A boyfriend!" She laughed. "No, not right now."

I'd jot this in my Venn diagram notebook. I said, "Oh, good. My dad hangs out with us at the pool. He needs some grown-up company. He runs his own business, you know. Tile. Does really well." I tried hard to think of other selling points—just like Dad did on a job estimate.

"It will be nice to meet him then," Wendy said.

I was trying not to smile too big. So far, so good.

She said, "Still working on your marriage project?"

"Wait, what?" Had she figured me out? "What project?"

"The marriage paper? You came in for some books."

"Oh, right, yes. Books." I relaxed. "It was fine. Two of them were so stupid. Like, how the wife should dress up before her husband comes home." We both laughed. "You know, the book you gave me, *Pride and Prejudice*. I liked it. And even though its way old, Jane Austen was the one who got it right, you should never marry without affection."

"Austen gets it right a lot. She's one of my favorites."

"Do you ever want to get married?" I asked.

"Sure, when the right guy comes along. For now, I'm footloose and fancy-free."

Halfway down the block for home, I turned back. I'd left the can of beans on Miss Wendy's desk.

That night, taking a bath, submerged in water, examining my newly sprouting pubic hair with my fingers—pleased, I counted them, five—a voice startled me making my hand fly up.

"What are you digging for? China?"

"Grandma!" I screamed. I hadn't even heard her turn the doorknob. I covered my naked body and shouted even louder, "Get out!"

She was like one of those giant Arguses we learned about in mythology, with hundreds of eyes always looking to catch me at something.

The next day Grandma asked me to go to the store again, and the day after that. After several days of this torture I complained to Dad.

"Ma, next time we should try to get everything we need on Saturday when I bring you food shopping. If you forget anything, I can get it on my way home. And if one of the kids has to go, Sam's Deli is fine. We have enough money to pay a bit more."

Grandma shook her head, mumbling, "So wasteful."

When Dad came in to kiss me goodnight, I put down my book on Galileo.

"Jody, here's some money to pay you for all those walks to the store. You can buy yourself some candy."

Did he know I'd stolen his change? I felt even more shame. A wanting to crawl under the bed and hide, another secret I had to bury.

"What are you reading?" asked Dad, sitting down on the side of my bed.

"About Galileo and the telescope. He was the first person to see that the moon wasn't smooth. Where's Claire?"

"Hopefully in the basement doing her homework. But more likely she's on the phone with James."

He put his finger to his lip, like he was sharing a secret. "Maybe you will be an astronomer or an astronaut. I'm sure you can do either if you set your mind to it."

"An astronomer, maybe. No way am I gonna be shot up into outer space in some nikkin' capsule."

"Always sensible, stringbean," said Dad.

"I got this at the library."

"You always find interesting things at the library."

"Like Miss Wendy."

"Miss Wendy?"

"The new librarian. She's super nice, smart, and has great red hair," I said. "You'd really like her."

"What did I tell you about matchmaking?"

"You told us you were lonely."

It seemed he found this funny—anyway, he laughed and hugged me and sat a little longer, flipping through the book to examine the drawings. And soon, just like when I was little, Dad leaned against my pillow and started reading: "It began four centuries ago…"

28

Out on the blacktop, Tracy and I leaned against the brick wall, waiting for the bell to ring. Me, with a brown bag filled with Bazooka gum and a couple candy bars. We were seeing who could blow the bigger bubble.

A ninth-grade girl sashayed over. "Hey, can I have one?" Kids never missed a chance to mooch gum. Word spread and soon boys I never spoke to before were talking to me. All but Charlie! Ever since ice skating he barely talked to me.

"Hey, can I have one?"

Oh my God, Jack Buckley, the new boy. He was super cool, wore cowboy boots, and never cared what anyone thought of him. With a swoop of his head, he tossed his dirty blond hair out of his eyes, letting me see the freckles—little sprinkles topping his nose. He even had a cool nickname: Buck.

Tracy elbowed me. Repeatedly. Why did she have to be so nikkin' obvious? I stood frozen, his eyes locked on mine, then quickly said, "Yeah, sure."

He leaned his shoulder up against the wall and crossed his legs.

I looked in the bag. "Damn, Jack. I gave the last piece away!" Then I remembered Claire telling me how kids in high school shared gum: ABC. Meaning, Already Been Chewed. I'd said that was disgusting. Not anymore.

"How about some ABC?" I asked, cocking my head the way Tracy did with boys.

He grinned, sending flutters through my stomach. Maybe Charlie wasn't so great.

I salvaged the wad, he opened his mouth, and I dropped it on his tongue! Several chews, then, slowly he blew and blew, my eyes widening as the pink bubble grew and grew and grew. *Pop!*

Tracy made a sound somewhere between a snort and a

raspberry. Somehow the sweet gooey stuff wasn't covering his face, just a smidge on his lip. What would it be like to kiss those lips? He was amazing.

Jack just gave me a slow, sly grin, turned and ambled off, cowboy jeans, cowboy strut.

❧

At home, I grabbed the permanent box of Cheez-Its and bolted for the basement. I switched on the TV, which took forever to warm up.

Billy, in his new Davy Crockett coonskin cap, was having a shoot-out with some bad guy. I picked him up to give him a hug.

"Put me down! I'm playing bad guys."

"Okay, okay." I gave him a kiss anyway and lowered him to the floor. No longer wanting to be my baby, he wiped off the kiss.

My favorite vampire show was on and some bozo was pulling the first chain off a coffin. He was looking for jewels, but I knew he'd find a vampire.

"Don't open it," I said as the thumping music played in the background, a sound that was in perfect sync with my beating heart.

"Open what?" asked Billy, looking at the screen.

"Nothing. It's just the show." Bozo unlocked the second chain.

"Jody, Jody! Bam, bam."

"You shot me," I said, not taking my eyes off the TV.

"Jody!"

"What?"

"You didn't fall down." The phone rang. Saved by the bell! I picked up. "Hello."

"Hey, it's Buck. Er, Jack. From school."

My heart thumped even harder. I took the phone, dragging the cord as far as it would reach into Grandma's bedroom.

Taking a deep breath, I tried to sound like boys called me all the time. "How'd you get my number?" I asked.

"Cinch. I called Information. What are you doing?"

"Watching a scary vampire show and my little brother Billy."

"I was just hanging with Scott," said Jack. Awkward silence. "What did Paul Revere say when he stopped his horse in Boston?" I asked him.

"I don't know. What?" asked Jack.

"*Whooaa!*"

Jack roared. Charlie would never laugh like that.

After ten minutes we hung up, my heart continuing to beat fast, giving a rhythm to the words, *Jack, Jack, Jack*.

The next day I rushed home from school, hoping to see the vampire bite bozo's neck, and sat not waiting or hoping for Jack's call. Finally, the phone rang. Forcing myself to wait, though not as long as I'd planned, I answered after three rings. It was him.

"Hey, Jody." How could just two words make me blush? "What ya up to?"

"Same vampire show. He just sucked the blood from yesterday's bozo. How about you?"

"I have to write that social studies paper for old Mrs. Oglesby. Witch." It was pretty obvious she didn't like him either, but I didn't say so. I also didn't tell him I had already written mine. "She's like one hundred years old."

"Yeah, her face powder is so thick and white she looks like a dead person." Jack laughed. I kinda liked her.

"Yeah, her ankles are as fat as an elephant," he said. "You going to the end of the year dance next week?" Jack said suddenly.

I screamed. Not really. But calmly as I could, I said, "Yeah, Tracy and I might go."

"Well, uh, Tracy? You want to go with me?"

"Um. What? Sure," I said. "I guess so." Silence. "I like your cowboy boots. They're really cool." It was then that I heard breathing in the background. A voice growled, "Why don't you go get yourself a paper route?"

I jumped right out of the chair. "Grandma, hang up the phone!" I yelled.

But she didn't: "What's a matter with you, young man, you got some kind of horror-mone problem?" Grandma said in her usual wry tone.

"*Grandma! HANG UP THE NIKKIN' PHONE!*"

"Don't be so salty, young lady."

"Um," Jack said.

Mortified, I mumbled an apology and slammed down the receiver, preventing Grandma Cupcakes from saying anything worse.

I stormed upstairs. "Grandma, don't you know it's not polite to listen in on people's phone calls?"

Grandma stood in the doorway waiting for me, arms across her chest.

"Well, you shouldn't be talking to boys. You are too young, missy. If you don't stop all this nonsense, all this doo-dah-doo-dah business, I'll send you off to the nunnery to live with Aunt Doris."

"Yeah, right!" That's not happening. "Maybe you should join her."

"What did you say, missy? Say that again," she taunted.

"Maybe you should go join her!" I wasn't sure if it shocked her or me more.

"Girls who talk to boys come to no good."

"Girls who don't talk to boys come to no good," I said, and stomped off to my bedroom.

She called after me, "Yes, missy, go to your room and say your prayers. And stay off the phone!"

I laughed snidely and called back down the hall, "You're not making *me* go to my room. That's where *I* was going! And I'm not staying off the phone, and I'm *not* going to say any stupid prayers. Except maybe *Make Grandma Cupcakes go away!*"

Yanking open my closet, I pulled out my plaid bell-bottoms, held them up to the mirror. *No, too busy,* as Mom would say. Tan ones, too boring like a packet of stale old Twinkies. Then, I noticed my purple pants. Perfect!

Laying them out on my bed, I imagined arriving at the dance, Jack leaning against the door waiting for me. Our eyes lock. He wraps his arms around me, dips me backwards, and kisses my glossed lips. In the gym, I wrap my arms around his shoulders as we sway back and forth. He's probably a much better kisser than Charlie. Though admittedly that wouldn't take much. I kissed the back of my hand to see what it might feel like. Nothing much.

In my mind I never get past first, maybe second base.

"Jody Moran!" Dad shouted down the hallway, home from work.

I slouched into the kitchen. Grandma was standing at the stove making some kind of slop.

"Jody, I hear you are talking to some boy on the phone," said Dad, more curious, than mad. I gave Grandma a dirty look.

He went on, all serious, "Maybe you're a bit too young to be dating. Sixteen is more like it."

"And maybe Grandma shouldn't be listening in on phone calls."

୨୦

That weekend Dad surprised us when he said he had invited a woman, Evelyn, to our house for dinner. A work friend had set them up on a blind date. Clearly Dad liked her. My ears perked up when he said she owned a beach house on the Jersey shore.

I did my best to clean up the house. Grandma Cupcakes wasn't going to. Not for some woman. She'd disappeared earlier, supposedly off visiting Aunt Sheila and my cousins. I guessed Grandma didn't want to see another woman at our house.

It was great to be rid of her.

I polished and dusted the furniture, in between ragging on my sisters to make their beds nice and neat and clean up their rooms. I scraped dried cereal off the kitchen table and made sure all the dishes were put away. Then I pulled out the vacuum hose and did what Mom use to call a "quick one-two" over the living room and fluffed up the pillows. We would be great kids to have around—no bother at all.

Close to five-thirty, wearing my daisy earrings, I stood watch at the living room window.

Claire moseyed in. "You're finally over your psycho cleaning." She flopped onto the couch, sending the pillows into disarray.

"Hey, you're messing up the couch."

"Why do you care?"

"She might be our next mother."

Claire stood up, straightened her shoulders and said, "I *have* a mother."

Through the fingerprint-smeared window, I noticed the crab apple tree was in bloom with glorious pink blossoms—one year without Mom. It was strange to think how something bursting with life now marked death.

I saw Dad's car pull up, saw him hurry around to open the passenger door, then saw Dad and Evelyn walking up the front steps. She was slim, wearing a pretty floral dress, pumps, and pearls. With streaked blond hair that fell to her shoulders and flipped at the ends, she was the perfect combination: a bit like Mom but with a bit of perky surfer girl. I wanted to run to my room and pull out my Venn diagram notebook, to record any overlapping circles.

"Kids, this is Evelyn," Dad said, smiling like a kid who brought home a perfect report card. "And, Evelyn, these are my girls. Claire, my oldest, then Jody, Mae, and Annie."

I curtseyed like a *Sound of Music* kid.

Dad laughed. "I've never seen you do that before."

"Sometimes I do," I said, a bit testily. And curtseyed again.

Dad said, "Where's the little guy?"

"Here I am," yelled Billy from the kitchen.

"I'm going across the street," said Claire. James. But she was stopped by Billy tearing into the room, his hands and face dirty, a half-finished Fudgesicle stick in his hand. Who the heck had given him that? Then I realized why he was grinning so proudly—he'd recently learned how to pull a chair up to the freezer and help himself.

"You look like the cat dragged you in," I said. I was starting to sound like Grandma Cupcakes.

As Billy inched toward Evelyn, I noticed a flicker of disgust spread across her face.

"And this here, under that chocolate, is Billy," said Dad. As Evelyn backed away, my anger fired up. Was it the fudge she was recoiling from or the thick, ropey scar that ran from his lip down the side of his face? There was nothing wrong with his sticky face!

Despite the mess, I swept the sweet boy off the floor, lugged him into the kitchen, pulled off his baseball cap, and held his hands under the faucet. On second thought, maybe Evelyn had only been taken by surprise.

Claire sidled up behind me and in a whisper said, "Think they do it?"

"Do what?" I asked, but I knew.

"You know."

"You're *sick*," I said. "They're barely even dating, yet." I didn't want to think of Dad having sex. "They're not even married."

"You don't have to be *married*."

"I know that!"

"You are *so* naïve." Walking off, she spun around and said, "And, anyway, they are *not* getting married."

Off she stormed, out the screen door.

Naïve: a lack of experience, wisdom, or judgment.

That night, drifting off to sleep, I heard a tap, then another. Something was hitting my bedroom window. *Tap. Tap.* I sat up to look outside. Claire was putting on her coat.

"What are you doing?"

"Shh! James is picking me up."

"You're sneaking out?"

She was dressed in jeans and a tank top. "Are you catching flies?"

I closed my mouth. Opened it again. "That's crazy," I said. "What if Dad comes in looking for you?"

"He won't. C'mon. He already said goodnight." She leaned in, looking me in the eye. "And don't *you* tell him." She knew I wouldn't. Then she plopped down next to me. "You know how James and I went to second base? Well, now he wants to go all the way."

"What does that even mean?"

"You know," said Claire, rolling her eyes.

"The dad puts his thing, his peepee, into the mom and they make a baby." We both laughed. "Do you think you're really going to?"

"Jody! That's none of your bee's wax. You shouldn't even ask me that." She popped back up, went all thoughtful. "Don't worry, I'm not going that far. *Yet*," she said, eyebrows raised as she tossed her sweater over her shoulder and tiptoed out of the room.

29

In social studies, Jack passed me a note, I unfolded it: *Walk you home today?*

When Mrs. Oglesby turned to write *Four causes of the Civil War* on the board, I wrote on back. *Yes!* Would I be Jack's girlfriend? Dad didn't have to know everything. Grandma would have a conniption. But Claire would love it.

Our notes continued back-and-forth till Mrs. Oglesby threw down her chalk, waddled over to my desk, her thick stockings bagging. "*Miss* Moran, just *what* do you have in your hand?" she said, and plucked away Jack's latest note before I could read it.

She unfolded it, studied it, wagged her finger in my face, and said, "Jody Moran, I don't know what all this nonsense is with you and Mr. Buckley, but I am *not* pleased. You are not that kind of girl!"

Kids near me were shifting in their seats.

Under his breath, Rob said, "Busted!" Was Charlie watching? My mouth went dry. I placed my pencil between my lips, pressing down, trying not to cry. My cheeks burned. I worried my face went all red, like I knew it could do. I hated the way my emotions were like a billboard across my face.

What kind of girl? I didn't want her to think I was a bad girl. She sounded like Grandma Cupcakes.

From behind me, I heard Jack's voice, tough and angry, "Hey, leave her alone." I felt a wave of excitement—he was standing up for me—then I wished that he'd be quiet. I'd never heard anyone talk to a teacher that way. Charlie? No way! Charlie would never talk back like that. Charlie barely talked at all. I studied my binder, his initials engraved in blue ink.

As Mrs. Oglesby droned on, I scratched out Charlie's initials.

❧

At the end of the day Jack was waiting for me, even though his house was in the opposite direction from chez Moran.

As we walked I wasn't hearing a word he was saying and barely said two of my own. With Mrs. Oglesby's harsh words ringing in my ears, Grandma Cupcake's do-dah-do rant, and Dad saying I wasn't old enough to date, I was on edge. With each step, my panic increased. What if Jack tried to hold my hand or kiss me?

Nearly home, as jumpy as a racehorse at the starting gate, I stopped abruptly and said, "You can't walk me all the way home. My dad will get really mad if he sees me with a boy."

Jack looked surprised. "Really? Okay, I'll see you at the dance."

"Jack." I flushed. "Wait. Never mind." I galloped off.

Once home, I checked to see if Grandma was anywhere near the extension and hurried downstairs to call Tracy. "I'm not so sure I want to go to the dance. Claire says they're boring."

"What? We've been planning this! You and Jack. You have to." Her voice rising. "I told Matt I would see him there and that Jack would be with us." I couldn't keep up with who Tracy liked—it changed by the day, by the hour.

"Well, I'm not a dating service. And I'm scared Dad will see Jack. Because of stupid Grandma, he says I'm too young to date. And I'm not sure I even like Jack."

"Oh, you like him all right."

"I just wish I was going with Charlie."

"Yeah, I get it," she said. "My mom will drive. We'll get you at seven-thirty. It won't be scary. It's just a stupid dance. We can't help if there are *boys* there!" I heard some clicking sounds. Grandma's listening! "And you don't have to tell your dad *everything*."

"Jeepers"—that was the code word I told Tracy meant Grandma was snooping. "I do tell him everything, Tracy."

"Yeah, we can just dance with each other and not those goofy boys," said Tracy.

I barely ate any dinner. Dad asked questions about the dance—who was going, what kind of music would they play—seemingly all okay with it.

"I'm glad you know that boys can be, what's the word, goofy," said Grandma.

"Were you listening on my call!" I opened my mouth in feigned shock.

"No. I have better things to do than listen to you and Stacy."

"I didn't say who I was talking to! And it's Tracy."

"Whatever."

As fast as I could, I slipped away from the table and sprinted off to my room. I pulled off my shirt and corduroys, replacing them with my purple pants, bra from Claire, white bubble top, and platform shoes. I pushed and pulled at my frizzy hair, trying to get it smooth. Impossible. Maybe my dangling daisy earrings would help.

I stared in the full-length mirror that hung on the back of the closet door. Not too bad. I only wished I had bigger breasts to fill out the bra. I practiced smiling and laughing. Jack saying, "I love your shirt." "Oh, this, thanks." Acting like it was just an old shirt.

Claire barged in.

"When did you grow up?" she said, as she curled up on her bed. "Those middle-school dances are so lame." Now that she was in high school, she thought everything about middle school was lame.

"Last year you liked them," I said.

"You actually look pretty decent. Wait." Then she jumped up and gripped my arm. "Come with me."

"Where?"

"You need some makeup." She steered me into Dad's bedroom. "Take your glasses off and sit here," she said, pointing to Mom's vanity bench. I did as told, hoping Dad was lingering over his coffee.

Mom had said we needed to wait till we were sixteen to wear makeup—two years away. What was the big deal about everything happening when you were sixteen?

In one swift motion, Claire pulled off her headband, yanked it over my head, and swept my hair back.

"Ow," I cried.

"Beauty hurts," she said, but with an impish smile. "First, we need to clean off your face. Do you even wash your face?" I stuck my tongue out at her.

Handing me Mom's Pond's cream, she said, "Okay, rub some of this on and then wipe it off with a Kleenex."

Claire pulled up the chair I used to sit on, back when I watched Mom get ready, turning me so she could reach my face but I could still watch her work in the mirror.

"What color eye shadow do you want?" She showed me the palette of colors.

I had asked Mom the same question, not so long before. "The blue, dear stringie," she'd said, sweeping the brush along the crease above her eye, concentrating. "It brings out the blue in my eyes, don't you think?" I so wished I had blue eyes like Mom, Claire, Mae, and Annie.

"I like the blue," I said, pointing to the shade in the collection, the color of my blue button.

"Green goes better with your eyes." And no more talk. Claire, gently holding my chin, swept the creamy green shadow along the crease of my eye with the tiny black brush. In the mirror, my eyes followed each and every one of her movements.

Then, with a clean angled brush, she blended a darker shade into the edges of my eyelid. She picked up a Q-tip from the countertop and wiped off some of the green shadow. Next, she dipped the pointed brush into the black liquid, carefully drawing the eyeliner along the line above my top lashes.

She sighed. "Do you think I should still go out with James?" My eyes shot open wide.

"Keep your eyes closed," she said. "You'll make a mess of it." With the same Q-tip, she removed a smudge from my right eyelid. The green and black merged together.

"Why would you break up? You love James."

"I don't know. I don't get to spend time with Michelle and other friends."

Wait. Claire was asking *me* for advice. I wanted to get this right.

"Is it because of the other night? Him wanting to, you know. It's okay not to. You don't have to dump him."

Claire pulled back. Silent, she carefully redrew the line. Quietly she said, "You know, maybe it is. How'd you get so freakin' smart about boys?"

"I mean, it's really okay."

"Yeah, James said that too. But maybe it did start me thinking we should break up."

"I kind of felt the same about Jack."

"What!"

"No, no," I laughed. "Not going all the way! Just this date. This dance. Once I knew he liked me, part of me didn't want to go with him anymore. But James is super nice. You'll want to be with him at the pool, he'll be lifeguarding."

"Yeah. You're probably right. I'd miss him." Claire picked up the tube of mascara. "Close your eyes again."

"And he lives on our street. Awkward!"

Claire laughed. "Okay, look up."

As Claire stepped back to eye her work I noticed the black licorice was gone from the tabletop. Billy or Annie had probably eaten them. Everything about Mom was disappearing.

"Remember when Mom got ready to go out. She'd sit here with her licorice on one side," I said, pointing to the left side of the vanity. "And her cigarette on the other, in that heavy amber ashtray."

Seeing Claire in the reflection felt like it gave me some protection. She was concentrating on my eyes—a bit more mascara—I wasn't sure she was listening. Then after a moment Claire asked, "What happened to that ashtray?"

"Annie uses it for her barrettes," I said.

Claire smiled, shrugged. I could so picture Mom reaching for the cigarette, her lips pulling in around the brown end of the cigarette filter. She'd blow the smoke out as the ashes dangled in mid-air. I'd waited for them to drop like glitter.

Claire said, "Sometimes I think about how Dad always

bugged Mom to stop smoking. And then she goes and gets killed by a van. It's so unfair. It makes me so angry."

"Ticked off," I said.

"Ballistic," she said.

"Good one," I said. "How about this: Afroth." *Afroth: filled with emotion.*

"Sounds like a dog with rabies."

"Pissed!"

"You know, when you came downstairs and found me with Mom, and thought we were *cuddling*," she laughed. "She was *talking*"—Claire made air quotes around the word *talking*—"to me about drinking. She caught Michelle and me with a can of Dad's stupid beer."

"You were drinking?"

"A whole half a beer each. Not like we were drunk. But Mom was *not* happy," Claire said. "Enough. Hand me the blush. Now smile." And with a sweep of the large brush, she brought some rose color to my cheeks, then rummaged through the little gold bag filled with Mom's lipsticks. Clearly, she had done this before. I told her I wanted a frosty white. Mom had once let me try on a little of her Cover Girl frosty pink lipstick.

Claire swiveled the tube. "Okay, pucker your lips like this." She looked like one of Annie's goldfish being fed. She ran the lipstick along my thin lips. Grabbing a Kleenex, she told me to blot them, "like this," as she smacked her lips together.

"Now brush your hair or you'll look like a freak." My hair, neither straight nor curly, was an in-between kinky that I hated, but at least it had grown back.

I pictured Mom teasing her hair, creating a high bouffant, then setting it in place with the white and red bottle of Aqua Net. I'd cover my nose, waving away the fumes that mingled with her cigarette smoke.

"Now for the finishing touch," Claire said, giving a twirl of her finger, just the way Mom did before she put on perfume.

Reaching for the cello-shaped bottle of Tabu, she gave a spritz behind my left ear, and then behind the right. I breathed in the familiar scent. Maple syrup on pancakes.

I held on to the edge of the vanity and leaned forward, getting a better look at myself in the mirror. It was like magic. I was a different girl. I smiled at Claire in the mirror. She smiled back. "Looking good."

A horn honked out front. "Tracy!" I said.

"Quick," Claire said. "Before Grandma sees you and says, 'Take all that schmutz off your face.'"

I laughed, grabbed my sweater and raced down the hall, shouting so that one and all could hear: "I'm going!" and ran out to Amelie's Citroën convertible, hopped over the door and into the back seat next to Tracy. She was in a new flowered top and cream pants.

"Whoa, mama," whispered Tracy, leaning across the back seat of the car. "Très chic! How did you learn to do that?"

"Claire did it," I said. "I can't believe I got out of the house without Grandma seeing me."

Arm in arm, we strutted into the building, the music blaring from the other end of the building. Isabel Farrow was parked at a cafeteria table, checking off names, just the right shag haircut.

"Are you ready?" yelled Tracy. "Let's find the girls."

"Wait, let's fill out the raffle tickets."

"There you are!" said Bettina. "You missed almost half the dance." How did she always look so perfect? On her arm was Todd's silver ID bracelet. A ninth grader!

I jotted my name on the ticket. Tracy did the same.

"Come on. Follow me." When Bettina summoned, you went. Why did Jack like me and not her?

Tracy and I shadowed her into the girl's room. There were five of us gathered around the sinks. Bettina in the center, sweet, gap-toothed Kate, and know-it-all Meg, half-leaning, half-sitting on the sink. I was glad to see there were none of those ninth graders that always smoked in the stalls.

"We've been waiting for you," said Meg, tapping the sink. She looked like a little girl in a silly party dress.

"Don't tell that I told," Bettina said, "but Jack got you a ring. A gold ring!"

"Ooh là là," said Tracy.

"He's going to give it to you tonight," said Bettina. "You're going to be his girlfriend!" Squeals of excitement erupted from our corner of the bathroom. My head was spinning taking in all this attention.

"You're so gorgeous," Kate said suddenly.

I shrugged. "Claire made me up."

"No," Bettina said. "It's you.

"It's true," Tracy said. It felt exciting and strange to be the center of all this attention.

Bettina pulled a comb out of her purse and ran it through her already perfectly combed hair, so long that it almost reached her behind. I watched the silver ID bracelet slide down her wrist. How did she feel so at ease with Todd? When finished she swapped it for a lipstick and lined her lips with a rusty red color. Effortless.

"Okay, let's go, ladies," said Bettina. "Jody, walk next to me."

We were barely out the door when Debbie Doidge brushed past, bumping into me. "Hey Moran," she said, stopping mid-step. "You clean up pretty good for a dork." She smiled.

"You too Doidge," I said, nudging her back. She laughed. We laughed!

Jack's best friend, Scott, stomped over. He was short and wiry, like a terrier always at Jack's heels.

"Buck wants you to be his girlfriend. Will you?" For a moment, I didn't know who he was talking about, but then I remembered the boys called Jack Buck. Every face was waiting to hear my response.

Before I could answer, Jack prowled over, his own gang of boys trailing closely behind. He swooped his hair back several times. He was nervous! I backed up a couple steps. Without a word he handed me a really nice small box. Cool. I flipped the black lid. Inside was a gold insignia ring with the letter *J* engraved on it. Was this for Jody or Jack?

His hair hung over his eyes, making him tilt his head to the side, to look through his long blond hair. He was waiting for me to say something. All eyes were on me. I wanted to ask him which one of us the letter *J* stood for, but I felt like a dork not knowing. So I nodded and glided the ring on my finger. It spun, too large for my finger.

Jack slipped his hand in mine and said, "Let's dance," as he led me to the auditorium. I was relieved when "Limbo Rock" started playing, not a slow song. I tried dancing like I'd seen the girls on *American Bandstand*.

One end of the room to the other was decorated with colorful balloons, crepe paper, and banners. Across the ceiling hung Christmas-style lights of reds, oranges, yellows, and greens. A cool huge silver moon hung from the center of the room. The Student Council was trying its darndest to add some color to the cold gray drab room. In one corner sat a lonely cafeteria table, wrapped in a bright striped paper table cloth and crammed with bowls of chips, pretzels, and an assortment of punches and drinks. Leaning on walls, around the room, were several teachers and parents keeping watch and telling kids they needed more space between them when dancing.

As a new song started, I continued shifting from foot to foot, my brain stuck, unable to think of anything to say. "This is a good song." How lame! I was nothing like the girl on the phone with him.

"Yeah, I like the Rolling Stones," said Jack. I stepped on his foot, again.

Across the auditorium I saw Charlie, head down, shuffling his feet, with his friends. He looked over, then pretended not to see me. Did he still like me? Maybe his heart was breaking.

Next we rocked to the Jackson 5.

"Scott kind of likes Tracy," said Jack. His eyes were twinkly. "Does she like him?"

Tracy had never mentioned Scott, but she loved whatever was new.

"She might," I said. "Give her a day." I didn't say, *Then give her another day and then another, and she would be three boys on.*

A few more fast songs played, then a couple of my favorite Beatles songs. Tracy swirled by with Scott, giving me a high five. She chatted away, making it look so easy.

At the end of the song, the DJ said, "Listen up. We have a

few words from your student council president, Isabel Farrow." The crowd went crazy, especially the boys.

"Thirsty," I said, and broke from Jack, dashing off for the refreshment table before he could protest.

I passed Isabel, who was bouncing her way up to the stage. I looked around the room and found Tracy and some of the other girls standing at the punch bowl, talking. Kate was wrapping crepe paper around Meg's head.

"I'm sweating," I said to Tracy. "Give me a sip." She handed me her cup.

"Let me see your ring again," she said hotly. I held up my hand. "You are so lucky."

"Am I?" I watched as two of the student council boys dragged a ladder into the center of the room and cut down the moon hanging from the ceiling.

"If you don't want it, I'll take it. *J* for Jack." She laughed.

"Jack said Scott likes you."

"Well," she said saucily, scanning the enormous gyrating room. "This could be trés interessant! Where is that hunk of burning love?"

"I thought you liked Matt."

"I do, but Scott's cuter."

The microphone crackled. Isabel first thanked her committee for all their hard work this year. "Now listen up," said Isabel. "It's time to pick the winning raffle ticket. The winner will receive this fab silver moon." She held it up high.

Oh, please, let me win. It would look so great over my bed.

"Here we go." She reached her hand into the large bowl, retrieving a ticket stub. "And the winner is: Tracy Bernard!" Figures. Tracy whooped and hollered. Our group of girls hugged her, cheering. I tried to look happy for her.

The DJ reached for the microphone, announcing, "Now for our last song of the night. A long slow one!" Someone lowered the overhead lights; the string of colorful bulbs now provided the only illumination. A familiar opening slide guitar blasted out of the gigantic speakers. Immediately, I recognized Lynyrd Skynyrd's "Free Bird," a song all the kids were obsessed with.

Eighth and ninth graders crammed together on the dance floor. I tried to catch Charlie's eye, hoping he would come and ask me to dance. Instead Jack popped up out of nowhere, took hold of my hand, and led me back on to the nikkin' dance floor.

The bass beat vibrated against my ear drums. He pulled me close, wrapping his arms around my waist, his hands against the small of my back. My face smushed against his neck, sticky with sweat. Not quite gross, but too real somehow.

We swayed back and forth, from one foot to the other. My insides vibrating with the music that echoed around the room. Jack drew back, his eyes on my lips. Something was going to happen, I could feel it. A warm feeling flashed through me— excitement or fear, I wasn't sure. I closed my eyes. His lips pressed against mine. Was that his teeth I felt, pressed against my lips? They felt warm, tasted salty. My heart beat so fast I thought it would pop out of my chest. I felt the ring on my finger. In *Valley of the Dolls*, after the man buys Neely jewelry he says, "You owe me." What if Jack wanted more than a kiss? Like James. Like all of them. Except Charlie.

How long could one song last? He kissed me again. This time his tongue, like some kind of worm, parted my lips and slipped in. My bra, annoyingly rose up as our bodies crushed together.

I stepped back, adding some space between us. Then the music picked up, and we unlinked, a bunch of familiar faces all around us. Reality. Finally the song ended, and the lights went up. I curtsied stupidly and said, "I need to find Tracy."

What a nikkin' dork I was!

It didn't take long. Tracy was talking to Charlie. My Charlie. Whispering in his ear! As I got closer, I heard her give one of her awful fake laughs. Why did boys fall for that?

I grabbed her arm a bit roughly and said, "Come on. It's time to go."

She pulled away. "I'm still talking," she said.

I gave her the Grandma Cupcakes squint and said, "I'll meet you outside."

Out front, I shuffled on the cement as parents pulled up,

collecting their kids. The late April air was unusually chilly, giving me goosebumps. Jack came outside and stood next to me, his hands jammed deep into his pockets, his gaze expectant. The light from the half-moon added a silvery shimmer to the sky. I couldn't think of anything to say. Apparently, he couldn't either. Why wouldn't he just go inside and leave me alone?

Tracy burst out, carrying the moon, just as Amelie pulled up, several boys following in her wake. "Hurry," she cried as she vaulted into her mother's front seat. I hopped in the back.

"Jack, I'm sorry," I said out the window.

As we roared off I heard him shout, "Wow, your mom drives a convertible!"

"My mom is dead," I muttered. How could Jack not know? My mom was dead and never would pick me up again from anything.

Tracy, up front, chattered to vivacious Amelie—the boys, the boys, the boys.

Vivacious: lively and attractive.

Late the next morning, Jack called. This time, when I heard his voice, rather than my stomach doing a flip-flop, I felt only dread. I wanted out. I liked Charlie. Not Jack. The dance had taught me that.

Before he could start talking, I gave my well-practiced line: "My dad said I can't go out with anyone."

When I hung up I pulled the *J* ring off my finger, tucked it away in one of my white boxes, like the button, the thimble, and Mom's Campfire girl pin. He'd kept the black box—let that be his souvenir.

Tracy called not five minutes later, sounding all sweet: "Want to hang out?"

"I don't think I can," I said coldly.

"Are you mad at me?"

"I'm disappointed," I said as calmly as Dad. But then I was Mom: "And you know why!"

"Fart-head, I wasn't flirting with Charlie if that's what you mean. He was asking me if you liked Jack. Who you're going out with!" Tracy let out an exasperated breath. "And why do you even care if I flirt?"

"So you *were* flirting!"

"Jody! I wasn't stealing Charlie."

"And I'm not going out with Jack!"

"Are you giving him his ring back?"

"No, he gave it to me. *J* is for Jody. I'm keeping it."

A little while later Tracy was at my door, the large glittery silver moon in her hands. "I think this was meant for you," she said.

30

As navigator, I sat in the front seat next to Dad. If Claire
had come, she and I would have had to take turns. Annie and
Billy clambered into the backseat, and Mae got the way-back
to herself and her book, *Little Women*. With exams coming, I
brought along my school books.

"Ready for blast off," Dad said, all official. "Mission control,
Commander Jody, I need instructions."

"Booster four, Captain," I ordered. Dad turned the wipers
on.

"Commander Mae," he called.

"Booster two, Captain." He flicked the car lights on and off.
We erupted in giggles.

"My turn, my turn!" yelled Annie.

"Commander Annie!"

"I don't know the numbers," said Annie.

"Just pick any number," I said. "It's a surprise."

"Number five," she yelled. "I'm five."

Dad revved the engine, honked the horn.

Annie's cackling laugh made the rest of us laugh even harder.

"Now my turn," said Billy.

"Commander Billy," called Dad. "What is your coordinate?"

"One hundred!"

"You know what that means," Dad said. "Blast off!" He
turned on the radio, flashed the lights, flicked the car lights on
and off, honked the horn, jammed the car in gear, and squealed
out of the driveway.

We roared through nearby towns, then we "dropped the
booster rockets" as Dad said, and headed south, through the
familiar outer-space smell of Newark, the smokestacks exhaling
black smoke.

I was imagining Dad and Evelyn's wedding, my sisters and I

wearing fancy bridesmaids' gowns. Evelyn would look great in one of the Moran Bunch family squares.

"Dad," Annie yelled. "I have to go to the bathroom."

"Real bad, Annie? Or can it wait?"

"It can wait," Annie said doubtfully.

"But if it's an emergency," I said, "let us know in enough time to pull over."

Dad said, "I spy with my little eye something that begins with the letter *D*."

"Is it in the car?" I asked, helping Dad out.

"Yep," said Dad.

"DOG!" yelled Annie.

"There's no dog in here!" Mae shouted from the back.

"Cat," yelled Billy. Dad and I laughed hard.

"No," said Mae. "Cats are so annoying."

Dad gripped the steering wheel heroically, a faint white stripe where his wedding ring should have been. When had he taken it off? Would that mean that Dad and Mom weren't married anymore? I wanted him to get married, yet still be married to Mom.

"Is it alive?" Mae asked.

"I sure hope so," said Dad.

I laughed. "It's Dad," I said.

"I was going to guess that," Mae said, pouting.

Fried seafood and salt air drifted into the car as we neared the beach. The roadsides were packed with restaurants, like Danny's Crab Shack, Captain's Famous Seafood Grill, and Sal's BBQ Pit. Billboards with pictures of a roller coaster advertised the boardwalk.

"Can we go to the boardwalk?" I said, pointing to the sign. "Please."

"Maybe next time."

I didn't mind, happy that he was saying there would be a next time.

We passed a church and then an old graveyard. I held my

breath the entire way, to be sure a spirit wouldn't steal my breath. I knew this was silly, but I did it anyway, just to be on the safe side.

Finally, Dad pulled into a driveway of broken shells.

"Gotta pee," Annie said.

Evelyn's house was the same as all the other pastel-colored beach houses on the road. Hers was baby blue with white shutters. A large white anchor hung by the front door. Small white pebbles covered the front and back yard, everything so clean and orderly.

"Hey, look, it's snowing," I said. Dad cracked up.

"Pee," Annie said.

Evelyn, in a pretty bright floral sundress, opened the screen door and welcomed us in. Her arms were lean and tan. Annie pushed past us. "Bathroom. Quick!"

Evelyn pointed down the hall, as Annie's flip-flops slapped the tile floors. The rest of us paraded into the tiny living room, dragging along our bathing suits and towels. Dad had a bag of sand toys hanging over his shoulder. A white ceiling fan swooshed overhead. Everything in the room was white—the wicker furniture, the rug, the curtains, even the coffee table. Dad gave Evelyn what seemed like an especially long kiss.

Evelyn escorted Dad into the kitchen as the four of us bounced like beach balls in Evelyn's tiny living room. Billy was grabbing an expensive-looking duck decoy off the side table as Annie brushed her fingers along the whispering strands of green and blue beads that hung in the doorway to a miniature dining room. Mae pulled down a book on orchestras from the shelf, looking for something to read. I gathered up couch pillows and made myself a nest, imagining Charlie was cozying up next to me. I couldn't get myself to open my science book.

When Evelyn returned with some sodas she looked horrified. "All children outside to play," she announced, not very kindly.

What the nikk? I wasn't some snot-nosed brat you sent outside to play! Evelyn, no matter how slim her hips, would not be bossing me around. Nothing about her or this place was in

the overlapping Venn Diagram circle. Well, maybe her smile—
she did have a lot of fantastic teeth.

Dad turned to Evelyn. "How about they stay in till lunch?
It's pretty sunny out there."

Evelyn said, "It's a beautiful day, and I'd prefer them outside
while I get lunch ready."

"I can help," I volunteered politely.

"Thank you, but your father can give me a hand. We'll call
you in when it's ready. Ten minutes." Her bright and enormous
smile didn't quite reach her wicked eyes, and as soon as she
ushered us outside with our buckets and shovels—*click*—
the screen door locked behind us. How dare she! Were they
planning to have sex in the kitchen?

Dad should have come to our rescue, should have said, "My
kids can't be shoved outside in this heat." But, no, he took Evil-
lyn's side and left us blocks from the beach with nothing to do.

The younger kids shoveled pebbles into their buckets, and
Mae sat on the ground with her book, while I remained posted
at the door.

Billy jabbered on about *The Lone Ranger*, his latest obsession.

"Jody, then Tonto said, 'Look, kemosaba. They took the
winter trail up to Fort Belknap.'"

"Yeah, Billy. That's a great one."

"Then the Lone Ranger sees a girl. She'd fall down on the
ground. He says to Tonto, 'We are going to find them.'" He
lifted his helmet off his head, and waved it around, and yelled,
"Hi-ho, Silver! Away!"

"*Uh-huh,*" I said. I tossed pebbles, aiming for the house,
trying to make as much noise as possible. No one came out to
stop me.

"Then, the Lone Ranger jumped on Silver and went and
shooted all the bad guys."

Annie asked, "Jody, why do people do that show?"

"What do you mean? The actors? They're paid money."

"But then they get shot. When you're dead, you can't spend
it."

I hid my laugh, explaining how they didn't really die. In the backyard under the blazing sun, we were hot and starving. Fist at the door, I was ready to save us when the door clicked and opened.

Dad looked relieved to let us in, and also looked, I don't know—*kissed*. Evelyn was standing behind him in her bathing suit, scowling but holding a fancy wicker picnic basket. Slowly her smile was glued back on to her face.

After a lunch on the boardwalk of cold cuts, chips, and pickles, I got naked myself in the ancient wooden bathhouse, shimmied into last year's blue-and-white polka dot swimsuit. Too tight, top and bottom both. Ek: stray hairs sprouted at my crotch, and no good way to tuck them back in.

I came out of the bathhouse, blinking in the sunlight, and took in all there was to see: a few families spread out under umbrellas, some building sand castles. Seagulls floated and clattered above, crying like babies.

Dropping our towels and toys on the sand, I trekked to the water's edge, tugging on my bathing suit, which rode up my butt. Things had definitely changed! Billy and Annie followed along as I scoured the beach for shells. I looked back at Dad and Evelyn sitting on a blanket, her hand on Dad's leg. Mae was on her towel, absorbed in *Little Women*. I wasn't sure I liked her reading so much. I was the reader in the family.

My feet touched the seething water. It was freezing! A couple of crazy-cute boys were on rafts, their shoulders oiled and bronzed. I had my eye on Annie and Billy. Dad often joked that I was like one of those herding dogs, always circling around the sheep, trying to keep them from wandering off.

Dad and Evelyn strolled down to the water's edge, hand in hand. She wore a green two-piece halter-top swimsuit not a stray hair out of place, but she didn't even wade in the surf. Why bother with a bathing suit? Mom would have been holding our hands and jumping the waves, no matter how cold.

I showed Billy how to fill the pail with wet sand and then turn it over to form a castle. "Let me do it," he said. I placed some small shells along the top. Then Billy saw a gull and started chasing it and I chased him. When I looked back, Annie, along with Evelyn, was wading into the water, rough foamy waves hitting at her legs. "You need to hold her hand, Evelyn!" I called over the sound of the surf.

"I got it," she said, waving her hand at me dismissively.

"Here, Billy. Look at this shell," I said. "Let's bring it back to our castle."

When I looked up, Evelyn and Dad were pulling Annie up from under the water. I scooped up Billy and ran over to Annie.

"I was swimming!" said Annie, shivering.

"See, if you'd been holding her hand, she wouldn't have been knocked over," I said. Billy climbed down from my arms, and Dad took his hand. "Like I told you."

"You don't tell me what I do and don't do, young lady," said Evelyn, her voice rising in anger.

Mae appeared at my side. "Don't yell at Jody!"

"Enough, Jody, Mae," said Dad, sternly. "Annie's fine."

I ran back up to our blanket, snatched up a towel, and swaddled Annie in it.

"Okay, let's go on back," said Dad, trying to sound lighter, cheerful. "How about we go for some ice cream before the long drive home?"

Slowly we packed up our belongings and trudged back to Evelyn's.

Back at the house, Dad said, "Okay, gang. Rinse off outside, get the sand off, and change into your clothes." He was hanging on to Billy. "Then you scream, I scream, we all scream for—" Mae, Annie, and Billy yelled, "Ice cream!" I didn't chime in.

Sunburned and still a bit sandy, I climbed from the middle seat into the front, my long and bony legs knocking into Evelyn's head. "Sorry," I said, giving her back a fake smile.

Squeezing myself between Dad and Evelyn, Dad's legs were pale and hairy, and Evelyn's were smooth and tan. I turned to my left, bestowing a smile on Dad, then a smirk-smile on Evelyn.

We drove a few miles to an ice cream shop, my thighs sticking to the hot vinyl seat. There we fell over each other, trying to be first in line to the walk-up window.

Cones in hand we found an open bench to sit on. Dad ambled over, licking his usual rum raisin.

"Where's your ice cream?" I asked Evelyn as she opened her compact and reapplied her lipstick.

"I don't like ice cream much," she said.

Figured. Mom would have ordered a strawberry cone.

"Let's finish our cones in the car. We have a long drive home," Dad said. "We'll drop Evelyn off and head right out."

Once again, I climbed in next to Dad.

Never liking the cone part, I used my long thumbnail as a tiny spoon. Slowly I licked the ice cream off my fingernail, making sure Evelyn was watching. When she looked disgusted, I gave a victorious smile. "Yum."

The following Friday, Dad went to have dinner with Evelyn, leaving Grandma in charge. After he left, Grandma listened in on Claire and James's phone call, heard something about sex, and popped her cork. When Dad came home early, Grandma met him at the door with news of Claire's "loose ways." Dad called Claire downstairs for a lecture, and Grandma said, "Joseph, maybe if you weren't out galivanting around, you'd be setting a better example."

"Enough, Ma. I already had a rough night."

The next day, Claire grounded forever, Dad invited me out on a sales call. As he drove, one hand on the back of my seat, he tried his best to chat, asking how finals were going.

He seemed glum, but I was glummer. Though finals had been fine, Charlie hadn't talked to me since the dance. And I worried that my not liking Evelyn had spoiled things for Dad, had driven her away.

"I have to make a couple of scheduling calls." Dad pulled into the Mobil station, next to a phone booth he could reach from the driver's seat, and made a second appointment for today. Then he dialed another number. "Mrs. O'Donell? Hi, it's Joe Moran. You asked me to call?" I heard him discussing a kitchen and bath redo for a couple minutes, then he said,

"Terrific. I'll see you at four o'clock on Monday then. Yes, I'll leave Annie at home. I don't think we could make heads nor tails of the job with her bouncing off the walls."

It wasn't until then that I realized he was talking to Mrs. O'Donnell. Dad chuckled and said, "I guess you've picked up on the fact that Annie is a bit stuck on you. See you Monday." He pulled the van up to the pump.

"That was Mrs. O'Donnell, wasn't it? You'll get to see her house. Wish I could."

"I'm a bit curious myself," said Dad. "Don't mention it to Annie."

"Dad," I said.

"Yes, stringie."

"I'm sorry I wasn't so nice with Evelyn," I said. "I mean, she has a great smile and a super beach house."

"Well, stringie, that's all true, but, well, we aren't dating anymore."

"I thought you liked her."

"I did. Now don't try to hide your disappointment."

"Dad, what? Was it our fault? My fault."

"Oh, for heaven's sake, kid. You saw it plain as I did. She wasn't right for us."

Us.

31

As I floated on my back in the deep end of the pool, the sun warm on my face, I stared up at the tree branches fluttering in the breeze, imagining their movements were perfectly timed with the sway of my hair under the water.

Tracy and I had been swimming, diving, and talking for hours—in our new, almost matching bikinis. Mine was bright yellow and Tracy's a deep red. It felt wonderful to be out of school and back at the Edgehaven community pool.

My quiet was broken by Mae shouting, "Marco!" and her friend, Lisa, yelling, "Polo!"

Then Annie called, "Jody, she's here. She's at the pool. Get out." I paddled over to the side, wiping the water from my eyes.

Annie, standing at the pool side, her chubby belly hanging over her orange polka dot bikini bottom, was waving her hands in the air. "Come see. Quick. She's here!" She was shouting and screaming as if Paul McCartney had arrived.

"*Who's* here?" I said as I climbed out.

Out of the corner of my eye, I spotted James balanced on the edge of the lifeguard chair and Claire sitting on a towel right below. I guess she definitely wasn't breaking up with him.

"Mrs. O'Donnell. Come see!"

I followed Annie along the pool deck, up to Mrs. O'Donnell, who was lounging on a plastic beach chair near the shallow end, reading a book. It was strange to see a teacher there, wearing a floral bathing suit with a bit of a skirt at the bottom. Her hair was longer than it was at *Alice in Wonderland*. And she was thinner than she looked in all her clothes. I guess she had a pretty nice figure for a teacher and a mom.

"Mrs. O'Donnell!" Annie called. Mrs. O'Donnell looked up, lowered her glasses, and seeing it was Annie, her face lit up.

Still seated, she gave Annie a big hug. I stood back, feeling kind of awkward without a towel or a cover-up. I glanced around the pool, trying to find Tracy. She was holding on to the side of the pool, looking up and talking to Colin, one of the other cute, tanned lifeguards. He was leaning forward on his tall wooden chair in his dark sunglasses, a whistle poised on his lips ready for a rescue.

"Nice to see you again, Jody."

"Annie!" called Mrs. O'Donnell's daughter, Patty, from the pool steps. Dripping water, she shyly tiptoed over.

"Hi, Patty!" Annie yelled.

"She's right here, Annie, you don't need to yell," I said. They grasped hands. "Hi, Patty." I gave her a smile. "I bet you're a good swimmer?" I asked. She nodded.

"Want to see?" she said, immediately.

"Sure," I said. "I'll watch."

"I'm coming with you," said Annie, running off after her, leaving me stranded with Mrs. O'Donnell.

"So how's the tile looking?" I needed something to say.

Mrs. O'Donnell smiled. "Terrific. Your dad certainly cares about his work. Every day he checks in, seeing how things are moving along. They should be finishing up at the end of the week."

I leaned over, trying to get a glimpse of the book on her lap. Mrs. O'Donnell held up the cover for me to see: *The Bluest Eye*.

"Ever hear of it? By Toni Morrison?" she asked. "Are you a reader?"

"Yeah," I said. "What's it about?"

"About a young Black girl, who feels she's ugly because of the color of her skin. The shame she feels, and the traumas she experiences." There was that word again—*trauma*.

"That's sad," I said, interested. Mrs. O'Donnell went on, like a teacher, telling me more about the novel. I guess I could see why Annie liked her. At *Alice in Wonderland* she listened so carefully to Annie, and today the way she hugged her. Plus she liked reading. Maybe Annie was on to something, she was pretty cool.

"Jody, come here!" yelled Tracy.

I said goodbye to Mrs. O'Donnell and dove in to the pool.

A week later, Tracy and I were tanning in her backyard. Eyes closed, Mom's sunglasses shielding my eyes from the sun, I was in my yellow bikini, leaning back on my elbows, taking in the line of my body. Looking over at Tracy's, comparing the curves of her body to mine. I was finally looking like a teenager.

Grandma Cupcakes startled me. She was standing at the fence. "Where's Billy?"

"How should I know?"

"You're naked. Put some clothes on." She clutched a hankie to her forehead, wiping away the sweat. I held my terrycloth cover-up over my chest.

"Last time I saw him he was playing with the boys from up the street. Jimmy and Petey Russo."

"Oh, playing, is he?!" Grandma said. "Well, I can't find him. He never came home for lunch. I've been looking all over. I'm getting worried."

The muscles in my body tensed. "Where's Annie?" I asked.

"Playing with one of her little noisy friends, what's her name, Pinky."

"Patty. Okay, I'll go look," I said.

"I'll help," Tracy said.

"You go that way." I pointed up the street. "And I'll go the other way."

"You too, Stacy, put some clothes on. You'll attract flies."

Claire, James, and Mae were already out on the street beginning to look.

Claire said, "You two ask the neighbors on that side of the street, James and I will cover this side."

Mae said, "What do I do?"

"You come with us and look through all the bushes," said James.

Tracy and I started at the Geigers' house.

"Hi, Mrs. Geiger. Have you seen Billy?"

"No, I haven't. He's missing?"

"Yeah, he didn't come home for lunch. Grandma's getting scared."

"Oh my God. Someone should run right over, quick, and check the Mason's pool." I shivered despite the heat. No way did I want to look in a pool. Two at a time, I ran down the steps, shouting for James.

"Your mom said you should run and check the Mason's yard. Right away." My stomach was hurting so bad, I didn't even want to say the word pool.

James took off. Tracy and I stood silent, in the middle of the cul-de-sac, until James came back around and yelled, "He's not there." Until I exhaled, I hadn't realized I'd been holding my breath.

Mae, who had picked up a large stick, was poking through Tracy's shrubbery.

We skipped Tracy's house and knocked at the Malone's front door. Their son, Robert, home from college, asked, "You think he was kidnapped?" What was wrong with these nikkin' people. I had just asked if they had seen Billy, not what might have happened to him!

Charlie's house was next. I was disappointed no one was home.

After no success on our side of the block, we met up with Claire, James, and Mae. Mae was clearly on the verge of tears. Me too.

"Jesus, where can he be?" said Claire.

"We'll find him," I said. "Tracy and I will check Prospect Woods."

"Tracy, I'll start at the top of the hill, you at the bottom. We'll meet in the middle." It was strange to be back in Prospect Woods, where we spent days building hideouts and tree forts as kids. Now we only went there to sled.

I fought my way through the brambles and fallen trees, repeatedly calling Billy's name. No Billy. "Let's go back," I said to Tracy.

Grandma was standing on the porch. I hadn't seen her looking this bad since Mom died. My scalp tingled. Claire and

James were huddled behind her, while Mae was on the cement step, now in tears.

"What do we do?" I asked. I couldn't think of any other places to look for him.

"I'm going to call the police," Grandma said, her voice shaky. This was serious. We followed her inside.

Mae and I perched on the living room couch, on the edge of our seats. Claire and James watched out the window. It felt so much like a year earlier, when Claire and Mae and I had huddled on the Geiger's couch the day of the accident. The memory was like one of those Chinese finger puzzles: the harder I pulled away from it, the tighter it clenched.

I heard Grandma in the kitchen. "Hello, Officer. I'm sorry to bother you, but my grandson is missing." She paused. "He's four." Her voice cracked. "Yes, yes, of course we looked there. We covered the neighborhood. He's not anywhere." She listened, saying, "Mm-mm," and then she gave our address. Grandma hung up the phone. "They're on their way." I stared at the wall clock. It had been over an hour since he'd been missing.

"Let's go outside and check again," I said. "Maybe we missed him."

Just as the police car pulled up, Claire yelled, "I see him!"

From around the corner, a formation of four boys marched on to Randolph Court. One of the older boys in front, shouting, "Hup, Hup," followed by a straight line of stragglers, returning from some military victory, each with a stick rifle resting on their shoulder.

And there was Billy, his camouflage army helmet on his head, his shirt tail hanging out of his shorts, Dad's Korean war dog tags around his neck, bringing up the rear. The tags jingled like angels being born. A huge grin across his face. Seeing us, the lead boy commanded, "Halt, soldiers."

"A police car!" yelled Billy.

I didn't know if I should cry or yell at him. Grandma crumpled down onto the bottom front step.

The officer climbed out of his car. "It's okay, we found him," I said.

The officer waved over to Grandma, "Everything all right, ma'am?"

She stood up, hanging on to the railing, and said. "Yes, everything's fine now. Sorry to trouble you, officer."

"Here, let me help you, ma'am." The officer took her arm and she hobbled up the front steps. She looked like she'd aged five years in an afternoon. "You been taking care of all the Moran kids, haven't you?"

"I'm not sure how much more of this I can take," she said.

"I understand." He nodded his head, his lips drawn in a line. "Here, let me get you a chair."

"No, no. I'm fine," Grandma said, pushing him off.

"You're looking a little gray."

"That's 'cause I'm old!"

He chuckled. "Can I call someone? Take you somewhere, the hospital?"

"Pff," she said, waving her hand at him.

The police officer bounded down the steps. As he passed Claire and me, he said, "You look after your grandma now. You hear."

Later, I was in Grandma Cupcake's bedroom helping her fold laundry, smooth out wrinkles, and match socks. She was plunked down in her rocker, with her feet up on the tiny footstool. She started coughing, a rattling, barking sound deep inside her chest. Steadying herself against the bedpost, she pulled a hanky out of her bra, where she stored everything, and wiped her mouth. A dark red glob of blood appeared on the fabric.

"Grandma!" I pointed to her hanky.

"Oh, a little blood—it's nothing. I've had it before." The creases in her face were deep, caked with white face powder.

I knew Grandma didn't have much faith in medicine, but I also knew coughing up blood wasn't nothing. "You need to go to the hospital. It's serious."

"Pff. If you let them go looking, they feel they gotta find something."

"Grandma, they only find something if there *is* something!"
Grandma continued folding laundry. "I'll go with you."

"Okay, you go and tell me what they say."

"Grandma! I'll call that policeman on you. He'll make you go."

"And I'll give him a donut and send him home."

Nothing I said convinced her.

"I'm going to tell Dad," I said and charged upstairs.

When I came back with Dad, Grandma stuck her tongue out at me. "Tattletale," she said. I stuck my tongue right back out at her.

Dad handed Grandma her coat and said, "I'm taking you to the hospital."

Grandma tossed it on her bed. "No, you're not."

Dad sighed, he knew there was no getting Grandma to do something she didn't want to do. "Well, if not the hospital, a doctor. Tomorrow!"

"You go to a doctor and they just find something wrong with you," she said.

"That's because there *is* something wrong with you," Dad said.

"That's what I said."

"All right, but I'm not taking my clothes off."

"On or off. Just go."

The next day, Dad dropped Grandma off at the doctor's office, and I went along to make sure she didn't sneak out the back door. Grandma saw the doctor. I sat with her as he asked lots of questions. He looked like he was barely out of high school. Every time he turned around, Grandma twirled her finger against the side of her head, the universal sign for someone acting crazy.

When he finally asked her to take off her clothes, I made a beeline for the waiting room. Eventually, Grandma joined me.

"What did he say?"

"He says we gotta wait."

"For what?"

"He needs to call his mother to find out what to do next."

We waited and waited, for what felt like hours. Finally the doctor came out. "Mrs. Cahill, please come on back."

"Jody, you better come too." Grandma leaned in closer and with a wry smile said, "He might get frisky. He did see me naked, you know." I laughed.

He brought us back into his office, where lots of diplomas hung on the walls.

"Well, Mrs. Cahill. It appears you have an ulcer."

"Of course I do. Headaches, too. Didn't I tell you already? I'm taking care of five kids." Grandma gave me a look, like, tell me something I don't already know.

"I'm going to order a few tests to rule out any other possibilities. We'll start you off with some antacids. But you'll need to live a less stressful life."

As we left the office, under her breath Grandma said to me: "He went to medical school for that."

Dad was outside waiting for us. "Well?" he said.

"Apparently, I'm too old for this," she said.

32

When I woke, I got dressed in my yellow bikini with shorts and a tank top on top, so I'd be ready for the pool. Above the toaster was the kitchen calendar, and I turned the page to June as my bread toasted. Another month without Mom. I remember when I was counting the days.

Tracy and I got to the pool when it opened at ten, and we didn't get out until the whistle blew for adult swim at noon. I spotted Miss Wendy moseying over to the snack bar. I wrapped a towel around me, retrieved some money from my sock, and followed a few paces behind, with just enough distance to assure I'd be next to her in line.

I said, "Oh, hi, Miss Wendy. I didn't know you were here."

"Oh, Jody! Great to see you." She put her arm around my shoulder, her hand pruned from swimming. "You caught me—a Good Humor ice cream sandwich." She winked. "Want to join me in being naughty?"

I grinned and nodded.

Mae and Annie came running up. "You didn't wait for us," said Mae. "You have the money."

"French fries," said Annie.

"My sisters," I said ruefully.

"I know just what you mean," Miss Wendy said brightly. "I have a younger one too."

I bought sodas and crinkled french fries for Mae and Annie, and an ice cream sandwich for me. I made sure I got the spot closest to Miss Wendy at the picnic table. She was drinking a Fresca, Mom's favorite.

"Do you girls like to read like your big sister?"

"Who are you?" said Mae. "I dove off the high dive for the first time."

"Impressive," Miss Wendy said. "I only jumped. I was too

afraid of diving. What do you expect—I'm the librarian." She laughed.

Annie made a ketchup mustache. "Knock it off, Annie," I said.

Picking up a napkin, Miss Wendy wiped off her mouth. The whistle blew.

"Adult swim is over," said Mae, grabbing her hand. "Come on, Annie."

"Bye, girls," said Miss Wendy. "Jody, what do you think of this idea for the fall? I thought I'd ask some of the moms if they wanted to start a mother-daughter reading club. You think you and your mom might want to do that?"

"My mom died," I whispered, as if it were a secret. Miss Wendy gave a slight jolt, trying to hide her shock.

"Well, maybe I should start a father-daughter reading club."

"My dad's not a reader. I should get back to the pool," I said, before she could go on.

She touched my hand, we stood and made our way back to the pool.

ᑤ

"Jody, Mae, Annie." Dad was calling. I swam over to the side of the pool and pulled myself out. Dad looked funny, the only person with all his clothes on—work pants, short sleeve shirt, socks, and tie shoes.

"Time to go, gang. Jody, collect your sisters."

Dripping wet I ran over, arms across my chest. "Dad, wait. I want you to watch, see how far I can go underwater without coming up for air."

Taking hold of his arm, I led him over to where Miss Wendy was sitting, pulled up a chair right next to her, and said, "Sit here, Dad. This is the librarian, Miss Wendy."

Dad laughed and shook her hand.

I dove in before Dad could stop me. After swimming a ways underwater, I turned back to the edge of the pool, close enough to hear them, and like a crocodile raised my eyes barely out of the water. Dad sat awkwardly, his arms dangling over the edge of the vinyl strap pool chair. I saw him check his watch. I couldn't hear Miss Wendy, but she was probably trying to get him to join her reading group.

Say something, Dad!

This wasn't going according to plan. Miss Wendy looked up, caught me eavesdropping. Dad looked me in the eye and tapped his watch.

Quickly, I swam underwater, seeing how far I could get with one breath. I popped up, pleased that I had almost made it the entire length of the pool. As I wiped the water from my eyes I felt someone grab my ankle. "Hey!" I yelped. I expected to see Tracy or Claire splashing up from the depths and into my face—but it was Charlie! He gave his small smile, then let it open all the way up. His braces were gone!

"Nice teeth," I said quickly, readjusting my two-piece, which was always riding up my too-skinny bottom.

He stood close. His blond hair touched the top of his earlobe. There were a few freckles on his nose. His dark, thick eyelashes were flecked with water drops. Without thinking, I leaned in and kissed him, my lips barely touching his, which were soft and wet. It sent tingles down my whole body. The rough patch on his chin surprised me. For a second, I remembered that kiss in his basement, his face had been smooth.

Charlie's thick eyebrows shot up. I wasn't sure which one of us was more shocked.

"One of us had to do that," I said. I took a breath and Charlie gave the cutest half-smile. I could see he wanted to do it again.

"And I'm glad one of us did."

He lifted my chin and this time he kissed me. His eyes, slightly open. From across the pool one of the older boys shouted, "Go, Cogs!" I took a step back and quickly looked over where Dad sat. He hadn't seen us.

Then I told him, "I'm watching my dad and Miss Wendy."

"Oh, your dad's here."

We dunked under together. Charlie took hold of my hand, gave a squeeze, and I swam for the steps.

✎

I paced in front of the window, waiting for Claire. Where was she! She's never here when I want her to be. I needed to tell her about Charlie and me at the pool. The kiss.

I turned away for a minute, still no Claire, but when I looked back, there was Mrs. O'Donnell and Patty strolling up the front walkway. I ran to open the door.

"Hi, Mrs. O'Donnell. Hey, Patty," I said. Patty had a Tubsy doll in her arms.

"Dropping off a check for your dad. And I brought along that book I told you about." She waved *The Bluest Eyes*. "I finished and thought you might like to give it a try."

"Thanks." I turned the book over in my hands. "Oh, Dad. He went with Billy to pick up dinner. But he should be here soon," I said. "Come on in. Is the kitchen all finished?"

"Almost." Her hair was pulled back with a butterfly hairclip. One curl escaped, falling loosely over her shoulder as she sunk into the living room couch. I sat in the gold armchair, across from her.

Annie, still in her polka dot bathing suit, slip-slided down the hall, throwing her arms around her Ms. O'Donnell. Mrs. O'Donnell hugged right back. Patty crept over and showed me her doll to admire.

"I have Tubsy too!" said Annie. "Come on, Patty. We'll go get mine and play dolls." And off Annie went, Patty trailing down the hall behind her.

"How long have you lived in Edgehaven?" I asked.

"Two years. We moved here from Weehawken."

"That's near where my dad grew up," I said, then added, "and my mom."

"Isn't that something?" she said.

"Did you go dancing at Schuetzen Park?" I asked.

"I sure did," she said.

"My parents won the Lindy contest there," I said.

"I'm impressed." Talking with her was as easy as talking with Juliette.

Just then Dad arrived home with a bucket of chicken, two bags of fries, and coleslaw—more than he usually got.

"Hi, Kay. A pleasure to see you," he said, offering her a big smile. *Kay.*

"I was nearby so I thought I'd drop the check off myself." She handed Dad an envelope. "Let me see those kitchen tiles you were telling me about."

"Yeah, the mosaics," Dad said, leading her into the kitchen and putting the food down on the countertop.

"Dad, guess what?" I said, breaking in. "Mrs. O'Donnell lived one town over from where you grew up and even went to Schuetzen Park!"

"I know," said Dad.

"You know?"

"I know. Turns out we have *lots* more than tile in common." Dad gave a wink.

"Oh, Joe," Mrs. O'Donnell said. "Well, I don't want your dinner to get cold."

"Stay," urged Dad. "I bought plenty of chicken. I mean look at this. There's easily enough extra for a second-grade teacher and a first grader."

I snagged a french fry from the bag. "What about Patty's dad?" Mrs. O'Donnell's eyebrows rose up.

"Oh, Jody. Patty's dad, Ted, passed away," said Dad.

"When she was two," added Mrs. O'Donnell. Jesus. Goosebumps rose up my arms. "What happened?"

"He had cancer." Her words ricocheted around my brain like a ball in a pinball machine. I pressed my tongue against the roof of my mouth, trying not to smile about him being dead and all.

I was still putting all this together when Dad called for all hands on deck for dinner, and Mrs. O'Donnell was taking off her jacket.

"I guess we do have something to tell you," Dad said. "Something to tell you all!"

"Well, this is serendipitous," I said, with a laugh. *Serendipity: finding something that was right there under one's nose the whole time.*

Or under Annie's nose.

33

I was sitting on Grandma Cupcake's front stoop, chatting with her old neighbors, watching all the people pass by.

Grandma had moved out of our house faster then she had moved in. In just two weeks she was living a few blocks from her old apartment on Tulip Avenue. She'd reclaimed most of her old parlor furniture from Aunt Sheila's basement, all the doilies right back where they belonged.

Her apartment building was filled with those same old familiar smells of garlic and onions.

"Hey, Grandma, there's your old neighbor," I said, pointing at the man across the street, lugging his groceries up the avenue." I was nibbling on a Twinkie that must have been over a year old.

"His wife passed away after I moved." Grandma pursed her lips and shook her head. "He doesn't look like he's had a good meal since then."

"You could make him pasta fazool," I said. "He looks kinda cute for an old guy." Now that I had success with Dad, maybe I was good at this matchmaking business.

"Him?" she said. "Oh no. He's no Charlie." Her eyes once again twinkly and smiling. Last night I had told her about him liking me. She didn't even get mad! "Anyway, he'd be too much for me," she said. "We'd wind up doo-dah-dooing and he'd get me pregnant." We cracked up.

"Your mother would have loved that one," she said. Mom did love a good laugh.

I had my old Grandma Cupcakes back, just a bit wearier.

The next morning, I went to Our Lady of Grace with Grandma, even getting there fifteen minutes early. When she lived with us she had given up trying to make us go. Now it felt kinda nice being back there. There were the same lanterns, rimmed in gold, hanging overhead. Father Murphy, with his Irish lilt, greeted Grandma like an old friend. This was her church, not St. Paul's. When we settled ourselves in her old pew, I pointed up at the crucifix. "Grandma, guess what Billy said. Mrs. O'Donnell brought us to church last week, and when Billy saw the cross, he said really loud, 'Why is that guy up there hanging on the lowercase *T*?'"

"I guess me plopping him in front of the TV to watch *Sesame Street* paid off," she said. We laughed.

"You know, I'm starting to like that lady," she said, pulling out her rosaries. "I suppose a man with five kids needs a wife."

"Grandma, did you go and read *Pride and Prejudice*?"

"What's that, *Prize and Pizzas*?" She chuckled.

I never knew half the time if she was teasing or serious.

Then she coughed, and coughed some more, so much that we had to leave the sanctuary, so much that Father Murphy came out to see if she was all right.

"I'm hoping it's not the big *C*."

"Oh, Nora," he said. His eyes showed such sympathy and love, nothing like Father Sullivan. "You'll be in my prayers," he said, and turned to go back inside and lead mass. Maybe I would pray for her too.

I took Grandma's arm and we proceeded back up the aisle to our seat.

"All those ciggies when I was young, buttercup," Grandma said. "Never ever smoke." She glanced over, noticed my worried look, and said, "Oh, don't go worrying. I'm not nikkin' going anywhere."

༄

Charlie and I were out in his backyard, almost like when we were kids again, but better. We talked about starting ninth grade, what courses we were taking, what teachers we wanted, and all about Mrs. O'Donnell.

"Remember the Venn diagrams I told you about for Dad? You can't believe how many things he and Mrs. O'Donnell share. Way more than anyone else he's met."

"Yeah, but," Charlie said, "the kids all have to like her, right?"
He was right. They could have everything in common, but if we didn't like her, she couldn't be the one. "We all do," I said, "except Claire's not so keen on her. But she wouldn't like anyone taking Mom's place."

"Yeah, who would." Charlie shrugged. "If it was me, I'd probably hate it." It made me feel good knowing he was trying to understand. "Does Patty like all of you?"

"Oh yeah. When Dad and Mrs. O'Donnell go out, she sleeps over. She always wanted to be in a big family. She and Annie spend hours playing dolls, school, and totally leave me alone."

"And Claire gets to make out with James?"

Suddenly I blurted, "My dad's gonna marry her."

"Venn magic," Charlie said.

"Well, he hasn't *exactly* asked her. Yet! But I can feel it in my bones."

"You can make one of those intention cards!" said Charlie. I smiled. He remembered me telling him.

He lay his hand on top of mine, my skin flushed where he touched, then he kissed me. I was no longer afraid I did it wrong.

"Charlie!" called his mother from the kitchen window.

"Uh-oh, I think she saw us," I said. We laughed.

"Come inside, Charlie. You have homework to do." He squeezed my hand and stood up. "Now."

"See you tomorrow, Jo."

I skipped down the street, ran into my room, wrote *Dad will marry Mrs. O'Donnell* on a business card, and placed it in my best little box.

Dad and Mrs. O'Donnell were off at Dick's Inn, Dad's favorite restaurant, where we went for really special occasions. The restaurant was famous for steak sandwiches—thin sliced tenderloin laid neatly on white bread and smothered with melted butter.

The younger kids, including Patty, were in sleeping bags

spread out across my bedroom floor for indoor camping. We'd got Dad to buy us marshmallows and chocolate bars so we could make untoasted s'mores. Dad even offered to pay me to babysit.

When I finally got the three little ones quieted down and in their sleeping bags, I started reading *Beezus and Ramona* to them. Three pages in, I heard the backdoor slam shut, and minutes later, Dad and Mrs. O'Donnell were coming in the front door. I guess James got out just in time.

Claire flew into the bedroom, leap-frogged over the little kid's sleeping bags, dove into her bed, and pulled the blanket up to her nose. "I'm asleep," said Claire. I chuckled.

Dad and Mrs. O'Donnell were making all kinds of noise in the kitchen. "Knock, knock," said Dad, as he and Mrs. O'Donnell flung the door open. Were they mad at the mess we'd left?

The four kids, like caterpillars, crawled out of their sleeping bags.

"Guess what!" said Dad, looking tired but happy. "We have exciting news."

"We're getting married!" said Mrs. O'Donnell, holding up her hand for us to see the glistening diamond ring.

"Yes!" I yelled. "Yes! I knew you would."

Annie and Patty grabbed hands, jumping up-and-down, yelling, "We're sisters! Sisters!"

Billy scrambled up on to my bed and started bouncing, higher and higher until he risked flying off. Mrs. O'Donnell caught hold of his pajama top.

"Let's settle down," said Dad.

"Some of us are trying to sleep," said Claire sticking her head out from under the blanket. A hickey on her neck! I caught Claire's eye and tapped my neck. She flipped over, once again pulling the blanket up further.

"I know it's complicated, Claire," said Mrs. O'Donnell.

"Wait, what?" Mae said. "You'll live with us?" She looked unsure whether she should be happy or sad.

"We'll be a family," I said, which seemed to be all she needed to hear. She tossed her pillow in the air. Then I asked Mrs. O'Donnell, "What will we call you?"

"I'm *not* calling her Mom!" said Claire, from under her pillow.

"My name's Kathleen, but my friends call me Kay."

Kay. I said it to myself. "Can I be a bridesmaid? When's the wedding?"

"Hold on," Dad said. "There's a lot to figure out."

Kay said, "We were thinking, maybe, this coming Labor Day weekend. It's not much time, so we'll keep it simple."

Dad put his arm around her waist. "We wanted to start off the school year as one new big happy family." He pulled Kay into a tight hug, then he said, "Come here, gang." And he pulled the rest of us into the hug. "Come on, Claire."

"Oh, all right," she said, popping out from under the blanket.

"Claire! Why do you have all your clothes on?" said Dad.

"You should be glad she does." Sometimes, I cracked myself up.

34

An old weathered gray dock in the black of night, alone. Clouds partially cover the full moon. Sea smoke rises as a foghorn blows in the distance. A small wooden rowboat, its lantern lighting the bow, drifts in. A cold dampness seeps into my bones. I'm terrified, unable to move or look away. As the boat creeps in closer, the water sloshes on the dock, and I spy a lone figure standing at the stern. My fear seems to propel the boat toward me, closer and closer. "Stop, stop!" I cry. A woman draped in a long black cape appears, collar turned up, strawberry-blond hair and sunglasses hiding her face, but of course even in the fog and dim light I recognize her. Mom has returned from the dead. My stomach lurches and my heart thumps wildly in my chest, my sheets twisted around my neck, my nightgown tangled around my legs. Dad! I cry. I have to warn him! He can't get married. Mom's not really dead!

༄

I couldn't shake the dream all morning, spooked the whole time we got in our wedding clothes. My dress was a beautiful lavender, covered in tulle, with small beading along the top and a bit of décolletage. That was last night's word. *Décolletage: a woman's cleavage revealed by a low neckline.*

"Be still," Claire said, painting mascara and shadow on my eyes. She was dressed in a silky blue strappy dress that matched her eye color, and the tallest heel shoes I had ever seen.

"The boat was pulling up to the dock and it was Mom—she was alive."

"Quiet," Claire said.

We'd been through it all. Despite both my wishes of the last year and my nightmare last night, the idea that Dad was getting married seemed surprising, even shocking—someone *was* taking Mom's place.

"I made this happen," I said.

"This is not about you," Claire said, as she put the last touches on my makeup.

In the balcony overhead, the organist played "Edelweiss," which Dad had chosen, him being the captain of our family and all, which Claire found stupid and I found beautiful.

Mae, Patty, and Annie were dressed in various shades of pastel and matching white shoes.

Billy wore his navy pin-striped suit, two sizes too big. Dad picked it out with Billy on a late-night outing to the mall. With his light blue shirt and a white boutonniere pinned over his breast pocket, he looked like a mini-gangster, especially with his scar. Dad said no to the fedora.

We promenaded up the center aisle in age order—Billy, Annie, Patty, Mae, me, Claire—stepping on a satiny white runner the whole way. Between each step, I counted out, "And-one-and-two," as Kay had coached us. Pew after pew, each with a satin white bow lining the aisle, each with a relative or friend. I smiled at Charlie, sitting at the end of the aisle, handsome in a blue sports coat. James, two rows ahead, had eyes blazed on Claire. There was Tracy with her mom, Amelie, looking as glamorous as ever.

The last time I had been in a processional at St. Paul's I was following behind Mom's casket. I tried to picture what my sisters wore that day and could only remember Claire's dress and Annie's shoes.

I'd let her slip away bit by bit. Standing there with the altar in front of me, I tried to call up her voice. Nothing. I thought of Juliette. A death doesn't happen just once. Mom's smell had long faded from the house and my memory. At least I could still hear her laugh.

As I got closer to the altar, I tried to grasp for something, anything, from the morning when I'd last seen her. What had she been wearing? What were her last words to me? Had I kissed her goodbye?

I didn't realize I was crying until the salty taste reached my lips.

I slipped into the first pew, my long dress gathering up at my feet, and sat among my sisters. The processional notes for "Here Comes the Bride" wafted through the air. This was the signal for Kay, in her cream-colored dress and matching bouquet of roses, to begin her advance. Everyone in the congregation rose to their feet.

When I turned to watch, I saw Grandma Cupcakes sitting in the pew behind me, her lips pinched tight, her pocketbook resting on her lap. She was staring straight ahead, as if she was waiting for a bus.

Kay joined Dad at the altar. He was grinning from ear to ear, a gardenia pinned to the jacket of a new black suit, clothes Mom had never seen. The smell of all the flowers was overpowering, the smell of a hundred brands of perfume, and for a moment I was afraid I might throw up. I took tiny sips of air as Kay's sister, Colleen, read some bible verse.

Father Sullivan cleared his throat. "We are here to celebrate a wonderous event, the joining together of two families. Of course, always keeping Margaret and Ted in our hearts."

I snapped to at the sound of Father Sullivan saying Mom's name, but I also liked that he'd mentioned her and Patty's dad. Dad and Kay were nodding.

"These children will never forget the parents who left them too soon. Their love is eternal and they cannot be replaced. But God shows us how to make room for more and new love too."

I'd been worried I was pushing Mom out of my heart, but what Father Sullivan said made sense for how I felt about Kay. My heart seemed to be swelling to make room for more love.

Dad and Kay clasped hands. Kay was staring at Dad with such joy on her face.

Dad said we had a choice about what we remember, and once again I scanned my brain for some seed of a good memory. Mom rubbing Vicks on my chest when I had a bad cough. She used the same strokes teaching me how to ice a cake. Her teaching me to write my name. I bunched my dress, ran my fingers along the rough hem, remembered being tucked in bed, supposedly asleep, but still wide awake, some kind of big day ahead. Restless, I tiptoed down the hall to the empty kitchen. From the basement came the soothing hum of Mom's new Touch and Sew, the one with the fancy zigzag stitches that Dad had given her for Christmas. I followed the sound downstairs and found her sitting there, hunched over her sewing machine, watching the line that was forming as she slipped the drapery fabric along the machine edge. The moon outside was bright and full, lighting the room with a pearly glow.

I could see her lightly freckled arm, her great poof of red hair, the tip of her tongue poking out from the side of her lips as she concentrated.

"Mom?"

She'd looked up, releasing her foot from the treadle, and gave me one of her crooked grins. She didn't ask what I was doing up, not a word, didn't mind about that. "Want to try?" she asked.

I pulled up a chair and leaned into her, pushed the cloth through the presser as she touched my arm, her foot powering the machine.

"You're a fast learner," she'd said when she looked at my seam.

Her breath smelled like Raleighs and black licorice, and her nails were pearly white against the silky fabric—Celestial.

Father Sullivan had been talking and now he was looking at Kay expectantly. Dad was too.

"I do," Kay said, and her arms encircled Dad's waist. We would be a new family now.

I do too, I thought. We all do.

ACKNOWLEDGMENTS

This novel would never have been written without the love and support of so many.

My thanks to Bob Winer and Sharon Alperovitz for creating New Directions in Writing, my writing home, and Sara Taber, my first teacher, who gave me the confidence to write.

Bill Roorbach for being my teacher, my first reader and my last. Bill, forever wise, connected me to my agent, Eleanor Jackson. Thank you, Eleanor, for your unending support and belief in my work. I am forever grateful.

Michaele Weissman who urged me to make the leap to fiction.

Thank you to my editor, teacher, and friend Mary Kay Zuravleff for offering me all the editing, insight, and warmth required to be a fiction writer.

My enormous appreciation to Anne Adelman, for reading every version of this story, offering enormously helpful feedback. I'm indebted to the many friends who read some portion of the novel: Dana Brotman, Martha Dupecher, Julie Eill, Susan Fitzgerald, Sara Groark, Caroline Hall, Linda Kanefield, and Rachel King. My gratitude to Warren Poland, for his generosity of spirit in encouraging me in all my writing.

Thanks to everyone on the Regal House team for publishing *Meet the Moon*. Special thanks to my ever-patient editor Jaynie Royal, and her auxiliary back-up editor, Pam Van Dyk. Special thanks to my friend, Lynn Rauch, for her meticulous last round of editing.

My deepest thanks to my daughter, Anna, not only for her encouragement, but her expertise as a grammarian. My sons, David and Peter, for being the wonderful young men they are. And my sister, Karen, for her support and enthusiasm at reading anything I sent her way.

And my biggest thanks to my incredible husband, Alan, who patiently sat each morning listening to me read early drafts, offering astute suggestions, and a metaphor when needed.